Trouble in Paradox
A Comical Time Travel Murder Mystery

Galactic Detective Agency
Book 7

Gary Blaine Randolph

ISBN: 978-1-7379299-8-7 (paperback)
ISBN: 978-1-7379299-9-4 (ebook)

Dedication

To O'Reilly and Jacob and Shadrach and Micah and Rachel and Solomon and Jonah. Friends on the journey.

Contents

Chapter 1

Something Borrowed, Someone Blue

Ding! Ding! Ding! I looked up from the taco I was enjoying. My friend Adam was standing at the table, stemware in one hand, his dinner knife in the other.

I chewed twice more and swallowed. "Wait a minute, Adam. Save the toasts for the wedding reception."

Sarah reached over with her napkin to wipe some guac from the side of my mouth.

Adam said, "I thought the point of a rehearsal dinner was to rehearse, Gabe. I was hoping to test out some of the edgier material from my best man's speech."

"Not in front of my parents and Nana, you don't. In fact, I'd like to review your material before you spring it on unsuspecting wedding guests." I made a gimme motion with my fingers.

"Here's your chance to review it right now." Adam pulled a stack of notecards from a pocket, tromboned his arm to bring them into focus, and began to read. "Ladies and gentlemen … and Gabe also, I've been waiting for this day for a long time."

That much was true. Adam had introduced Sarah and me a few years ago and brought her into our I.T. crowd coffee circle, not so subtly trying to fix us up.

"Hold up," I said, "The only speeches tonight are the ones Sarah and I are going to give."

"Suit yourself. I guess you can hear all my jokes tomorrow afternoon … live before an audience of thousands."

"More like a hundred," Sarah said.

"Whatever." Adam lifted his glass. "Then all I'll say is this: to Sarah and Gabe, Mr. and Mrs. Gabriel Lake. Wait, that sounds old-fashioned. Gabriel and

Sarah Lake. Or are you going with Sarah Gallo-Lake … or just Sarah Gallo? Well, whoever you are, I wish you all the best." He took a sip, followed by murmurs of agreement and sips around the table, and sat back down.

I said, "Then I guess that's our cue. Sarah, do you want to —" I smiled at my bride-to-be, and she shot me a wink, which left me unable to finish the sentence. She was wearing an olive-green wrap dress, a favorite of mine that she had picked up on an alien planet while we were trying to catch a criminal.

Now, there's a sentence you don't see every day. Before I go any further, I should explain the whole crime-fighting in outer space thing. My regular gig is software development, putting together programs for various clients on a contract basis.

My super-secret side gig started a little over two years ago when I was recruited by the Galactic Detective Agency to help them with a case on Earth requiring local talent. One thing led to another, and I've been sort of on-call with them ever since, buzzing around the galaxy fighting bad guys and solving murders. In truth, I do more legwork than crime solving since the agency is headed by a certified genius named Oren Vilkas.

Sarah had even accompanied me on a couple of my investigations. Sarah and I and her seven-and-a-half-year-old son, Lucas, who had also been off-planet with me, were the only humans who knew for sure that we aren't alone in the universe.

"Do I want to speak first?" Sarah asked with a coy glance over her glasses that told me she figured out I had been left tongue-tied from her wink. She stood and gazed over the room. "Thank you, everybody, for coming out tonight. I hope you come out tomorrow too." Chuckles swept around the table. "Gabe, I can truly say you have opened new worlds to me." Lucas giggled, getting the inside joke. "We have had adventures and excitement, and I look forward to so much more. As some of you know, I've been unlucky at love before, but Gabriel Lake gives me hope that this time it will stick. He makes me laugh and calms my soul. And on top of all that, isn't he a cutie?"

Adam said, "I think you need to see an eye doctor."

I didn't have to defend myself. Sarah, my mom, and Nana all gave Adam a dirty look.

Sarah raised her glass. "At last, I feel like I have someone who will always stand at my side and never leave me. I feel like the luckiest girl on Earth. To Gabe, to Lucas, to family and friends, both here and far away."

Everyone joined her in raising their glasses. She sat back down, and I stood. I looked around at the circle of smiling faces. Wow, was this actually happening?

"Um … I'm not going to say much either. I only want to acknowledge some special people around this table tonight. Sarah, of course, my lovely bride, and one of the smartest and most talented web designers around. Until I met Sarah, I thought all I.T. people were as dumb as Adam."

"Hey now," Adam said. "I was smart enough to introduce you two."

"Yeah. And aren't you looking pleased with yourself this evening because of it."

"I was right, wasn't I, Gabe?"

"You were, Adam. Thank you. I also want to say thank you to Lucas for giving me permission to join your family. I can't wait for all the fun times we'll be sharing." Staring at the tablecloth in school-kid embarrassment, Lucas gave me a thumbs up.

"To Sarah's parents, thank you for raising her right. To my mom and dad, thank you for raising me right. And I can't forget Nana Lois, who, along with Grandpa, played endless games of Candy Land and Clue and gin rummy with me."

Nana, who was pushing one hundred but still as sharp as the safety pins she always kept handy, said, "Frank would be so proud of you."

Which stopped me in my tracks. I pressed my lips together and dropped my head, blinking a few times. I looked back up with a stiff upper lip. "I think that's it. Everybody, have another taco."

An hour later, after more conversation and laughter, everyone had left except Sarah and me … and Lucas, whose head was down on the table.

She squeezed my hand. "I think we're done here."

"Yeah, get that boy in bed. He has a big day tomorrow. We all do. Do you need help with him?"

"No. I've been training for seven years." She lugged Lucas out of the chair and flopped him over her shoulder.

I opened the restaurant door for her and walked them to their car, unlocking the door so she didn't have to fumble with it while holding sixty pounds of kid. It had rained while we were inside, a not uncommon occurrence in Indianapolis in May. Virginia Avenue glistened black under the streetlights.

Sarah gently dropped Lucas into the booster seat and strapped him in. Straightening, she draped her arms around me and gave me a kiss that raised my resting heart rate. "You still want to go through with this?"

"My feet are completely warm," I said. "Why? Do you have doubts?"

She smiled. "I don't think so. You do put the cap back on the toothpaste, don't you?"

"I prefer the kind that flips open and closed. Makes it simpler."

"I can live with that. Can you live with Legos everywhere?"

"We've been dating for a while now. I think I'm used to Legos and everything else."

"All right then." She pulled away and patted my cheek. "See you at the church."

What a night, I thought, watching her drive off. Great friends, a beautiful soon-to-be-wife. Everything was coming up Gabriel.

I walked back inside the restaurant, one of my favorite Mexican places here in Indy's Fountain Square district, to grab my fedora. I decided to visit the washroom before walking the few blocks home.

As I was washing my hands, I took a moment to stop in front of the mirror and check myself out in my suit. Or rather, my grandfather's suit. Navy blue pinstripes, double-breasted, the necktie gray and baby blue in art deco lines, and a matching pocket square. Grandpa Frank had taken excellent care of the outfit. He wore it only on special occasions, calling it his "marrying and burying suit."

After he passed, Nana Lois said I could have anything of his I wanted. I chose the suit because ... well, for a lot of reasons. I could picture him wearing the suit and the jaunty way he invariably carried himself when he had it on. And seeing it always swept me back to the 1940s, a time I had fallen in love with through old film noir detective stories and war movies. Plus, Grandpa, at least the younger version of Grandpa, was the same size as me.

I kept the suit stored in a garment bag in the back of my closet. This was one of the few times I had worn it. I thought wearing Grandpa's marrying suit to my own wedding would honor him. Besides, it looked mighty sharp with my fedora. Gazing in the mirror, I felt like I had stepped out of a Raymond Chandler novel.

Hearing the washroom door open and close, I busied myself with disposing the paper towel.

"Admiring yourself?"

I turned at the sound of the voice. The person, shorter than me, was shrouded in a hoody, the hood up and pulled low over a ballcap. The evening was chilly for late May, but not that cold. Who was this weirdo coming into a bathroom and starting a conversation? I didn't answer.

4

"Or should I say congratulations?" the figure said. "This is your matrimony ritual, isn't it?"

"My what?"

The face raised, the blue skin finally catching the light.

"Jace?"

Jace Gilead was the ship's engineer on the *Shaymus*, the spaceship used by the Galactic Detective Agency, the ship that had taken Sarah and me to the planet where she had picked up the dress and I had proposed. Jace was from the planet Rheged Prime, where everybody's skin was a shade of blue.

"Hi, Gabe."

"I'm … I'm glad you came, Jace." Over the course of a half dozen mysteries with them, I had grown close to the crew and operatives who made up the team. "But I can't let you come to the wedding. This is Sarah's day, and having someone there with blue skin — or Zastra, for crying out loud — would kind of steal the spotlight."

"That's not why we're here. We need you for a job."

"Sorry. I can't take off. Tomorrow is my wedding day."

"It's more of an errand really."

"Jace, I can't."

"We just need to pick up somebody. Quog."

"Quog wants to return now? That's great, but his timing couldn't be worse."

I had met Quog on one of my adventures out in space. He was a human who had been kidnapped by aliens as a boy back in the 1960s. Sold and re-sold as a slave, he had eventually earned his freedom. But by then, so much time had passed he was hesitant to return to Earth, afraid he would no longer fit in or that everyone would think he was bonkers if he ever mentioned extraterrestrials to explain his years of absence. By the time we had met, Quog was in his late sixties and had been gone from Earth so long he had even forgotten his real name, which we finally figured out had been Doug. I had tried without success to talk him into returning to his Indiana home.

"He asked for you, Gabe. You're the only Earthling he knows. And the only one who understands his situation. All you have to do is ride along on a chrono jump to Anyi and escort him back to Earth."

"Anyi? Have I been to that one?"

"I don't know. I haven't kept a journal of your travels. Binary suns. Huge outcroppings composed of diamonds."

"I think I would have remembered diamond boulders. You know, I wish Quog all the best, but right now I can't nursemaid his reentry to Earth society. I have a honeymoon planned, and three's a crowd."

"You won't have to, Gabe. It's one night. You'll be back before morning."

I felt for Quog, separated from his family when he wasn't much older than Lucas was now, finally finding the courage to come back after all this time. How could I say no? "We just pick him up and bring him back? There's no case to solve, no criminal to apprehend?"

"There and back again."

"That's what Bilbo said. And look what happened to him."

"Who?"

"Never mind. You wouldn't know since Earth literature is quarantined."

All of Earth was under a galactic quarantine, which was why no one else on Earth knew anything about the amazing worlds and weird species out among the stars. I never had gotten all the details on the hows and whys, but essentially humanity had been placed in the interstellar equivalent of time-out. If you've read the news lately, can you blame them?

"Okay, okay. I'll go." I knew I should be getting to bed for a good night's sleep before my wedding day. Then again, I figured I was probably too worked up to sleep much anyway. Besides, I thought, it was one quick trip to pick him up. What was the worst that could happen?

Chapter 2

Interstellar Uber

"So where did you park the ship?" I asked Jace.

"Not far. Follow me."

He led me a few blocks west of Fountain Square to where ramps for Interstates 65 and 70 loop around each other like spaghetti on a plate. Nestled under a dark overpass sat the *Shaymus*.

I couldn't help but smile to see it again. To me, the *Shaymus* was like the starship *Enterprise*, James Bond's Aston Martin DB5, and Scooby-Doo's Mystery Machine all rolled into one. I'd ridden to the stars and back in that ship — egg-shaped, red with a black stripe sweeping the length of its side, landing struts underneath, short wings, and a low dome on top.

As Jace and I edged down the grassy embankment toward it, the ramp began to lower from the side with a *whir*. A line of red lights beckoned us inside. We climbed into the gleaming white crew deck corridor that ran around the middle of the egg.

Jace said, "Close ramp," and it began to rise. "I need to get down to engineering for the flight. Do you want to go up and say hi to the gang?"

"Sure." I stepped to an open shaft opposite the ramp and said, "Deploy stairs."

A spiral staircase emerged from the side of the central shaft. Jace climbed down. I climbed up. I emerged into an oval room, its deep hunter green walls decorated with works of art. Closest to the stairs were two desks. One was mine. At the other sat a human-sized lizard person wearing a long, hooded duster coat.

"Zastra," I said. Zastra is the number one operative of the Galactic Detective Agency, a fact she rarely lets me forget.

"Hi, Gabe," she said in her raspy voice. She was from the planet Sratha, and about as prickly as you would expect for someone from a reptilian species. On the other hand, she was an awfully handy person to have on your side in a fight.

Across the room, what you might incorrectly call two little yellow birds perched in a habitat. One of them said, "Well, looky here. If it isn't meathead."

"Hi, Buad. Hi, Blan." They also were operatives, brothers from the planet Avan. Their small size and ability to fly made them excellent at surveillance. As for their ability to be smart alecks, they excelled at that as well and loved to give me a hard time.

The face of Dwayne "The Rock" Johnson appeared on the large video screen on the front wall. "Welcome back, Gabriel."

This was Oren Vilkas, the boss of the Galactic Detective Agency. Oren only appears to look like Dwayne Johnson. He can use any face he wants since he exists digitally. He used to have a physical body, but hundreds of years ago when his body was dying, he had his consciousness transferred to circuitry. They can do that sort of thing out among the stars. Of all the faces Oren could use, he generally prefers to take the appearance of The Rock with a tinge of blue added as a nod to the fact that in his physical life he was Rhegedian like Jace.

"Hi, Oren. It's been what? Six or seven months?"

"Yes. Thank you for coming. I'm sure Quog will appreciate having a fellow Earthling escort him back to Earth.

"What kind of getup do you have on?" Zastra asked me.

"It's called a suit. You guys pulled me from my wedding rehearsal dinner."

"I don't know what that is."

"Do you have weddings on Sratha?"

"Not as such."

"Well, we do, and we dress up for the occasion."

Blan cackled. "You look like you're done up in a package, ribbon and all."

By the way, if you're wondering how I was able to communicate with Avanians and Srathans and Rhegedians, it was through a nifty piece of galactic tech called translator bots — nanobots that take up residence in your brain to translate any known language into your native tongue. With translator bots, you could converse with anyone, provided they also had them. Which everybody except Earthlings apparently did. It's only one of the mind-blowing technologies Earth is missing out on because of the quarantine.

"Yeah," said Buad. "How do you breathe with that cord around your neck? What is that — a leash or something?"

"It's called a tie, and Sarah says I look handsome."

"Uh-huh. Well as we all know, if she had good taste, she wouldn't be hanging around with the likes of you in the first place."

"Boy, it's great to be back," I said with sarcasm. "Let's get this show on the road. I'm on a deadline. The wedding is tomorrow."

Oren said, "Kah-Rehn, we are ready to launch."

Kah-Rehn was the ship's AI pilot. Her synthesized voice sounded through the speakers. "Everyone, strap in."

I slipped into the chair at my desk opposite Zastra. Straps sprang from the seat and fastened around me in a five-point harness. Just then my phone dinged. I fished it from my pocket to find a text from Sarah.

Love you

I figured I had better answer it, seeing as how I would be out of network for a while. I tapped in:

Love you too

I snaked an arm around the harness to get the phone back into my pocket.

With a rumble, the *Shaymus* lifted off from Earth and soared toward the heavens.

"Welcome back, Gabriel," Kah-Rehn said over the speaker.

"Hi, Kah-Rehn. I hear we're going to a planet with diamonds sticking out of the ground."

"That is correct, Gabriel. The planet Anyi is composed largely of carbon. For centuries Anyians blasted away huge diamond outcroppings to allow houses and roads to be built. Farmers struggled with tilling their fields because the diamonds kept damaging their equipment. Miners were frustrated by striking veins of diamonds when they were looking for metals. When Anyi joined the galactic community, they were shocked to find out those nuisance rocks held considerable value to other people."

I said, "Wow. I wonder if my home planet has anything other worlds want. We have plenty of mosquitos we'd love to export." Surely there was a bat planet somewhere.

We were now in orbit over Earth. Oren's face disappeared from the view screen, replaced by an image of our amazing planet. A *buzz* started up. That was the chrono drive.

As you may have heard, the galaxy is huge. I mean, colossal plus enormous times humongous huge. Think of it this way, the fastest you've ever traveled is probably in a commercial jetliner. If you could take one of those at its normal speed to the nearest star over from our solar system, it would take you fifteen million years. With my luck, the guy in front of me would have his seat leaning back into my lap the whole time.

Fortunately, another technology the alien civilizations have worked out is the chrono drive, which works on the principle that the universe used to be a much smaller place before the cosmos started expanding and gravity began pulling matter together into stars and planets. The chrono drive travels back in time to that cute, little newborn universe, speeds across the much-reduced space to where your destination planet will someday coalesce, then finally returns to the present.

As I watched, Earth deformed. Our sun dissolved. The stars broke apart and blended together. When we reached the time of the early universe, the *buzz* stopped. We sailed across the primordial soup for a minute. Then the chrono drive started up again to take us forward in time. We soon found ourselves orbiting a gray and green planet glittering in the sunlight of twin orange stars.

The *Shaymus* headed down through the atmosphere toward one of the metropolises. We landed in a plaza in front of an impossibly tall skyscraper. Zastra and I left the ship and bounced through surprisingly low gravity toward the building. As we approached, the building's side panels sparkled in the light of the suns.

"Is that made out of what I think it is?" I asked.

"I never have a clue what you're thinking," Zastra said, "but it's diamond."

"Wow! I should have come here for the engagement ring. Is this where Quog lives?"

"This building is his workplace."

We entered the lobby. No front desk or receptionist was there to direct us to Quog. But on a wall opposite the door hung a camera eye with a mouth-like speaker below it. Between the two, positioned like a nose, a microphone extended from the wall.

"May I help you?" asked a digitized voice coming from the speaker.

In sci-fi shows robots are always rolling around or plodding along on awkward legs. But, of course, if a robot doesn't have to move, why build in that functionality?

Zastra said, "We're looking for Quog."

"Did you say Mogh? We have no one by that name."

"No, Quog."

"You are looking for a toad?"

This was working as well as some of my Amazon searches. Either this bot needed a software update, or it had installed a few too many updates.

I gave it a try. "Quog. Quog. Old guy, white beard, about my height."

"Oh, Mr. Quog. What is this regarding?"

"It's a personal matter."

"I am sorry. No personal visitors are allowed during work hours."

"But … um … hasn't he turned in a resignation?"

"One moment please … Yes, he has."

"So then this isn't during his work hours, is it?" I thought my logic was impeccable.

"Quog's status is irrelevant. No personal visitors are allowed during the company's work hours."

Zastra shot me a glare. "My friend here was wrong. This isn't a personal matter. We're here to see Quog on business."

"Thank you. I will inform him. You may wait in the seating area."

We moved across the lobby. While the reception bot was fixed to the wall, plenty of other bots were rolling past us. In addition, I saw species I recognized from other planets — a green Dieren, a copper-colored Bononian, two stubby Delusians.

"What do the Anyians look like?" I asked Zastra.

"There aren't any."

"I'm sorry, what? Kah-Rehn talked about farmers and miners here."

"They don't exist anymore."

"What happened to them?"

"A century ago, their environment was falling apart, so they built an AI designed to save it. The AI determined that the best way to improve the ecosystem was to get rid of the people."

"You mean it …?" I swiped my thumb across my throat in a slashing motion.

"No, of course not. Directly harming people would be counter to its programming. Don't you know anything about AI?"

"Probably not enough."

"The AI simply let the planet become uninhabitable, knowing that once the people died off, nature would recover relatively quickly."

"Yikes."

"What? The AI was right. This place is a paradise now."

I wasn't so sure about that. I monitored an approaching cleaning bot with growing alarm. "What's to keep these bots from killing us?"

"As long as people don't come in sufficient numbers to harm the environment, it's no problem."

We spotted Quog riding an inclined conveyor belt down to the lobby. His eyes lit up when he saw us.

"Gabriel, Zastra, you came." He stroked his bushy white beard, a match to the wispy, snowy hair on his head.

I said, "Hi, Quog. Ready to go?"

He leaned toward me and lowered his voice. "Am I making the right decision here?"

"Earth is your home world, Quog."

"Is it? I don't know. I haven't lived there since I was a boy, and now here I am an old man. I'm going to be lost. I've forgotten nearly everything I ever knew about Earth. For instance, your money, is it called dollies?"

"Dollars. You were close."

He rubbed his forehead. "Dollars. Dollars. And I have no idea about what technologies they have on Earth now."

"Quog, you can figure it out. And you can always call me."

"Call you." His face lit up. "Telephones. I remember telephones."

"There you go. We'll talk everything through. We have the flight and the morning at my house before I have to get married."

"Oh, dear me, am I interrupting your wedding day? I'm so sorry."

"Don't be. Everything is going to work out fine."

"I hope so." Quog gazed around the lobby. A small furry alien with an armadillo shell and wide sloth-like eyes waved to him. He waved back without enthusiasm. "All this has been my life. To leave it and return to quarantined Earth and never speak again of this to anyone …"

His voice trailed off. I hadn't realized until then what a massive disruption this would be for him. I gave him a minute to re-convince himself.

Zastra said, "Do we need to do anything to convert your savings into Earth money?"

An expression close to cockiness wiggled its way across Quog's face. "Oh, I think I have that worked out." He pulled a pouch from a jacket pocket and opened it to show us a mound of sparkling diamonds. "They tell me this is worth around one million Earth dollies … I mean, dollars. I'm a millionaire." He pulled his shoulders back with a gleam in his eye.

I said, "Well, a million bucks isn't what it used to be in the sixties. Don't get me wrong, it's still quite the nest egg. You'll be fine. You just won't be running in the same circles as Bill Gates and Oprah. I didn't know you were loaded, Quog."

"Retirement account, severance pay, reimbursement for sick days not used. Goodness gracious, it all adds up."

"Let's head back to the ship. I'm on something of a tight schedule."

"Relax," Zastra said. "You know the chrono drive can take you back to within a couple of hours of when you left."

"Yeah, I know. But I can't afford to blow this. The sooner I get back, the better I'll feel. Quog, do you have any luggage?"

He glanced down at his outfit. It was a satiny tunic as orange as an Indiana sunset. It hung down to the middle of his thighs over bird's-egg blue pants. "You mean more clothes like this, Gabriel? Do you think they would fit in on Earth?"

"Hmm. Not unless you score a guest spot on *The Mandalorian*."

"Is that what's on TV now?"

"Boy, is it! But no problem. We'll find you some duds when we get back. You might be able to wear some of my stuff. C'mon. The ship is this way. I'll brief you on modern times while we fly."

Chapter 3

Two Tickets to Paradox

Just before dawn, the *Shaymus* dropped out of the Indianapolis sky into a parking lot off Shelby Street behind the line of shops facing Fountain Square.

Quog and I stepped from the ship under a pastel blue sky shifting to orange low in the east, the air pleasantly cool. My plans were to walk to my bungalow a few blocks away and teach him to use my computer and the Internet. He could continue learning about twenty-first-century Earth as I worked through my pre-wedding checklist. He was welcome to crash at my place and housesit for me while I went on my honeymoon until he could find somewhere of his own.

Quog took a deep breath and peered around. "Ah, Earth. After all these years."

"Take it in, buddy," I said. "You're home at last. How does it feel?"

"I admit, Gabriel, I am both elated and terrified."

"Me too, but then, it's my wedding day."

We crunched across the gravel parking lot in the pre-dawn silence. Halfway to the street, I stopped and turned in a circle.

"Is something the matter?" Quog asked.

"I don't know. Something doesn't feel right. I thought the backs of these buildings were painted with murals."

"Maybe they needed a fresh coat of paint."

"Except the paint isn't fresh." The cinder block walls were grayed with soot. I looked at the parking lot below at my feet. "I don't remember this being gravel either."

Quog bent down and came back up with a dime in his hand. "This is money, right?"

"A dime, ten cents. Can I see that?" He handed it to me. "This one has to be old. Dimes have FDR's picture on them … I think. I don't use change much anymore. This one has some Greek god or something."

"Is that a date on it?"

I squinted in the weak light. "Yeah, 1940. This old thing could be worth something." I held it out to him.

"You keep it," Quog said. "I have the diamonds, remember?"

We walked on up Shelby toward the square, which despite the name is triangular as it's where the streets of Virginia, Shelby, and Prospect come together.

Quog asked, "Tell me again about those note thingies."

"Post-It notes? Quog, we talked about cell phones and GPS and social media and streaming TV, and it's Post-It notes you find most amazing?"

"I just don't see how they can stick to something and then come off and still stick again."

I didn't respond. We had reached the corner, and the bottom had fallen out of my stomach. The sun was now coming up along Prospect Street, and I could see all along it.

On the side of the big Fountain Square Theater building hung a movie marquee, which wasn't there last night. The storefronts were different — hardware, a dry cleaner's, a furniture store, even a Hook's Drugs, which hadn't existed since I was a kid. None of these businesses were supposed to be here. The few cars parked along Prospect Street were sedans with rounded fenders, tall roofs, and more colorful paint jobs than I was used to in my era. I was starting to get the impression we weren't in the twenty-first century.

"Oh, no! No, no, no, no."

Across Shelby, where the e-bike rental should have been and wasn't, I spotted a bundle of newspapers tied up in twine in front of a shop. I darted across the street and stood looking down at it. The headline above the fold announced:

HITLER LAUNCHES OFFENSIVE AGAINST YUGOSLAVIA

The date under *The Indianapolis Star* masthead said: *Thursday, May 20, 1943.*

My heartbeat was thundering in my ears. I blinked away black spots from my vision. "C'mon, Quog. We gotta get back to the ship before they leave."

I swiveled like a door on a hinge and darted back up the street, my mouth dry, my stomach swarming with butterflies, not giving a thought to poor old Quog who was lagging behind. To my relief, I saw the *Shaymus* still there in the parking lot. I ran up to it and said, "Lower ramp."

The ramp lowered, but way too slowly for my taste, and I ended up jumping onto it while it was still two feet above the gravel lot. I dashed inside. Deploying the stairs, I swept down to engineering.

"Jace, something messed up. You missed the target. We're not in the right time. I'm lucky I got back here before —"

I stopped short. Something here wasn't right either. Jace had one of the panels open. Several of the components inside were covered in scorch marks. He was poking into the circuitry with a high-tech space tool.

He glanced up with a wrinkled blue brow. "You didn't need to rush. We aren't going anywhere … or any when. The chrono drive is broken."

Quog clanged down the steps behind me, leaning against the railing and breathing heavily.

"What do you mean by broken?" I asked.

"What do you mean what do I mean?" Jace said. "It isn't working. It's malfunctioning. Something blew as we were passing through the last couple of hundred years."

I nodded. "Yeah, I know. We're in 1943."

"We are? That's not bad."

"Not bad?"

He held up his thumb and forefinger a centimeter apart. "On the scale of thirteen billion years, we missed it by this much." He shot me a grin. "At least you have plenty of time before your wedding."

I wasn't amused. "You can fix it, right?"

He waggled his head back and forth in an extremely non-reassuring way. "Yeah, I should be able to. But first, we need to have a meeting with everybody."

I didn't like the sound of that at all. I wanted Jace to tell me it needed only a quick adjustment of the flux capacitor or the phase inhibitors or some such sci-fi gadget to take me back to my real life. Instead, he was standing there grim-faced. We trudged up the spiral staircase to the office, Quog in front of me, Jace bringing up the rear.

Quog said, "Oh dear, I feel terrible about this. It's because of me you're in this predicament. I should never have come back."

Jace said, "Take it easy. Odds are this would have broken on our next trip in any case."

16

"Yeah," I said, "this is not your fault." Inwardly, however, my stomach was doing cartwheels.

As we stepped into the office, Oren came on the view screen. "What is going on?"

Jace reported the situation to him. Zastra, Buad, and Blan listened in concerned silence. Quog stood. I paced.

"Do you have any idea how this happened?" Oren asked.

Jace launched into a monologue of technobabble worthy of an episode of *The Flash*. It had to do with solar flares and fluctuations in the neutrino compensator matrix … or something like that. As I said before, I don't understand how any of this works.

Oren said, "This is regrettable."

"Regrettable?" I said. "I'm going to miss my wedding by virtue of dying of old age a decade or two before it happens. Yeah, it's regrettable all right. Besides, I thought you guys always told me going back in time was bad because it would lead to a loop thingy."

"A causality loop," Jace said.

"Right. A causality loop, which is a bad thing, right?"

"Theoretically, it can be," Oren said. "A causality loop occurs when the future becomes the cause of the past. It creates a temporal paradox, a self-contradictory sequence of actions in which a past event triggers a future event that in turn triggers the past. The universe does not like temporal paradoxes. Until Jace gets this fixed, everyone needs to stay on board. Any act could have unforeseen consequences."

He didn't have to convince me. I've seen *Star Trek* and *The Umbrella Academy* and *Loki* and all the sci-fi shows. Time travel was one of my favorite storylines … until now, that is. I wondered if I needed to slip down the ramp and pitch the dime back into the gravel. But seriously, a dime?

"There's something else," I said. "There's a war going on right now. The whole world is fighting. If either side should find out about this ship and all of you, they would either blow it up immediately or else try to convert it to a war machine."

Oren said, "Then we need to find a better place to hide the *Shaymus* while Jace makes repairs. We should relocate to a less populated part of the world. Gabriel, do you have a suggestion?"

Jace said, "Hold on. We can't fly to the desert or the jungle. I don't have replacement parts for everything that blew. I'm going to have to build some components, which means somebody needs to go out for parts."

Everyone turned their eyes toward me.

I said, "You mean I have to go out and risk destroying the future?"

Zastra rolled her yellow eyes. "Well, obviously, it can't be me."

She had a point. With her lizard face, she would cause riots in the street. I envisioned all those old sci-fi movies with scenes of crowds running in terror from a giant radioactive ant or the blob or evil space aliens.

Oren said, "It has to be an Earthling."

I said, "But what if I … I don't know … step on a flower a butterfly was going to feed on, and the beating of the butterfly wings or lack thereof causes some weird weather event to change life as I know it. I don't want to land back in the present and find this has become the planet of the apes."

"The what?" Blan asked.

"It's a movie."

Buad said, "You know now that you mention it, apes might be an improvement."

I gave him an angry stare. I wasn't in the mood.

"Oh, for Zahn's sake," Zastra said. "Time isn't as sensitive as all that. The broad sweep of history is shaped by social forces, not by freak occurrences."

"Yeah?" I said. "Tell that to the guy who knocked a spring off a shelf and invented the Slinky. Or the doctor who accidentally discovered penicillin by forgetting to clean up after himself. What if word gets out about all of you, and fear sweeps the nation, and President Roosevelt has a heart attack before we get over the hump of this whole war thing?"

"That's why you're going out, not me. Just buy what Jace needs and interact with people as little as possible."

"On the other hand," I said, "maybe I could try to improve the timeline a little while I'm here. I mean, it's probably too late to kill Hitler, but suppose I drop a hint about the Battle of the Bulge or the Kennedy assassination. What if I could do something to keep Sarah from marrying that jerk of a first husband who broke her heart? But wait, then Lucas wouldn't be born, and he's a fantastic kid."

Oren said, "Quog, I think you should go with Gabriel and keep an eye on him."

"I was kidding," I said.

Quog said, "Perhaps I could be of more use here. My first job after my kidnapping was fetching parts at a spaceship repair depot. I was cheaper than a bot since they didn't feed me much. Granted, my knowledge is dated, but I do know a phase inverter from an ionic capacitor."

Blan said, "It's more likely Gabe needs somebody to babysit him."

"Hey, this is my planet," I said, "and I happen to know a lot about this period from old movies. I'll do fine. But you can come, Quog. It might help you reintegrate into society. What do you need, Jace?"

"Some programmable integrated circuits and wiring."

"Yeah, about that. Integrated circuits haven't been invented yet."

"How about transistors? Surely, they have transistors."

"If I recall correctly, we're a few years too early."

"Then what do they have?" Jace asked.

"I think they did most things with vacuum tubes and magnetic relays."

"You're kidding me."

"Sheesh," said Buad, "we're in the stone age here. How are you guys fighting this war? Spears and arrows?"

That earned him a dirty look from yours truly. Nobody insults the US military of World War II. "Can't you replicate what you need?"

"Some of it, yes," Jace said. "But some of these pieces are proprietary and have anti-replicator chips built in."

"What? I thought it was only us Earthlings who let the lawyers set rules to make life more difficult."

"Get what you can. I can construct it. This could be fun," Jace said with a chuckle. "It will be like my primary school science fair project."

"Your science fair project was building a chrono drive? All I did back in school was demonstrate that Skittles dissolve in water."

Zastra said, "That's why Jace is doing the repairs, and you're just shopping."

Chapter 4

My Life as a Counterfeiter

So the plan was set. I would purchase parts, Jace would fix the chrono drive, and we would get back to the twenty-first century in time for my wedding.

"Gabriel, do you have Earth money to procure the repair parts?" Oren asked.

"Ooh. Not as such," I said. "Credit cards haven't come around yet. And they've changed the look of cash over time. The few bucks I have on me would never be accepted here … I mean, now … I mean, in this period. Man, this time travel stuff is confusing."

Quog said, "We have the dime I picked up in the parking lot."

"Sure, but I don't see how ten cents is going to help us much. Things are cheaper back in this time, but I doubt we can buy everything Jace needs for a dime."

Oren said, "Perhaps not with a single dime, but what about many dimes?"

"What do you mean?"

"You can use the replicator."

The *Shaymus* had a replicator sitting down in the galley. Mainly we used it to make food. It had Rhegedian recipes for Jace; seed recipes for Buad and Blan; and squishy, squirmy dishes for Zastra. I had programmed in such Earth delicacies as coffee, donuts, tacos, and pizza, all of which proved to be surprising hits with the aliens. To program it, all you had to do was sacrifice one example item. The replicator broke it down to a molecular level and stored the information in a file. From then on, it could make an exact copy for you at any time using a supply of quarks and electrons it kept on hand, whether you were talking hamburgers or hand tools … or dimes.

Jace, Quog, and I went downstairs to the crew level and around the hall to the galley. I placed the dime on the counter underneath the replicator.

I said, "Program replicator, please. File under the name dime."

With a *hum*, a beam scanned the coin, and it disappeared. A minute later, the replicator dinged, indicating that the instructions had been worked out and stored.

"How many are you going to make?" Quog asked.

"I don't know. If I were buying electronic parts in my time, I might need fifty or a hundred bucks. Back here, who knows? Maybe twenty dollars' worth?"

"That's an awful lot of dimes, Gabriel."

"You're right. Let's start with ten bucks. Replicate one hundred dimes, please."

The pile appeared on the counter nearly the size of my fist. I shoveled them into my pants pocket where they made a knot on the side of my leg. I walked around the galley a little to make sure I wouldn't list to one side or jingle-jangle when I moved.

"We'll go with this," I said. "I feel bad about undermining the wartime treasury of the United States government, but I need to get back to my own time."

Quog asked, "Should I go with Gabe or help you, Jace?"

Jace said, "I have things under control here. You go."

"What about my clothes?"

I gave him the once over. "Yeah, that orange number isn't going to fly in this era. You look like George Jetson."

"Ah yes, George Jetson. Ha!"

"The trouble is, these people won't meet him for another twenty years. I think your pants will do all right. How about we replicate my shirt for the top half?"

I slipped out of my suit jacket and pulled off the tie. We offered my shirt to the replicator along with a specification to remove any dirt and DNA from the recipe. Storing the pattern under the name Gabe's Shirt, we then ordered a double and received two clean shirts back. The shirt clone was a little too wide in the chest for Quog's thin frame, but it made up for it by having sleeves a bit too short.

Jace asked, "Do you know where you can pick up the parts?"

I shrugged. "I'm guessing a hardware store or a radio repair shop. Hopefully, there's something nearby. We'll have to walk around and see."

"Be extremely careful, Gabe. Zastra is right about the timeline being resilient, but only to a degree. You are unlikely to do anything to change the outcome of this war or the shape of the world as you know it, but you could easily change an individual's life."

"You mean like when Scotty went back to the 1980s and gave that guy the formula for transparent aluminum?"

"Scotty who? Did something like that happen?"

"In a movie it did. But don't worry. I have dimes to pay for what we need." I patted the side of my leg.

"This isn't a movie, Gabe. Be careful."

"I will. I will."

While I had been counterfeiting, Kah-Rehn flew the *Shaymus* to a more secure location, a clump of spruce trees down in Garfield Park. Which meant we had a thirty- or forty-minute walk to return to Fountain Square. The morning had warmed into a beautiful Indiana spring day. When we reached the square, Quog sat down at the fountain to rest. While he did that, I continued up Shelby and pitched one of my dimes into the gravel parking lot more or less in the spot where we had found the original. No sense in tempting timeline fate.

I returned to Quog and gazed up at the fountain. It was completely different from what stood there in my time. This had a statue of a pioneer family, the dad in buckskins with a rifle in hand, Mom clutching a Bible to her chest, the son holding an ax, and a little girl carrying — well, I couldn't tell what it was — flowers? Knitting needles? A spindle for a spinning wheel? The sculpture seemed anachronistic, pioneers here in the middle of a city with cars and buses whizzing by. What varmint was the dad going to shoot around here? Still, the statue was pretty cool in an old-timey, slice of Americana kind of way.

With Quog rested, we walked along Prospect Street checking out the shops. I got a kick out of looking in the window of the barbershop, which by the way, still existed in my time and miraculously had changed little over the decades.

We first tried the hardware store I had spotted earlier. I was encouraged to see radios in the front window alongside brooms, electric fans, aluminum coffee percolators, and garden tools. A bell over the door dinged as we entered. We strode across a squeaky wooden floor to a display case where a man about Quog's age in a vest and bow tie said, "How may I help you?"

Quog was gawking at everything inside the store, probably using the sights to reconnect long dormant neuron pathways in his brain. He gaped at a display of fishing rods. He poked his finger into an open bin of machine screws. To me, this old shop was a long way from Home Depot. For Quog, after spending decades in an advanced alien society, it must have been mind-boggling.

22

I said, "We're looking for electronic parts to fix an old radio. Tubes, relays, wires, things like that."

I felt a thrill to be back in the game, thinking on my feet, coming up with cover stories on the fly. Other than visiting strange planets and meeting weird aliens, this was the most fun part of working with the Galactic Detective Agency. Even now when technically we weren't investigating a case, it was an adrenaline rush — like improv but with higher stakes.

The man behind the counter ran a hand over his chin. "I have supplies for house wiring — light sockets, outlets, lamp switches, wire, and such, but not tubes or relays. How about instead of getting parts, you buy a whole new one? Our latest model has amazing sound. It would be music to your dad's old ears."

"My dad?"

He bobbed his head at Quog.

"Oh, yeah. My dad. You know, Dad's ears are fine. His eyesight too. We only need the parts. Do you have any idea where we could find them?"

"You might try Sharp's Radio Repair down the street."

"Okay. Thanks." Quog and I turned to go.

With an edge in his voice, the man said to my back. "How come a young man like you ain't in uniform?"

I hadn't thought of that. I was well within draft age by Second World War standards. Turning, I instinctively said, "What?"

He repeated himself. "I said, why aren't you serving our country?"

"What?" So much for thinking on my feet.

"What's the matter with you? Are you deef?"

"Yes. Yes, I am." I nodded and pointed at my ear. "Sorry. It's my hearing. I tried to enlist but failed the physical. Dad's hearing is hunky-dory, but mine isn't. Weird, huh? Probably because of that summer job I had working with a threshing machine."

The clerk raised his voice. "Maybe you want the new radio for you then."

"No, no. We'd rather fix it. Father and son project. Waste not, want not, am I right?"

We left the hardware store and walked down the block.

"Whew!" I said. "Fitting into another time is as hard as fitting in on a different planet. Now, where's that radio repair shop?"

Quog pointed across the street at a storefront with a big console radio cabinet the size of a washing machine sitting on the sidewalk. We walked inside to shelves loaded with radios, electronic testing equipment, and stacks of components all in little cardboard boxes.

A small, balding man in tortoiseshell glasses looked up through a puff of smoke from a soldering wand. "Morning." His necktie was tucked inside his shirt, presumably to keep it from dangling in his work.

"Morning." I eyed the dangerously frayed electrical cord on the wand and made a note not to get anywhere near it.

The man held up the piece he was working on, a heavy metal chassis with a dozen components sticking up from it like some alien cityscape. "Look at that. Good as new. I found this in a junkyard. Only needed a new capacitor, but somebody had thrown it out." He shook his head, his upper lip curling. "You'd be surprised at some of the things people throw out. It's like junking a whole car when it runs out of gas."

"That's people for you," I said.

"It's because nobody understands modern electronics. Electronics, do you know that word?"

"I've heard of it."

He gazed down at his pre-silicon circuit board. "Their loss, my gain. I can use this myself. Or sell it. Do you want to buy a refurbished radio?"

"So that's what this is — radio innards."

"Sure. What did you think it was, a cantaloupe? Here." He slid off his stool and plugged the skeletal radio into a fabric-covered extension cord. Returning to the steel chassis, he adjusted his bifocals and twisted a knob. A *click* sounded, followed by static. The man thumbed another knob, producing bits and pieces of voices and other sounds fading in and out as the tuner slid along the radio dial, finally settling on a big band number with a jazzy clarinet part.

"Wow," I said. "Far out."

"Sure is. This station is coming in all the way from St. Louie."

I made a mental note to watch my use of slang and moved the conversation along. "We need some parts."

He switched off the radio. "We have parts, all right. What are you looking to fix?"

"Not fix as such. We're … um … we're teaching a troop of cub scouts about electronics. We want to build a radio with them."

The man wobbled his head. "Good for you. That's the future. Yes, sir."

"Don't I know it? Let's see what you have."

We loaded up on an assortment of vacuum tubes, some resistors and capacitors, a few electromechanical relay switches, and several feet of wire. The guy tried to add a bunch of testing equipment to the order, but I knew Jace already had tools much more advanced than anything there.

When all was said and done, the total came to seven dollars and eighty cents. The guy wasn't happy to be paid in dimes, but he swept them off into his hand, dropped them into the cash register, and bagged our purchases. We headed back toward the ship, supplies in hand.

On the street, we passed a man with a three-day growth of beard and a hole in his jacket, leaning against a pole outside the drug store. He touched me on the arm and said, "Brother, you have a dime for a cup of coffee?" I had nearly two bucks of dimes left, all of it free money to me. I dug in my pocket and came out with a coin. "Gee, thanks." The man wandered off.

As we passed the movie theater, my eyes automatically went to the poster on the A-frame sandwich board sign out front to see what was playing. In swirling colors, the shadowed face of the heroine recoiled in fear from creepy hands reaching in from the side of the frame.

"Hey, Quog, check it out. They have Alfred Hitchcock, *Shadow of a Doubt*. That ought to be good. Have you ever seen it?"

Quog said, "Goodness no. Nothing like that. I was a kid when the Thomians grabbed me, remember? The only movies my parents took me to were Walt Disney. I recall seeing *Son of Flubber* … oh, and *Bambi*."

"How cool would it be to see a 1940s movie in a 1940s theater? I wonder how much it costs?" I scanned around and found the prices posted on a sign beneath the ticket booth window. "Thirty-cent matinee." I jangled the change in my pocket. "We have the cash and the time. We can drop off these parts with Jace and then come back after lunch. What do you say? We surely can't mess up the timeline sitting in a movie theater."

A grin spread across his face. "You know, Gabriel, that would be fun. It might help me in my adjustment to Earth culture."

Of all the dumb ideas I've had in my life, that one may have been the dumbest.

Chapter 5

You Won't Believe What Happened at the Movies

Jace, on the other hand, didn't approve of our idea at all. "Now, Gabe, we went over the danger to the timeline. You yourself said —"

"Yeah, but now that I've been out, I can see there isn't much risk. Seriously, what am I going to do? Accidentally kill Kurt Vonnegut? Break up David Letterman's parents before he's born?"

"Who are these people?"

"Only Indianapolis's favorite sons. The point is it won't happen. How could it? We'll be snuggled down in movie seats minding our business. I love this time period. This is a tremendous opportunity to experience it."

"I don't know, Gabe. I think you should stay here, keep out of the way of this society."

"We *will* be keeping out of the way. We'll be sitting there in the dark. It'll practically be like hanging around here. Besides, Quog's time wasn't that different from this time. Watching a movie will help him remember the culture. Then all I have to do is bring him up to date on how things are different today. Well, not today. I mean, the present. Not this present, but my present. My point is we can't simply drop him back into twenty-first-century Earth without some enculturation. Back me up here, Quog."

"I do need a reorientation into Earth society," Quog said. "I'm only now realizing how much I've forgotten. Good gravy! They have automobiles, radios, toasters. Those are all mere vague memories to me. I haven't seen any of those things since my kidnapping."

Jace made a face and directed his attention back to his repair work. "I guess. But be careful."

26

"I'm always careful," I said.

He looked up with doubtful eyes. "Your experience in past cases would suggest otherwise."

I had no comment for that. I flicked my head in a c'mon gesture to Quog, and we left engineering for the galley. Quog replicated two bowls of noodles for us, an Antarean dish he found in the replicator. After eating, we set out, taking advantage of the lovely day to admire the flowers and fountains in Garfield Park's sunken garden.

I was taking my time, but Quog asked, "Shouldn't we be getting to the theater, Gabriel?"

"I don't know. I forgot to check what time the movie starts. Not to mention, I don't have any idea what time it is. There isn't a single cell tower on this entire planet to push the time out to my phone. I thought we'd just go there and trust our luck. Do you feel lucky?"

Quog chuckled with a glum look in his eyes. "I haven't felt lucky since the Thomians grabbed me."

"Ah, right. Sorry." What do you say after that? I tried to be upbeat with, "Well, I'm feeling lucky enough for both of us. C'mon. This is going to be fun."

We left the park and headed north, walking through quiet neighborhoods. At one point, while crossing the street, Quog stepped off the curb without looking for oncoming traffic. A white delivery truck blasted by inches from him, horn blaring.

I put a hand on his shoulder and crossed the street with him. When we reached the sidewalk, I said, "Traffic drives on the right. Look to your left when you cross. Well, look to your left first, then the right too. They come from both directions."

He shook his head with a shiver. "Oh my. I forgot all about the dangers of traffic. I'm used to flying cars and hover vehicles that go over you."

A blue and yellow bus swept past us and pulled to the curb at the next corner.

"How about we ride?" I trotted ahead and caught the bus. I told the driver, "My dad is coming right behind me."

The busman, wearing a tie and a peaked cap, scowled. "Make it snappy, bub. Do you have tokens?"

"No, we're … um … we're new in town."

"Seven cents each then."

I dug out two dimes and handed them over. To my absolute delight, the driver popped out my change from one of those cool old-timey, belt-based money changers with tubes for each size of coin. By the time I had the nickel and penny in hand, Quog had joined the party, and we found seats. The bus pulled away, rumbling along the streets to the pungent smell of diesel.

The passengers were a diverse lot. A black mother with a small child, who stared at Quog's full white beard as we entered. A white woman embracing a shopping bag on her lap. A teenage couple holding hands and whispering in each other's ears. Two women in their twenties wearing overalls and bandanas over their hair, no doubt heading to or from wartime factory work. Finally, a white businessman in a sharp, tailored suit, who was ignoring everyone and everything around him behind a newspaper.

Quog leaned over and whispered to me, "This takes me back. In my younger days, I was a tram conductor on a Kahari mining asteroid. It ran back and forth to the mines, back and forth all day long."

"Was that before or after you got your freedom?"

He scratched his bearded chin. "You know, I can't remember. It doesn't much matter, not if you know anything about Kahari mining colonies."

"What about them?"

"Have you heard the saying 'work hard, play hard?' With the Kahari it's 'work hard, work hard.' The tram ran continuously, as did I."

Above the bus windows, colorful posters reminded people of their duty in the war effort. One urged people to buy war bonds. Another showed a Navy destroyer going down in the sea with the caption: *Loose Lips Sink Ships*. Another admonished people to stamp out black markets by using ration coupons. But the one that struck my eye had a guy driving a convertible with an outline of the German Fuhrer in the passenger seat. It said:

When you ride ALONE you ride with Hitler! Join a Car-Sharing Club TODAY!

Wow! They sure knew how to pile on the guilt.

One of the women in overalls said to the other, "Have you heard anything from Kenny?"

"I got a letter," the other one said with an excited smile. She pulled a piece of tissue-thin paper from a pocket and unfolded it carefully. The page had so many cutouts snipped from it, it looked more like a paper snowflake than a letter. "He's in England somewhere. After the censors got through with this, it didn't say much. But he did say he was thinking about me."

The child started singing to himself *Who's Afraid of the Big Bad Wolf* as he gazed out the window at the passing sights. I remembered the song being in a Disney cartoon from about this time. I thought the kid was adorable. So did the factory girls, who grinned and waved at him. The businessman, however, folded down his newspaper to sling a scowl in the boy's direction before making a show of shaking his paper back into place. The mom patted the kid's leg and got him to stop.

We hopped off at Fountain Square and approached the ticket booth. A man accompanied by two young women stood ahead of us at the window. Lucky guy, I thought, especially when the women turned to the side to examine a poster for a coming attraction, and I got a look at their faces.

Not that I, engaged to be married, was checking out other women. But for the sake of the story, it's relevant to remark that if a 1940s cartoon character was standing where I was when they turned, his eyes would have shot a foot or two out from his face with a *boing* sound.

The pair looked enough alike to be sisters, both with black hair and dark eyes. One had more of a Mediterranean complexion. I typecast her as the shy one of the pair since she kept her head down and spoke behind her hand. The other held her chin high and laughed with confidence.

They entered the theater with their tickets, and I ambled up to the window. The teenager behind the glass wore a red jacket with two rows of brass buttons and yellow stripes at the wrists. Perched on his head was one of those caps without a bill that look like a round tin of holiday fudge.

And like the bus driver and the shopkeepers we saw earlier, he wore a tie. Did everyone in this era wear ties? It was hard to believe that over the course of eighty years, we had gone from people selling movie tickets in this kind of garb to buying them from a guy in a t-shirt to finally having them pop out from a computer kiosk with no human interaction at all. Then again, we'd gone from powdered wigs to Civil War sideburns in fourscore and seven as well.

I said, "Two tickets for *Shadow of a Doubt*, please."

The kid chuckled. "That's your only choice, mister."

I had forgotten this was in the days before sprawling cineplexes. In this decade, they had one auditorium and played one movie at a time, except for when it was a double feature.

The kid pulled two tickets off a gigantic roll. "Sixty cents, please."

I dropped the necessary dimes on the counter. "Snappy uniform you have there."

He looked down at it with a half-hearted shrug. "It's okay, I guess. But soon as I turn eighteen next month, I'm trading it in for olive drab. I wanna go punch a Nazi." He raised his dukes and shadowboxed. "Boy oh boy, I'll give 'em the old one-two. Right in the kisser."

"Good for you, kid. Punch one for me too."

Quog and I proceeded through to a spacious lobby as grand as a fine hotel. We trod across ornate carpet so plush it practically invited you to stretch out and take a nap. People were milling about. At the concession stand, a group of three soldiers were buying popcorn and chatting together. The scent of the popcorn wafted on the air. We passed through swinging doors into the large auditorium and cool darkness.

A newsreel was playing, showing scenes of the Axis powers surrendering in Tunisia and victorious American and British troops celebrating. The people were watching it intently. One middle-aged woman sat there in tight-lipped concentration as if hoping to spot a familiar face somewhere in the battalion of American soldiers. The announcer intoned, "And it's on to Europe."

Quog and I moved toward a group of empty seats in the middle of a row, whispering, "Excuse me," as we sidestepped past people. Halfway to the seats, I spotted the trio of soldiers, each holding a popcorn box, sidestepping in from the other side. We stopped and nodded to each other in smiling embarrassment.

"Sorry," the soldier in front said in a stage whisper. "You take the seats."

I swept a hand to offer the spots to them. "Nah. For our boys in the service."

"No, we insist. My mom taught me to respect my elders."

Elders? I didn't think of myself as an elder. Quog yeah, but not me. But looking at them in the flickering light of the newsreel, I pegged them at only eighteen or nineteen. I supposed to them, I must seem like an elder. With the expansion of the military for the war, they probably had colonels my age.

The soldiers backed out of the row and found seats near the front. One of the soldiers leaned forward to say something to the people in the row ahead of them.

Quog and I dropped into the thick upholstered seats, which squeaked as they slid into position. The newsreel ended and was followed by a short episode of the serial, *Adventures of Red Ryder*, which, though it had nothing to do with Christmas, nevertheless reminded me of my favorite holiday movie.

Then came the happy sounds of a Merrie Melodies cartoon. This one had Bugs Bunny battling a gremlin who was trying to sabotage a military plane.

Quog leaned over to me and whispered, "I've seen this one."

"Me too," I whispered back.

At last, the feature film started. Hitchcock had made it dark and brooding, the atmospheric black-and-white of the film itself setting a foreboding tone. Joseph Cotton was alternatingly charming and menacing as both a favorite uncle and a scheming murderer, leaving you both rooting for him to be caught and yet hoping he could somehow get away with it. Or maybe I was sympathetic because I had recently begun my own criminal career as a counterfeiter.

Surprising to me was the steady stream of people getting up in the middle of the flick, leaving, and coming back. I saw the skinny cloth caps of the soldiers popping up several times as they stood to let people pass.

We were in the middle of a scene full of dramatic tension between the characters when the silhouette of a woman jumped up, taking me out of the movie once more. With annoyance I thought, here we go again, another one heading for the bathroom. Except this silhouette didn't move. She stood there and screamed.

My first thought was to wonder why. I mean, the movie wasn't all that intense. Of course, bloody horror movies with teens splitting up for no discernable reason and bad guys who refuse to die hadn't yet been invented. Maybe people in this time weren't used to suspense the way my generation was.

My second thought was surprise that women really did scream like that back in this time. I had always figured it was merely a movie trope. Why would women of this era be so much more screamy than men?

But then the woman spoke, shouting out. "Murder. She's been murdered. My friend. She's … she's dead."

Murmurs spread like a wave across the theater. The movie stuttered to a halt, and the lights came up. Everyone stood and craned their necks. Everyone, that is, except one woman about ten rows ahead of me. She was slumped forward, her clothes drenched in blood, a knife sticking out from the base of her skull.

Chapter 6

What Happened Next

For a few moments, everything was chaos — people shouting, pushing past others, straining to get a glimpse of the dead girl. The ones nearest the body moved as far away as they could, as quickly as they could.

The man I had seen in the ticket line with the two women moved to comfort the woman who had screamed. I recognized her as one of the ones he had been with, the confident one. She appeared far less self-assured now. With a gut-wrenching feeling, I realized the dead woman was the other of the two, the shy one.

Meanwhile, movie patrons were simultaneously flocking either toward the dead body to rubberneck or toward the doors to flee, creating a traffic jam in the aisles. A few may have made it out before a squad of uniformed ushers burst into the auditorium, blocking anyone else from leaving. Armed only with flashlights, the teenage ushers took command of the situation as best they could.

"If everyone would please return to your seats," one of the ushers said in a cracking voice. "Please sit down. Those of you sitting near the … the … person, you can move somewhere else, but please remember where you were sitting. The police are on their way. They'll want to interview everyone."

"Now just a minute," a man in a straw boater hat said. "I need to be going home."

"You can't keep us here," a woman said. She pursed her lips and clutched at her handbag like a life preserver.

The ushers glanced at each other, uncertain of what to do. The one who had spoken whispered something to one of the others, who rushed out. He returned a minute later along with a pear-shaped man of indeterminate age in a well-made dark suit, whom I presumed to be the theater manager.

He had a severe face, a thin mustache, and a nearly bald head, which he held erect like a prairie dog scanning for predators — a prairie dog holding a cigarette between two fingers. Yanking off round wire-rim glasses, he pulled himself up to his full height, which wasn't saying much, and scowled around at the crowd with fierce determination. "Return to your seats, please." His Ss came out as Zs, and the whole thing came out like a threat. The crowd settled down into submission.

Quog and I sat down along with everyone else. He said, "Now I'll never know how the movie ended."

"Don't worry," I whispered. "If we ever return to the present … *my* present, you can probably stream it."

Now, I like solving crimes, but dead bodies are not my cup of tea. I slouched into the seat and tried to ignore the scene straight ahead of me. I took the opportunity with the lights up to appreciate the starry night scene painted on the plaster ceiling high overhead, the fake box seats built along the side walls, the red velvet curtain hanging behind a graceful arch to frame the movie screen.

The manager stationed three ushers at the back door and marched the rest of the squad forward to take up positions around the body. The scowl never left his face.

Before too many minutes had passed, two cops in blue uniforms and peaked caps showed up. They strode forward to the body, relieving the ushers of guard duty.

A voice in the crowd said, "At last, we can get out of here."

One of the cops turned to the crowd with raised hands. "I'm going to ask everyone to remain seated until the detective comes to take your statement."

"When's he getting here?" someone asked.

"I don't *have* a statement," a man said. "Look, I was sitting here in the dark. I didn't see a doggone thing."

A woman said, "If I don't have supper on when my husband gets home, I'll never hear the end of it."

"Remain seated," the cop said with a firm tone. "This is a murder inquiry. It takes priority over supper."

"Not to my husband," the woman said bitterly. Her line drew a laugh.

The two cops leaned over the body, examining it with their eyes, pointing at things. I peered around the hat of the lady in front of me to watch. To me, this was the interesting part, the investigation.

After discussing things over in whispered tones, the cop who had spoken straightened up and said, "Who was sitting in the vicinity?"

The woman who had screamed stood from across the aisle. "I was sitting with her. I'm her roommate."

She seemed more composed now. Something about her — the dark hair, the bright penetrating eyes staring out from a somber face — reminded me of the actress Hedy Lamarr, an early crush of mine when I started getting into old movies back in high school.

"Your name, miss?" the cop asked.

"Muriel Marshall." She kept a white-knuckle grip on the seat back in front of her. "What am I going to do?" She looked across the theater as if asking the crowd for help. "I need to tell her family. I … What do I do with her things?"

"Let's not worry about any of that right now, miss. We'll make the notification, and the rest will work itself out."

"Thank you," she said in a quiet voice. She sat down.

"I was with them," a man's voice said.

"Who said that?" asked the cop. "Stand up."

It was the man I had seen with the two women. He was thin and had slicked-back hair. I put him down for late thirties. "Peter Ryan. I lodge at the same rooming house with them."

The cop noted the name and then scanned the crowd again. "Who else sat near here?"

One of the soldiers stood, the one I had spoken to when we were finding seats. "We were in the row behind." He was a good-looking kid, and with the lights up, I thought something about him seemed familiar, though I couldn't place it.

"All right," the cop said. "The detective will want statements from you too. Who else?"

"This guy," the soldier said, pointing to another man. "He was beside us, a couple of seats away."

The man being pointed at gave the soldier a cold stare. He was young, though the glower made him appear older, dressed in a suit and fedora like me. He wore a hard, sour expression, the kind of face Bogart used in his early gangster movies.

"And who are you?" the cop asked, the tone in his voice telegraphing the fact that he pegged the guy for a ne'er-do-well.

"Ray Noonan," the man said as if it was supposed to mean something.

"Noonan," the cop said, making a note of it.

An older man stood with a groan and rocked back and forth from one foot to the other. Stringy gray hair hung down around a round face. He squinted and spoke with a creak in his voice that reminded me of the actor Walter Brennan. Not the younger Walter Brennan of this era, but the old Walter Brennan from 1960s Westerns.

"I reckon I should tell you my wife and I — my name's Lester Potter and this is my wife, Nellie — we were sitting in the same row with Irene, down a bit."

"Irene?" asked the cop.

"The dead girl, Irene … Giordano."

The other cop leaned over to his partner and said, "You shoulda asked her name first thing."

The first cop ignored the comment. "How do you know her, Mr. Potter?"

"Hmm?"

The cop spoke louder. "I said, how do you know her?"

"Who?"

"The deceased."

Potter looked confused. "I don't know any Denise."

"The dead girl."

"Oh. You mean Irene. That's her name. We own the rooming house where she lives … um … lived." He nodded toward Muriel Marshall and the slick-haired Peter Ryan. "She roomed at our house along with those two."

"Okay, thanks," the cop said.

Lester Potter stared at the cop for a moment. Then he scratched at his cheek in a distracted manner and sat back down.

"Did he say Irene Giordano?" A voice sounded from the back of the theater. He stood, an older man, maybe early sixties. Unlike Lester Potter, his white hair was perfectly combed.

"Yes, sir," said the cop. "You knew her?"

"She worked for me."

"And you are?"

"Dr. Arthur Hatch. Irene was my office nurse."

"Did you come to the movie with her?"

"No. No. We didn't have any patients scheduled, so I gave her the afternoon off. I had no idea she was here."

"Thank you, Dr. Hatch."

We were putting together an all-star cast here. The dead girl's roommate bore a resemblance to Hedy Lamarr. This Noonan guy was impersonating a tough, young Bogart. Lester Potter, the old guy was Walter Brennan. If you squinted, the white-haired doctor could pass for Christopher Plummer. And the theater manager had the kind of chilling looks to be cast in a movie as the evil scientist. I strained to catch a look at Nellie Potter and was pleased to find her wearing a faded housedress and a hard, judgmental expression reminiscent of Margaret Hamilton, the witch in *The Wizard of Oz*.

I couldn't think of any celebrities the guy with the slick hair resembled — Peter Ryan he had said — though I figured if I knew my 1940s character actors better I could probably have come up with a match. So I was totally expecting the detective, when he showed up, to be a double for Spencer Tracy.

In that I was disappointed. The guy who walked in and approached the uniforms had dark bushy eyebrows and jowls forming around a soft, tired face. His suit hung loose on him as if the pressures of the job had somehow shrunk him from a once larger size. He wiggled two fingers at one of the cops. "What 'cha got, Sergeant?"

They conferred for a couple of minutes, then the tired man scanned the audience and said in a weary voice, "Folks, I'm Detective Vukovich. Okay, here's what's gonna happen. These two officers are going to take everyone's statements except for …" he consulted a notebook. "… Dr. Hatch, Muriel Marshall, Peter Ryan, Ray Noonan, the three soldiers, and Mr. and Mrs. Potter. I'll talk to all of you myself." He bobbed his head at the mustached theater manager. "Also, you. Your name is Beck?"

"Yes. Carl Beck. Carl with a C." There was that accent again, a German accent.

A grin tried and failed to find its way to the detective's face. "Right, a C. Not a K, which would be way too German, right?"

Beck pursed his lips without replying.

Vukovich said, "Everybody, as soon as you give your statement, you'll be free to go."

We sat and watched the interview process begin. The uniformed cops started at the back of the theater, presumably because those people had the least information and could be dismissed quickly. Vukovich went to work on Beck.

Meanwhile, a team of three in white lab coats entered and congregated around the body. While two of them stood around hanging onto a stretcher, the other one leaned over the dead woman, adjusting thick spectacles for a better look.

After a minute he called Vukovich over and talked to him in hushed tones. The detective bent over the body himself. When he straightened up, he held something in his hand inside a handkerchief. The lab coat guy in glasses nodded to the other two, who lifted the body to the stretcher. The trio left while all of us watched in silence.

In their wake, Vukovich spoke to the crowd, "Does anyone here have the initials F. L.?"

Murmurs swept around the theater. One of the soldiers, the one who looked familiar, stood. "My name is Francis Lake … Frank Lake."

That's where I recognized the guy — from playing catch with him and sitting on his lap while he made funny faces. Frank Lake was my grandfather. I was wearing his suit. He had been a soldier in World War II. He sure didn't look the way I remembered him with silver hair, glasses, and slightly overweight. But now that I knew, I could see it in his eyes and nose and chin. And because of me, because I had taken his seat, he had ended up sitting right behind the murdered girl.

Muriel Marshall stood and glared at my grandfather. "Frank Lake, you low life. You killed her." She turned to Vukovich. "Frank Lake kept asking Irene for a date and wouldn't take no for an answer."

The detective opened his hand to reveal a pocketknife with a brown handle nestled inside the handkerchief. "Well, Private Lake, if you were looking for your knife, I found it. Funny thing, it was in the victim's neck. You're under arrest for the murder of Irene Giordano."

Chapter 7

I Pick up a New Alias

Quog whispered to me, "Did that man say his name was Lake? That's your name."

"I'm well aware of it. It's my grandpa."

"Dear me. What do you think —"

"Shhh." I patted his arm. I wanted to watch the proceedings. The cops were cuffing Grandpa's hands in front of him and leading him up the aisle. Our eyes met briefly as he passed our row. He looked embarrassed, frightened.

After the swinging doors closed behind them, someone called out, "Well, with them leaving, now who's going to interview us? When are we getting out of here?"

"Keep your shirt on," Vukovich said. "We'll get to you when we get to you. They'll send a couple more officers over in a few minutes."

"Really now, Detective. You have your man. Surely, you can let us go."

Vukovich glared the person into silence.

I placed a hand over my mouth and muttered to my translator bot connection. "Oren. Oren, we have a problem." Yeah, translator bots can be networked together over intermediate distances for remote communication. I told you they were cool.

His sonorous voice sounded in my ear. "What is it, Gabriel?"

"I can give you all the details later, but for now, the gist of it is that I may have changed the timeline and caused my grandfather to be arrested for murder. I mean, I don't know for certain that he wasn't charged with murder in the timeline I always knew. He told me a lot of stories but never anything like that. But is getting arrested the kind of thing you tell your grandkids?"

"Gabriel, you're babbling. Return to the *Shaymus* immediately. We need to discuss this."

"I can't. Well, not yet anyway. The police are taking statements. We'll be there as soon as we can."

"Understood."

I leaned toward Quog. "Wait here. I'm going to snoop."

I stood and stretched my arms with a twist of my back. Gazing around at the architecture as if I were still interested in it, I murmured, "Kah-Rehn, tie into my visual translator bots and record an image of the people." That was another cool thing the bots could do.

I sidestepped through a row to get a better view of Dr. Hatch. Then I came back and meandered a few rows toward the blank screen, eyeballing the Potters, the two remaining soldiers, and Muriel Marshal and Peter Ryan. I checked for signs of blood splatter on each of them but didn't find any.

Detective Vukovich was interviewing Ray Noonan only three rows ahead of me. I propped one shoe up on the armrest of an aisle seat and retied the lace while straining to hear what they were saying.

"What can I tell you, Detective?" Noonan said with a shrug. "I had the afternoon off, and I came to the movies."

"The afternoon off from what, Noonan? Where are you working nowadays?"

"I work security at the Kit Kat Club."

"You do? Maybe you can help us. We had a report of bookmaking and loan-sharking going on there. Know anything about that?"

"No, Detective. I think you must be misinformed. Terrible how some people gossip, isn't it?"

"Or maybe this Irene Giordano was on the hook to you, and you followed her here to send a message."

Noonan made a sour face. "Why are you trying to pin this on me, Vukovich? You already arrested that soldier. I came here to watch a movie. I love Hitchcock, don't you? Have you seen *The 39 Steps*? Let me tell you, Detective, I was on the edge of my seat. The guy in that movie, he could really outfox the cops."

"Yeah, yeah. I'd love to talk cinema with you all day, Noonan, but I have things to do. Did you know the girl?"

"Never saw her before in my life."

"She's not the daughter of someone from a rival gang? Or related to someone in the Chicago mob?"

"Mob? Gang? Detective, I don't move in those circles. And I don't appreciate what you seem to be implying about this unfortunate young woman."

"Listen, Noonan. I'm going to check everything out about this girl, and if I find a connection to you, you'll be sorry. You hoods all think the heat's off now with the FBI focused on war espionage. But, let me tell you, the Indianapolis Police Department still has their eyes on —"

I looked up when Vukovich cut off. He was staring straight at me. "You need something, bud?" he asked.

I smiled. "No, Officer. Just stretching my legs. I've been sitting awhile."

"Well, beat it."

I returned to my seat beside Quog.

"Learn anything?" he asked.

"Not much, but it sure was entertaining. Like watching an old cops and gangsters movie."

"A movie where your grandfather is arrested for murder."

"Don't remind me."

I watched the two soldiers across the aisle from us and up a couple of rows. They huddled together, their faces wearing grave expressions. One of them was a skinny kid with red hair and freckles. The other was muscular with dark Latino eyes. I stood and moved in their direction. When they looked up, I nodded to them. The dark one nodded back, which I took as permission to approach.

"Boy, this is something, isn't it?" I said as if just making conversation. Their faces were young and innocent. I would have bet good money that neither of them needed to shave on a regular basis. They looked like high school kids waiting outside the principal's office after being caught in a teenage prank. "Sorry about your buddy."

The redhead merely stared at me, eyes like fried eggs in a skillet.

The other one said, "I'll say. The sergeant is gonna bust our chops when we get back. To say nothing of poor Frankie. What's gonna happen to him? He could miss out on the whole war, wasting away in a jail cell." His gaze dropped as if he were trying to read the future, as with tea leaves in a cup, from the pattern of smashed popcorn kernels strewn across the floor.

I asked, "You don't think he did it, do you?"

"Frankie? No. I'll give you the dope on Frank Lake. He's as honest as the day is long. This whole thing stinks." The redhead was still mute, letting the other one do all the talking.

"Will the Army intervene?" I asked. "Will they send a lawyer for him?" I strained to remember the plot details of *A Few Good Men*.

"Who knows, mister? We're buck privates. The only thing they tell us is what to do."

The red-haired soldier finally spoke. "What are they gonna do with him, the police?"

I said, "They'll interrogate him. They'll talk to you too. You can put in a helpful word for him. If you can swear he didn't stab that woman, tell them. But don't lie."

"This is bad business. This is crummy."

I asked, "What about his folks? Will somebody be telling them?"

The dark one shook his head. "Beats me, but I hope somebody gets him off the hook." He eyed the redhead.

I patted him on the shoulder and walked away, wondering what their futures held. Would they hit the beaches on D-Day? Would they live to hold a grandchild on their laps like Grandpa did with me? Or would that even still be Grandpa Frank's future? I walked back across the aisle and dropped into my seat.

Detective Vukovich had released Ray Noonan. Now he moved toward us. Evidently, my eavesdropping had warranted priority treatment. Stepping into our row, the detective leaned against the back of the seat in the row ahead of us and crossed one ankle over the other. "Okay, what are your names?"

I started to give my real name but stopped when the thought hit me that having the same last name as the accused would be suspicious and raise way too many unanswerable questions. You try explaining to the cops how you're older than your grandpa.

My brain flashed through the names of all the fictional characters who hadn't yet been hatched in this time period. Luke Skywalker, James Kirk, Arthur Dent, Jim Phelps. I landed on one of my favorite fictional detectives from TV reruns. "Columbo."

"So you're Italian like the dead girl. Did you know her?"

I was almost offended for my pretend ethnicity. As if all Italians know each other. Should I ask Detective Vukovich if he was acquainted with all Serbians or whatever his ancestry was? It was a reminder to me of how people tended to view identity in this era.

"No, we've never met."

"First name, Mr. Columbo?"

With a fluttery feeling, I realized I didn't know the fictional Columbo's first name. Did the TV character even *have* a first name? I blurted out, "Lieutenant. I mean … Lou Tenant … Louis Tenant Columbo. Call me Lou."

"This your dad?"

"Yeah. Quog … I mean, Doug." I faked a laugh. "Boy, this murder has me all discombobulated."

"Doug Columbo. Douglas?"

"That's right," Quog said.

"Address?"

"We're not from around here," I said.

"Visiting for the day?"

"You guessed it."

"Where from?"

"Tearho Indeena," Quog said.

"He means Terre Haute, Indiana," I hurried to say, covering up for his muddled memories of Earth. "Dad's had a few health problems. It affects his speech sometimes."

Quog nodded sheepishly.

Terre Haute was Quog's boyhood home. I thought it a smart idea to name it as our hometown. That way if there were follow-up questions, Quog could answer from memory … maybe.

"They don't have picture shows in Terre Haute, Mr. Columbo?" the detective asked.

Quog said, "My, you do ask a lot of questions, Detective."

Vukovich gave him a dead stare. "I'm a cop. You expect me to yodel?"

I said, "We were here on business — picking up some specialized electronic parts."

"What for?"

I grinned at him. "Can't say. Army business."

That slowed him down. The war took priority over everything, and secrecy was essential. Scowling, Vukovich dug in one of the pockets of the baggy suit and came out holding a green tin the shape of a lipstick tube. The word *Tums* was written on the side. He unscrewed the lid and popped a tablet into his mouth. As he chomped on it, he said, "Okay. I'll let it go … for now … unless I find out something about you I don't like. What did you see of the murder?"

"Not much," I said. "We were too far back. But here's what I did see. A whole bunch of people were getting up and down and passing through there during the movie. Any one of them could have stabbed that lady. It didn't have to be the soldier. The soldiers were about the only people who weren't going in and out, shuffling along there."

"You think somebody else reached into that soldier's pocket while he was sitting there, stole his pocketknife, and used it to kill the girl?"

"It might have been stolen before he ever sat down. We saw the soldiers standing around in the lobby getting popcorn, isn't that right, Quog … I mean, Dad?"

"Why do you keep saying Quog?"

"Sorry. It's an old Sicilian word for daddy."

Vukovich looked skeptical. "I thought Italians said papa."

Quog jumped in, navigating the conversation toward safer waters. "Yes, the soldiers bought popcorn. I must say, it smelled delicious. I haven't had popcorn since I was a kid."

"You haven't? Why don't you get you some? It's cheap enough. Are you two going back to Terre Haute tonight?"

"Um … probably," I said. "We haven't decided. There's a lot to see here in town."

"Sure. Well, I guess we're done here. Wait. In the unlikely event, I need to follow up, what's your address in Terre Haute?"

I said, "Seven forty-two Evergreen Terrace." It was the first address that came to mind.

Vukovich jotted it down. "All right. You're free to go."

I asked, "Did any of the witnesses actually see the soldier stab her?"

He squinted at me. "And why should I tell you, Columbo? Am I supposed to report in with you?"

"No, but I have an interest in the case."

"You do? And why is that?"

"Well … it happened right here in front of me. Besides, the soldier is just a kid straight off the farm. I can't imagine —"

Vukovich interrupted me. "How do you know he came from a farm? Do you know him?"

"I … I mean, he looks like a farm kid, right? Strong bones from all that milk."

"Hmm." He waved his arm toward the door. "Go."

We left the theater and headed back to Garfield Park and the ship. For the sake of speed, I kept my eye out for buses as we walked but didn't see any. Meanwhile, my mind kept replaying the events. I should have backed out of the row when I saw the soldiers coming. I shouldn't have even been at the theater in the first place. What was going to happen to my grandpa? How big of a mess had I made? I desperately needed to discuss this with Oren.

"C'mon, Quog. We need to hustle."

I picked up the pace. The more I stewed about the situation, the faster I walked. Before I knew it, I was leaving my older companion huffing and struggling to keep up. I tried to slow down, but I was too worked up.

"Gabriel, wait … Gabriel, if you could just … Okay … Okay, you go on … I'll catch up."

Chapter 8

It's About Time

"What is the penalty for murder on this planet?" Oren asked.

We were again gathered in the office — Oren on-screen, Buad and Blan in their habitat, Zastra and me at our desks. Even Jace had taken a break from working on the chrono drive to join the confab. He and Quog sat in the red leather chairs that faced the view screen, Quog still red-faced and breathing heavily from our dash back.

"Death," I said. "They execute convicted murderers. I think they're using the electric chair at this time."

"What is this electric chair?" Zastra asked. "It sounds like some kind of massage recliner."

"Not even close. They strap you in a big wooden chair and zap you with enough electricity to kill you."

Her yellow eyes blinked. "And here I thought my species was harsh. What is wrong with you people?"

I said, "If it helps, we don't do that anymore." Truthfully, I wasn't at all sure about that being the case in every state.

Oren said, "From what you described of the events in the theater, it sounds as if the case against your grandfather is strong."

Quog said, "The police detective seems to think so."

"But he couldn't have done it," I said.

"What makes you believe that?" Oren asked. "What evidence do you have?"

"The evidence of my whole life. He's my grandfather. I knew him. He was a kind man. He used to carry spiders out of the house rather than step on them. Grandpa Frank couldn't murder anyone."

Oren said, "You might be surprised, Gabriel, by what people are capable of if sufficiently motivated. Remember, he is a soldier. He has been trained to kill."

"No, I can't accept that."

"Has your father already been born?"

The implications of the question worried me. "No, not in 1943. My grandparents didn't marry until after the war. My dad was born in the fifties. Why do you ask?"

Buad whistled. "Classic grandfather paradox."

"What?"

Buad shook his feathers. "You've never heard of the grandfather paradox, doofus? What do they teach you in school on this screwy planet? It's a classic example of temporal physics. Do you want to explain it to him, Brother?"

"Sure," Blan said, "let me educate you, pinhead. Suppose you have a time machine. You travel to the past and somehow manage to kill off one of your grandparents before they have any offspring. That changes the timeline as you know it, including your own birth, which would then no longer happen. Thing is, if you don't get born, then you can't travel back in time and kill your grandparent. In which case you *are* born, so you *can* travel back in time and kill your grandparent. Do you see the paradox here? It's like a ... a worm with no end."

I spun my finger around in a circle a few times, thinking it through. "Yeah, but I haven't killed him."

Jace said, "You may have set events in motion that cause his death. It amounts to the same thing."

I stared at Jace. He stared at me. At least he didn't say he told me so. He didn't have to. Those words were already running on a loop inside my head.

"Does this mean I'm going to start fading away like Marty McFly?"

"What?" asked Jace. "Who? Is this another of your movie references?"

"Yeah, and a great one too."

"It doesn't work like that, Gabe. You do realize Earth movies are not your best source of information on temporal physics ... or any kind of physics, for that matter."

I was relieved, if only slightly, to find out that at least I wouldn't be turning into a ghost anytime soon. But I was still concerned. "You guys always told me this sort of paradox thing could confuse the universe so much it just kind of blows up."

Jace bobbled his head up and down. "It can."

"Then why are we all still here? Does that mean Grandpa won't be convicted, and my dad and I will still be born?"

"It is possible," Oren said. "However, a much more likely explanation, given the evidence against your grandfather, is that the universe resolved the paradox by splintering the timeline."

"Splintering the timeline. You mean like with a multiverse, parallel universe kind of thing — one where I do exist and another one where I don't?"

"Not complete universes, I'm afraid, Gabriel. The splinter timeline would only exist from this moment to the time when you left Earth with us on this last trip. It would exist only long enough for you to be born and travel to this time where you cause your grandfather's arrest."

"What are you saying? The timeline I exist in, the one I know and love, ends the moment I stepped on the *Shaymus*?"

"If I am correct, yes."

I swallowed. Hard. "But I liked that timeline. All my stuff is there. Sarah and Lucas are in that timeline."

Jace said, "They're in the other timeline too — the one that continues. But most likely you aren't."

My head was spinning. My chest felt compressed like that time in grade school when Joshua Watkins had knocked the air out of me with a dodgeball. My stomach had taken a dive off the high board. "Then if I go back to my time … then what?"

Blan said, "You go poof."

I stared around at Jace, Zastra, and Oren, waiting for someone to contradict him. Nobody did. "How do we fix this?"

Oren flipped up a hand. "One option is we don't fix it. While you can't return to your old life, you could live the next eighty years in this timeline. I think that would cover your normal lifespan, wouldn't it."

"Yeah, and then some. But the thing is … I had plans back in that other timeline. A wedding. Nonrefundable tickets for a honeymoon. There's a couple of new movies I was looking forward to." I hopped from my seat and began pacing. "There has to be something we can do."

Zastra said, "Calm down, Gabe."

"Calm down? Calm down? I don't want to be stuck here … or now … or however you say it. They won't have the Internet until I'm an old man. Television hasn't even been invented yet. I'd have to talk to people on the phone instead of texting them."

Quog said, "It won't be so bad."

"It won't be so bad? I should look on the bright side here? Is that what you're saying? Sure. Sure. I mean, I guess I could get in on the ground floor of software programming. I could pick up some IBM stock now, some Apple stock when the seventies roll around. I could bet on the 1970 Cincinnati Reds and the 1985 Chicago Bears. Man, I wish I had memorized more sports trivia. Wait, could I find myself as a little kid and warn me not to take this trip? If I live that long, I mean?"

Jace said, "No. Whatever you do, you can't meet yourself. That's one of the axioms of temporal physics. Besides, it wouldn't do *you* any good. It would only create another splinter timeline. Because you did board the *Shaymus*, any you who doesn't come aboard wouldn't be you. It's a different you."

I dropped back in my seat. I lowered my head and pounded it on the desk a few times. Taking a breath, I looked up. "Okay. You said that was one option, Oren. There's another one?"

"We can solve the murder. It is what we do, you know."

Now, that was a plan I could get behind. I had never seen Oren Vilkas fail to solve a case. "Why didn't you say that to begin with? Right. Sure. Let's find out who really did it. Would that restore the timeline?"

Jace said, "Possibly."

"What do you mean, possibly? Why wouldn't it be definitely?"

"There's no way of knowing if in the original timeline the police caught the real killer. We might end up changing more things. But at least it would return your grandfather to his prior trajectory."

"His approximate prior trajectory," Oren said. "This experience of being arrested will change him in ways we can't predict."

"I'll settle for that. My existence lies along that trajectory. Let's do this."

Oren said, "For obvious reasons, Gabriel will have to shoulder most of the responsibility of the investigation. If need be, we can use Buad and Blan for surveillance and Quog to some extent."

"While they're doing that, what am I supposed to do?" Zastra asked.

"Unfortunately, very little other than advising on the case. No one on this planet has ever seen anyone like you. And they shouldn't."

She crossed her scaly arms in front of her and scowled. "Fine. I'll just sit here." She said it with a bitter tone. She wasn't used to being kept on the sidelines.

"So what's the program?" I asked.

Oren said, "Let's go back over the suspects you mentioned. Tell me more about them. Start with the two people the murdered woman was with."

"Muriel Marshall was the roommate. I don't know much about her except she screamed when she discovered the body and helped cast suspicion on Grandpa by saying he was pestering Irene for a date. I suppose the scream is an indication she isn't the murderer."

"Unless it's an act," Blan said. "If you ask me, the bigger the show of grief, the more likely it is the person did it."

"Could be. The man with them was named Ryan. Peter Ryan, I think. He said he lived at the same boarding house as the women. He could be a suspect."

Zastra said, "And didn't you say the house owners were there also?"

"Yeah. An old couple. The Potters. The old guy seemed barely with it. The woman looked like she could take the fun out of a circus."

"What about this Noonan person?" Oren asked.

"Ray Noonan. He's a tough guy. Or at least he thinks he is. I think the cops thought so too. Murder might be right up his alley."

"Anyone else?"

"Those were the ones sitting closest to Irene. Lots of other people were in the theater, including the doctor she worked for, which as coincidences go, is stretching it."

"I don't trust coincidences. Let's add him to the list as well. Did you see the doctor moving around during the vid?"

"Everybody who moved — and there were plenty of them — were no more than silhouettes in the darkness. I couldn't tell who was who. For all I know, one of the ushers could have slipped in and done it. Or that manager. He was creepy enough. If I were casting a war movie, he would be the Nazi bad guy."

"If the man seems disreputable, start with him. Go back to the theater and talk to him along with any of the ushers or anyone else you can find. They may have seen someone acting suspiciously. After that, visit the boarding house."

"Okay. Okay." I rubbed my forehead, trying to find a way to focus.

"Hey, Gabe." It was Buad. He had flown over to my desk and was looking at me with what appeared to be compassionate eyes. "Don't worry. We'll get you home, got it?"

I nodded, feeling better.

"Knucklehead." There it was.

Despite being worried about getting back for my wedding and borderline terrified about being wiped from existence, I found within myself a fair measure of excitement about this investigation. I was going to be a real 1940s detective. I was going to be like Philip Marlowe and Sam Spade, following clues through the city. Granted, Indy wasn't San Francisco or Los Angeles, but it was my city, or at least, an earlier version of my city. I was going to solve this case — with Oren's help, of course — and send somebody up the river to the big house. It would have been fun if the ante hadn't been raised so high.

"We can do this, right?" I asked. "We can catch the murderer and free my grandfather so he can safely go off to war?" There's an odd phrase for you. But I greatly preferred him fighting his way across Europe compared to sitting in prison.

Oren said, "We'll solve it. Bring me the evidence."

"Oh, I will." I pulled my fedora lower over one eye, ready for action. "You bet I will."

Chapter 9

My Grandpa the Jailbird

Oren wanted me to start the investigation at the theater. But there was another place I needed to go first. However, to find it, I would have to do some asking around.

Walking up Shelby Street, I stopped a man. "Hey, pal, if somebody got arrested, where would they take him?" The guy gave me the stink eye and walked on.

I ducked into a shoe store on Prospect and asked the same question. The clerk took a step back and raised his chin. "You just keep moving along, buddy. The criminal element is not welcome here."

"I'm not a criminal," I said. "I have a friend in trouble."

"Yeah, and I have a shotgun under this counter."

I raised my hands and backed out of the store. Finally, I received some help from a guy heading into the side entrance of the Fountain Square building.

"Yeah, mister, what you want to do is go to police headquarters. It's on Alabama Street."

"Does a bus go there?"

"Sure does."

I walked to a bus stop and waited. When a coach pulled up, I told the driver where I wanted to go. He said I had the wrong bus but told me what number to watch for and where to catch it. I did. That bus dropped me off in front of an elegant three-story structure fronted with gray Indiana limestone. I was pretty sure the spot was a parking lot in my time, which I thought was a shame.

I entered and approached a uniformed officer at a tall counter. He looked me up and down before asking in an accusing tone, "Can I help you?"

"Hi," I said. "I would like to speak to a prisoner, Frank Lake. He was brought in this afternoon."

"What business do you have with him?"

I had already decided not to say I was a relative. Sure, it might get me in to see him, but I wouldn't be able to explain myself to Grandpa if someone relayed that information to him.

"I'm his attorney."

The officer made a face as if he had bitten into a lemon marinated in vinegar. Apparently, he wasn't a fan of the legal profession. "Name?"

"Louis Columbo." I had been tempted to go with Matlock or Jack McCoy, but I thought I might run into Detective Vukovich and didn't want him to catch me using a false name ... or rather, a different false name.

"Okay. Follow me."

He led me down a hall to an interview room. The walls were cinder block. A wooden table with metal chairs sat in the middle. And an honest-to-goodness metal pendant light with a high-wattage bulb hung from the ceiling. I couldn't keep from grinning. I had seen this same room in so many old movies. This was where they gave somebody the third degree.

"Have a seat," the cop said. "We'll bring him in in a minute."

It turned out to be more like fifteen or twenty minutes before they finally escorted Frank in. His Army uniform had been replaced by a blue work shirt and jeans. His hands were handcuffed in front of him. The guard pushed him down into the chair opposite me and stood over him with his arms crossed. Frank slouched into the chair like a balloon with a slow leak.

"Can we have some privacy?" I asked.

The guard laughed. "A wise guy." So much for attorney-client privilege.

Grandpa squinted at me, closing one eye. I had seen him do it a thousand times. "Do I know you, sir?"

"I was at the theater. We were jockeying for the same seats."

"Oh. Right. I thought you looked familiar." He didn't know the half of it.

I reached out to shake his cuffed hands. "My name is Louis Columbo. I'm an attorney."

"I don't know if I need an attorney. This is all a misunderstanding. Did my parents send you?"

Which told me he had talked to them. It also meant another lawyer might be coming. That wasn't a problem as long as I left before the real lawyer arrived, or if I at least had a story to explain my presence. "No. I'm ... um ... here on my own. I take an interest in defending our boys in uniform."

Grandpa nodded. Then, as if I had reminded him, he peered down at the jail clothes he wore instead of his khakis.

"First," I said, "did you do it?" That probably should have blown my cover story. In the movies, a lawyer never asks a client if he did it. But Grandpa Frank didn't seem to notice.

"No sir," he said with emphasis. "You gotta believe me."

"I do. Let's review the case. The victim was stabbed with a pocketknife carrying your initials."

"Yes sir. But I didn't do it."

"Do you have a knife that matches that description?"

"Yes, sir. Or I did. I don't know where it is now."

"When was the last time you remember having it?"

"I ... don't know."

I blinked at him. "Frank, you're going to have to do better than that." It felt weird calling him Frank. Even weirder was seeing my grandfather as a teenager.

He didn't say anything. I could tell he was holding something back, which wasn't a good look for someone facing a murder charge.

"What is it you're not saying?"

He shrugged. "Nothing."

"If you say so. Do you recall the knife being in your pocket while you were on your way to the theater?"

"It's always in my pocket, sir."

"Evidently not."

"No, sir."

"Also, you don't have to keep calling me sir." That was weird too. "Could the knife have fallen out of your pocket while you were sitting in the theater?"

"It might have." I could tell it wasn't the truth.

"You don't remember it being gone during the movie?" In my head, I could hear a prosecutor saying, "Objection. Leading the witness." But we weren't in a courtroom, and I was grasping for any lead I could get.

"No. I was focused on the movie, sir ... Mr. Columbo."

Stupid engrossing Hitchcock film, I thought. Why couldn't it have been some dumb B movie?

Where are you stationed, Frank?"

"Camp Atterbury, sir."

Ah, right. My mind flashed back to one time riding in the car near the base, and Grandpa saying he had taken basic training there.

"Basic training? They let you out on a Thursday afternoon during basic training?"

He sat up straighter. "We just finished basic and got a day of leave. Tomorrow, we start specialized training." He slouched again, staring into the handcuffs as if they were a crystal ball. "Everyone except me."

"How did you get to town?"

"Bus. A whole bunch of us came from the base."

"On the bus did you see anyone acting oddly?"

He broke into a crooked grin on one side of his mouth. "It was a bunch of soldiers on a day pass. They were all acting oddly."

"Frank, you need to take this seriously." This was the man who taught me how to tie my shoes, and here I was giving him advice. "There are lives on the line."

"Lives? Plural? Besides mine?"

"I mean … if the real killer strikes again. You were a friend of the victim?"

"A little. We met at a dance a couple of weeks ago."

"What about this story that you were pestering her for a date?"

He shook his head. "I asked her out once or twice. She said she couldn't date me because I wasn't Catholic, and her mom insisted she stick with her own kind."

"Meaning Catholics?"

"Meaning at least Catholics. Preferably Italians. You know how the older generation is. She wouldn't go out with me. She wouldn't go out with Red. She might have gone out with Dean, but he has a girl back home and wasn't interested."

"Did you and Irene argue about it?"

"What was there to argue about? She couldn't go against what her mom said. Sure, it bothered me. I tried to talk her into it. But there's a lot of fish in the sea if you know what I mean." He winked.

Which bothered me a little. Here was my grandpa acting like a lady's man, a Casanova, a player. Nobody wants to see that.

I blurted out, "What about Nana?"

"Nana?" Frank asked. "You mean my grandmother? She's okay. Why do you ask?"

54

"Sorry. Did I say Nana? I meant … banana … bananas. Are they feeding you all right in here?"

"I don't know. I've only been here a couple of hours."

"Well, let me know if they don't. Let's talk about your soldier friends. You said Red and Dean. Are those the guys who went to the movie with you?"

"Yeah. Red Fraser and Dean Costa."

I wished I had a notebook and pencil. Generally, I use a notetaking app on my phone to keep track of case facts, but I couldn't exactly pull an Android device out of my pocket in 1943. I repeated the names a couple of times to memorize them until I could write them down.

"Where are you from, Frank?" I thought I might as well take the opportunity to learn more about his early life.

"Clinton … Indiana … or thereabouts. We live on a farm out that way."

"What do you raise on the farm?"

"Corn, wheat, hay for the horses, a few pigs. Is this relevant?"

"It paints a picture. Are you a close family?"

"Sure. Mom, Dad, my brothers, and sister."

"Did your dad fight in the last war?"

"He wasn't the right age. They're stacking these wars too close together nowadays."

"You're right about that," I said. "By the way, is your dad bald?"

"Pardon?"

"I was just wondering if baldness runs in the family … your family."

"Dad has hair. Some. Why do you ask?"

"Never mind. You know, I have some distant relatives over by Clinton. Do you know a Lois … um …" I struggled to remember Nana's maiden name. "Jordan. Lois Jordan."

"Sure, I know Lois. She was a schoolmate of mine. She wrote me a letter, which kind of surprised me. I never knew she was interested."

"You don't say."

He reached into the front pocket of the shirt and pulled out a photograph. He gazed at it a moment before turning it toward me. A black-and-white image of a teenage girl with a ribbon in her hair smiled back at me. Nana was so, so young.

I had to pull my eyes from the photo. "Back to the case. Did Irene say anything to you to make you think someone wanted to kill her?"

He shook his head. "We only spoke a few times. Mainly we talked about whether she would go out with me."

I nodded. "Okay, Frank. Thanks. I'll see what I can do."

"What about bail?"

The guard scoffed, which I took as a sign that bail wasn't likely. I shook my head, and Frank melted a little more. I stood and extended my hand. Grandpa rose and shook it.

"Nice suit, Mr. Columbo. You know, if I ever get out of this and come through the war and all, I'd like to have an outfit like that."

"I bet you will, Frank. One just like this one here. I'm going to do some investigating. We'll meet again."

Grandpa stood, and the guard gripped his arm. I followed them out of the room. We headed in different directions, him back to a cell, me toward 1940s Indianapolis where I needed to find a murderer. I had my hand on the push bar of the outside door when I heard Detective Vukovich behind me.

"Hold up there." He approached while popping a Tums. "Columbo, right?"

"Yeah."

"What are you doing here?"

"I'm an attorney. I came to see a client."

"You told me you were working for the Army."

"What can I say? Attorneys get involved in all kinds of things."

"What client brings you here?"

"Frank Lake."

Vukovich stared me dead in the eyes. "An ambulance chaser, huh? I arrested him, and all you saw was a score."

"It's not like that." Yet without explaining my relationship to Frank, that's exactly how it would appear.

"What? Is his daddy rich?"

"No, he's a farmer."

"Then you must be in it for the headlines. Attorney defends fighting man accused of murder. You think you're going to be the next Clarence Darrow?"

"I don't think he did it."

"Based on what, Columbo?"

"Insufficient motive. Have you talked to him? He wasn't concerned about the victim not going out with him. Good-looking kid like that could land a date with any girl in the city."

"Then how do you explain his knife in her neck?"

"I can't … yet. But a lot of people have the initials F. L. Can you prove it's his knife?"

"I can. The fingerprint analysis just came back. The only prints on the knife were Lake's. We got him dead to rights."

"No," I said. "The killer could have worn gloves … or held it with a handkerchief."

"Or maybe Lake killed her, which is the simplest explanation."

"I don't buy it."

"You don't have to," Vukovich said with a smirk, "but the jury will."

"I'll find more evidence."

"You do that. But stay out of my way. I find you interfering with my investigation, and I'll slap you with obstruction of justice." He gave me one last dirty look and moved on.

So the cops weren't going to be any help. They thought they had their guy. It was up to me to catch a murderer and save the timeline and rescue both my grandpa and myself. The glow of a streetlamp shone through the frosted glass of the double-door windows. I pulled my fedora lower and walked out into a warm, spring Indianapolis night.

Chapter 10

The Not So Thin Man

I decided to employ my feet in returning to Fountain Square. I walked down Virginia Avenue, a route I had walked and ridden my bike along on many occasions. In my time, a wide bike path bordered shops, craft breweries, and apartment buildings all along the way. In 1943 it had more of a neighborhood feel, and walking it, I felt like a real old-time gumshoe.

The hike gave me a chance to think through what Grandpa Frank had said and what I would be doing next. I wanted to talk to the theater manager and anyone else there who might have seen anything at the time of the murder. I also wanted to have a conversation with the roommate, Muriel, to see if she could be pried away from her conviction that Frank was an angry jilted lover. It would be helpful to speak with Grandpa's Army buddies again. However, flying the *Shaymus* to a military installation sounded dangerous, and trying to find two soldiers out of thousands in the camp and getting permission to talk to them seemed doubtful.

I passed a shop on a corner, fittingly named Corner Drugstore. I peered in through the glass door and realized I was looking at a real vintage drugstore, which meant this was much more than a place to fill prescriptions and stock up on snacks and hair care products. It was the beating heart of mid-century America. How could I resist?

I walked inside to tinkling from a bell over the door. To my right stretched a long pharmacy counter in white marble and dark stained wood. In front of it stood a wooden barrel with a poster announcing: *Save Your Cans — Help Pass the Ammunition*. The barrel was nearly full of tin cans of all sizes, each washed and flattened. Across from the counter stood wooden and glass display cases holding ointments, candy, magazines, soaps, and about everything else. Further in gleamed a red countertop lined with built-in chrome swivel stools topped in red vinyl — a real old-fashioned soda fountain.

I swung a leg over a stool and waved to the soda jerk, who stereotypes notwithstanding, was a young woman in an ankle-length black skirt. She wore her blonde hair in tight curls around her face with a white cloth cap on her head.

"What'll you have?" she asked me.

I studied the oversized menu hanging over the mirror along the wall. A milkshake was just thirty cents. "Chocolate shake, please." It left my available funds at less than a dollar, but a dollar seemed to stretch a long way in this era.

"Coming right up."

I watched her make it from scratch with ice cream and milk, blending them in a tall jade green mixer. When she brought the drink, I said, "Did you hear about that murder at the theater?"

Her eyes widened. "Sure did. They say some soldier did it. I tell you, what's this world coming to?"

"Did you know the girl? Her name was Irene Giordano."

"Mister, it's a big city."

"Yeah."

"Besides."

"Besides what?"

She stared at me for a few beats. "I don't think we ran in the same circles."

"What do you mean?"

"Mister, there are two kinds of girls in this country right now. Some of us are working hard to keep things together while the boys are fighting — taking factory jobs, slaving away behind soda counters, even joining the WACs or whatever."

"And the others?"

"Boy crazy. They only want to party, go to dances, compete for the limited pool of men."

"And you think she was the second type? What makes you say so? You said you didn't know her."

She trudged to the other end of the counter, snatched a newspaper from the top of the cash register, and brought it over. "Page three. You can tell by looking. Anyhow, that's the kind of girl who gets herself killed, right?"

I took the paper and turned to the page. The picture was a photo booth shot, Irene mugging for the camera, her bushy dark hair pressed against the shoulder of some boy whose face had been cropped out of the photo.

This was the evidence of her being a party girl? Talk about judgy. This lady really put the jerk in soda jerk.

I said, "She was a nurse."

The server made a face and didn't answer.

I reached the bottom of the milkshake and gazed down the counter where a slice of apple pie sat all by its lonesome inside a glass display stand. I was still hungry.

"I could clean up that piece of pie for you."

She brought the pie and a fork and added fifteen cents to the check. After polishing it off, I dropped some dimes on the counter to cover the check and a tip.

I walked back out onto the street. The night had chilled, and when I buttoned Grandpa's suit jacket, I found it a little tight. The prescription called for more walking and less pie and milkshakes.

I reached the Fountain Square Theater and bypassed the ticket window. The usher at the door, a lanky black teenager, blocked my way between two velvet-roped stanchions.

"You need a ticket to come in, mister."

"I'm not here to watch a movie. I want to talk to the manager."

"What's this about?"

"I'm investigating the murder this afternoon."

He eyeballed me for a few seconds, then called to the kid at the refreshment counter. "This gentleman wants to talk to Mr. Beck."

"So?" the other kid asked.

"So I can't leave my post. Can you fetch him?"

The kid sighed dramatically and plodded off. Music swelled from inside the auditorium.

"What's your name?" I asked.

"Billy, sir."

"Billy what?"

"Billy Taylor, sir."

"You were here when the murder happened, right?" I remembered him among the squad of ushers.

"Yes, sir."

I wanted to tell him he could knock off with all the sirs, but I knew a black kid needed them to survive in the America of 1943.

"Is there anyone else working tonight who saw it?"

He rubbernecked about the lobby. "I don't think so. Only reason I'm here is I need the money."

"This afternoon, did you see anyone acting suspiciously?"

"Before it happened, you mean?"

"Before or after."

"I don't know." He studied the floor.

"You won't get in trouble, Billy. I'm a private investigator, not a cop."

His eyes flicked up. "Like in that *Thin Man* movie?"

"Something like that. Just tell me what you know."

"Excuse me." Billy nodded at a middle-aged couple coming in. I sidestepped to let them pass. Billy took their tickets, tore them in half, and returned the stubs. "The movie started about fifteen minutes ago, folks."

"Told you," the man said to the woman as they passed on in.

Billy turned back to me. "I don't know if this is suspicious, but this one man was standing around in the lobby for a while like he was waiting for someone. He finally went in by himself."

"What did he look like?"

"Older white gentleman. White hair. It might have been nothing. Maybe his date stood him up, but he looked too old to be dating."

It sounded like Dr. Hatch, though the description could fit a lot of other people too.

"Anything else? Did you notice when the murdered lady came in?"

"Yes, sir. She came in with a man and another girl. They were all chatty and laughing. And to think only a few minutes later … Such a pity."

"Did you get the impression the guy was with one of the girls in particular?"

The usher shook his head. "He was sort of making eyes at both of them."

A stern voice sounded from behind him. "That's enough, Billy." Carl Beck stood there, his black suit impeccable, though I couldn't help noticing how his vest was straining a bit at the buttons and how his chin was starting to grow a companion. Not that I should criticize after loading up on pie.

"I am Carl Beck. May I help you?"

I said, "I hope so. My name is Lake. I mean, my name is Columbo. I'm here on behalf of Private Lake, who was arrested here this afternoon."

He raised his chin. "Murdering someone in my theater. The impudence. We're only glad justice was served quickly." The Ws came out as Vs.

"I'm not sure it was. Can we talk?"

"I suppose. Not here." He nodded at Billy, who unhooked the velvet rope to let me pass.

Beck led me across the lobby to a small door. Inside, a long set of stairs led up past the projection booth to an office with a smell like a cigarette factory. He shut the door behind us. The room was not large, but it was neatly kept. He waved a wrist toward a chair while he walked around the desk to his.

I sat. "I'd like you to tell me everything you saw this afternoon."

He leaned forward, elbows on the desk, his fingers tented. "I've already gone over this with the police."

"I'm not with the police. Private investigator."

He sat back and straightened his vest. "I didn't see much. I was in my office here. I heard a scream. I assumed it came from the movie. But then one of the ushers ran in and told me there had been an accident."

"Except it wasn't an accident."

He shook his head in tiny motions. "No, it wasn't." He took a breath and let it out.

"Do you know if Irene Giordano was a regular here?"

He opened a desk drawer and reached in for a cigarette, lighting it from a dark green marble cylinder sitting on a corner of the desk. The thing was twice as large as a coffee mug and no doubt heavy enough to be a murder weapon itself. "Was that the poor girl's name? How should I know how often she came?"

"I can ask the ushers."

"No. They have jobs to do. I won't have you pestering them."

"This is a murder investigation."

"Which, as I understand, has been solved." He puffed, and smoke billowed in my face.

"Are you acquainted with any of the other people the detective singled out?"

"No."

"Dr. Hatch?"

"Yes, I am familiar with Dr. Hatch."

"In what way?"

"In that we are both business owners here in the building."

"His office is here?"

Beck produced a curt nod of his head. "It is a sizeable building."

"What about the Potters?"

He adjusted his wire rims and ran his hand over his nearly non-existent hair. "Who?"

"They own the house where Irene Giordano lived."

He stroked his mustache with thumb and forefinger as he shook his head. What was with all the personal grooming? Was he vain, or was he nervous about something?

I said, "I need to talk with them. I don't suppose you know where they live, do you?"

"How could I if I don't know them?"

"Right, right. How about Ray Noonan?"

Beck shifted in his chair. "No. I don't know him either. Now, I have been more than generous with my time, Mr. Columbo. I have work to do."

"Sure," I said, rising from the chair. I moved toward the door and opened it. Then I paused and swung around to pull a Columbo on him. "Oh, one more thing. You said you were in your office at the time of the murder. As it happened, I was in the theater myself. And after the girl's roommate screamed, the ushers rushed in right away. But, you see, the crowd was acting unruly, and one of the ushers ran out and returned with you not a minute later."

"Yes?"

"Well, I'm wondering about the timing. How did an usher run through the lobby and up those stairs all the way to your office, and then you come back down all in less than a minute?"

Beck sniffed and ran a finger across one eyebrow. "Ah, yes. I remember now. I had already come down from the office to check with the ticket booth about the receipts."

I flipped up a hand. "There you go. That explains it. Thank you for your time, Mr. Beck. I'll show myself out."

I descended the stairs. The door I came out of into the lobby was less than ten feet away from a side entrance into the auditorium. Billy's back was turned. I decided to slip into the theater to do an experiment.

No one was sitting in the last two rows except for a teenage couple who were paying more attention to each other's lips than to the movie and obviously would take no notice of me. While Joseph Cotton and Teresa Wright verbally fenced on the big screen, I glided into a seat in the last row.

I figured my car key fob was more or less the same size and weight as the pocketknife. I unhooked the fob from my house key and stuck it back into my pocket. Of course, I had no idea how tight my suit pant legs were compared to Frank's Army uniform, but this was the best I could do. I stood up and sat down several times, but the fob didn't slide out.

I slouched in the seat. I tried propping my legs on the back of the seat in front of me. I moved my legs to the floor and then back to the seat repeatedly. On the third or fourth time, the fob plopped to the floor. I glanced at the kissing couple. They didn't seem to have heard it ... or in any case, been disturbed by it, which was a good sign that the pocketknife might have fallen out undetected.

Phase one was completed. Now for phase two. I sat up straight and scanned the floor with my eyes trying to see where the key fob had landed. It wasn't easy to find in the dark, and I peered left and right, prompting the teenage boy to glare at me and whisper, "What are you looking at, creep?"

I finally spotted the fob near the seat in front of me. If the knife had fallen from Frank's pocket, which was at least possible, then it could have slid down the inclined floor, putting it in the path of anyone passing through. Someone could have stepped on it or accidentally kicked it, and that person or someone else might have become aware of it and picked it up and used it for murder.

With all those might haves and could haves, it seemed like a long shot. Certainly, it violated Occam's razor about going with the simplest answer. However, it gave me a sort of reasonable explanation for how somebody else could have killed Irene Giordano with Grandpa's knife.

Chapter 11

Let Your Fingers Do the Walking

I walked back along dark streets toward Garfield Park. I kept thinking about how I should have been married by now. That is, if by the word *now* I meant the night after this adventure began. Not by now if I meant the evening of May 22, 1943. In this weird situation, the word *now* had nearly lost all meaning.

What was Grandpa Frank holding back, and why? What was with the nervous grooming of Carl Beck? Could the drugstore waitress have been right about Irene Giordano being a party girl? If so, what did that mean to the case? And what about the mysterious white-haired man waiting for someone in the movie theater lobby? I wanted to hear Oren's insights. He was the genius, after all. But first I needed some shut-eye.

In the darkness, I got turned around in the huge park, and it took me an extra half hour to locate the clump of trees where the *Shaymus* was hiding. Finding it at last, I opened the ramp and lumbered around the crew deck hallway to my cabin, cabin eight.

The last time I was in the cabin, I was with Sarah and Lucas. She had been cuddled up in the spacious cockpit lounge chair in the middle of the room. Lucas had been stretched out on the bunk. I hung up Grandpa's suit on the closet bar, slid my wallet and keys into one of the drawers, and dropped myself face first onto the bunk. I conked out somewhere in the vicinity of straight away.

For obvious reasons, the cabins on the *Shaymus* have no windows. I mean, it's not like you would want to throw one open for some fresh air while traveling through the vacuum of space. So when I awoke, I couldn't tell if it was still night or the next morning.

"Kah-Rehn, what's the local time?"

The synthetic voice answered me. "I don't know, Gabriel."

"You don't know? You always know that stuff."

"I can find no electronic network with which to connect."

"No Internet. Right. Well, tell me this. Is it light outside?"

"The sun rose a short time ago."

"Excellent. Thanks."

I rolled off the bunk and stumbled into the tiny, attached bathroom for a sonic shower. You can't expect a spaceship to lug around tons of water to wash people. Sound pulsations can vibrate away the dirt and get you just as clean, though it doesn't do nearly as much to wake you up.

I shaved using the razor and shaving cream I always kept on the ship. Then I dressed and moved to the galley where I replicated a waffle and a cup of coffee. While I ate, I organized my thoughts for talking with Oren.

I mounted the steps to the office. Buad and Blan were pecking at seed cakes in their habitat. The view screen was blank, and Zastra's desk was empty.

"Oren," I said.

The screen came on with the face of Dwayne Johnson. "Hello, Gabriel. How is the investigation progressing?"

"I'm here to report in."

"Satisfactory. I am asking Zastra to join us. She's been restless, and we could benefit from her input."

"Should I wait for her?"

"I'm having the conversation piped to her translator bots. Proceed with your report."

I proceeded, giving him the rundown on my conversations with Grandpa Frank, the waitress, Billy Taylor, and Carl Beck.

By the time I finished, Zastra was climbing into the office. She pointed a green, clawed finger at me "Talking with your grandfather was dumb and dangerous."

"She's right," Oren said, "though it sounds as if you handled it adequately. However, you must not reveal your identity to him."

"I won't, believe me. I couldn't explain it to him anyway without sounding insane. What do you think about the case, Oren?"

"The theater manager does seem suspicious."

"Yeah, and he could be a spy. We're at war with Germany."

Oren raised one eyebrow. "First, none of *us* are at war with any of Earth's nation-states, not even you. We do not belong here. We are here only to solve a murder. We must do nothing to influence the course of the war. Second, assuming Carl Beck is a spy, which seems unlikely, why would he risk his cover to kill a young woman?"

"Maybe she found out about his secret," I said.

"It is a possibility, one you should test by trying to find out more about her. The next step would be to visit this house where she lived. Talk to anyone who knew her, especially those who were at the theater at the time of the murder. Do you know where the house is located?"

"No, but I have an idea how I can find it."

"Excellent. It might be advantageous for you to take a room at the house yourself."

"Okay. I'll pack my shaving kit and make some more dimes."

Zastra said, "I have a question. After talking to your grandfather, do you still believe he's innocent?"

"Absolutely ... for several reasons. One, remember he was sitting that close to Irene only because Quog and I took their seats. He should have been rows and rows back. Plus, he'd have to be an idiot to stab someone using a knife with his initials carved into it."

Buad cackled. "Well, he is related to you, dummy."

"At least I'm not a birdbrain."

"Hey, who are you calling a bird?"

Oren said, "You said you thought your grandfather was withholding some piece of information."

"Yeah."

"Any ideas about what it might be?"

"None."

"What about his soldier friends? Could one of them have committed the murder?"

"Could be. They certainly weren't acting normally at the theater, but of course, their buddy had just been arrested. Oh, I see what you mean. Was Grandpa holding back something about his friends?"

"It's worth seeing if we can find out more about them. Where is that Army base?"

"Camp Atterbury? It's somewhere south of here. I don't know where exactly."

"Find out. I can send Buad and Blan out on surveillance."

"Will do."

Zastra said, "Gabe." I turned to face her. She was staring at me like a predator sizing up its prey. "Gabe, does it seem likely that an Earthling wanting to kill another Earthling would stab them in the back of the neck where they have their spine? Wouldn't the soft front of the neck make a more enticing target?"

I instinctively raised a hand to my throat. "I don't know. If it were me, yeah, I might reach around. Then again, I don't murder people."

Oren said, "This Dr. Hatch, he might have some insight into that. When you interview him, be sure to ask."

"I will. Is that it?"

"Yes."

I breathed out a sigh.

"Is something the matter, Gabriel?"

"No. No. This is just a lot. My future, the future of my whole family is riding on this. And then there's all these people. Any of them could have done it."

Oren's eyes met mine. He spoke softly. "One step at a time. Gather the facts. Discover the motive. We'll get there."

I returned to the galley to replicate more dimes and found Quog there eating a bowl of something that looked like pumpkin guts.

"What's that, Quog?"

"Spiny Ivy Gourd. It's an Arsawan dish."

"Is it good?"

He paused before answering. "Not particularly."

"We ought to get you re-introduced to Earth food. The ship can make pizza, tacos, hamburgers —"

He cut me off. "Ooh. Hamburgers. I used to love those."

"Odd choice for breakfast, but why not? Coming right up." I issued the command and saw the sandwich appear before my eyes on a plate. I carried it to him at the table. "What did you do last night?"

He shook his head. "I went to bed early. Long, emotional days like yesterday wear me out anymore. Today, I don't know what I'm going to do."

"Did you bring along any books or vids?"

"No. I thought I needed to leave everything from the wider galaxy behind. I planned to pick up some twenty-first-century Earth books when I arrived. Then all this happened."

"If you like to read, I can loan you my phone. I have some books on it. Granted, most of them are from the twentieth century, but they're classics. Nero Wolfe, Perry Mason, Sam Spade, Philip Marlowe."

"Sounds interesting. I used to watch the *Perry Mason* TV show as a kid."

"Me too, but in reruns."

I handed him the phone and showed him around the icons. Being used to advanced technology, he caught on quickly. Then I replicated another ten dollars of dimes. I wasn't sure that would be enough for a room in the boarding house, but I hated to walk around with any more change in my pocket. Before I left, I decided it would be helpful to replicate a clean shirt as well.

The morning was bright and beautiful. May in Indiana is the best … well, except when rain falls in buckets … or when you're finally feeling like summer is on the way, and then somebody flips the switch back to March weather. But this day was great.

I was feeling optimistic. I hadn't learned much from the people at the theater, but I hoped for more from the residents of the boarding house, those who knew Irene best. With any luck, I'd pick up a clue that would let Oren solve this crime before lunch.

Heading out of the park, I caught a bus and rode back to Fountain Square, then walked up Virginia Avenue to the Corner Drugstore, where I had stopped the night before. The female soda jerk had been replaced by a teenage boy, but that didn't matter. I wasn't there for food this time … or to fill a prescription … or to weigh myself at the huge upright scale just inside the door.

My destination was a trio of thin wooden cubicles just beyond the soda counter. I had spotted them last night while sipping the milkshake. A person from my time could be forgiven for mistaking them for closets or changing rooms. Fortunately, I had seen movies containing these ancient artifacts and knew what they were. Also, a sign over each one proclaimed: *Telephone*. A good detective picks up on clues like that.

I entered one of the booths and sat on the little wooden stool shelf built into the side of the box. I located the telephone book and flipped through the alphabetical listings. I remembered phone books from my childhood and the slogan that seemed to always be printed on the front: *Let your fingers do the walking*. The phone book was like a non-computerized search engine for every family and every business in the city.

I found three entries for a Potter, L. One was up on Kessler Boulevard. Another was out on West Michigan Street. Neither seemed likely starting locations for someone to come to a movie in Fountain Square. The third was an address on Olive Street, not much more than around the corner from the theater and only a few blocks from the bungalow, which one day would be mine.

Committing the address to memory, I then flipped around through the book attempting to find Camp Atterbury. It wasn't under C or A. I tried U.S. Army. I even browsed the yellow pages. Nothing.

Leaving the booth, I stopped at the counter and asked the soda jerk, "I have a question. How can I get to Camp Atterbury?"

"Enlist," he said with a grin.

I grinned back. "What is this? A drug store or vaudeville?"

The kid said, "I think it's on the bus routes. Do you want a cup of coffee?"

"I've had some, thanks. Suppose you were going to fly ... I mean, drive ... to Atterbury?"

He scrunched up his nose to think. "It's down near Edinburgh I believe. Highway 31 runs close to it. How about a cream cheese Danish?"

"No thanks. So south," I said.

"South-ish. As the crow flies."

I chuckled. Buad and Blan would throw a conniption if they heard anybody compare them to crows. "How far?"

"I don't know from distance, mister. Thirty, thirty-five miles? We also have those little boxes of cereal and milk."

Was this kid paid on commission or something? Maybe his pop owned the place.

"Thanks ... for the information." I took a step, then paused. "Oh, maybe there is something you can sell me. Do you have pocket notebooks for sale ... and pencils?" I figured writing down clues would be easier than trying to memorize everything.

"We sure do. The stationary section is right behind you."

Ten cents later, I left the drugstore and ducked around the corner out of sight. "Buad, Blan," I said to my translator bots.

"What do you want, numskull?" Blan answered.

The greeting irked me, but I let it pass in the interest of getting the job done. "I have the information you need for your assignment. There's a major highway running south out of the city. Signs along it will have the number thirty-one.

Follow that until you see a huge military base. It will be somewhere around thirty miles."

I didn't have to worry about them knowing how far thirty miles was or recognizing a number on a sign. Translator bots convert alien written language as easily as spoken language. And they automatically convert any unit of measure to whatever units the hearer would understand. So whether Avanians use kilometers or parsecs or bird-lengths or what have you, Buad and Blan heard it in their native terms.

"Got it," Buad said.

"Do you know who you're looking for?"

"Yeah, the two soldier guys. Who else would we be looking for on a military base? Red Fraser and Dean Costa. We have their names, and we have their faces from the images you got at the theater. Don't worry, meathead, we'll track 'em down."

With Buad and Blan briefed, it was now time for my part in the morning's program. I resumed my walk, spotting Olive Street just beyond the massive Fountain Square Theater building. Out of curiosity, I walked on, taking a small detour to check out the bungalow I would own in several decades.

The footprint of the house was essentially unchanged. The paint color was different, a plain white instead of the sage green of my time. What the 1940s version of the house had, which mine lacked, was some cool fretwork around the top of the covered porch. I wondered how much it would cost to add that back. I might run the idea past Sarah … assuming, of course, I could put history right and get myself back to her.

Chapter 12

Rooms to Let

The large two-story on Olive Street was painted light gray, a color which conveniently disguised, to the passing eye at least, how badly the place needed a fresh coat of paint. The house stood separated from the sidewalk by a narrow strip of grass intersected by a path of ancient, uneven brick. A cardboard sign in the front window announced: *Rooms to Let.*

Climbing the steps to the wide, covered front porch, I found a button beside the door and pressed it. A grating mechanical buzz echoed inside.

Nellie Potter answered the door in a floral housedress with white trim on the front pockets. She brushed a strand of gray hair behind one ear as she peered at me through the screen.

I said, "Hi. I was wondering if you have any rooms available."

Mrs. Potter sized me up with her eyes. "How did you hear about us?"

"You have a sign in your window."

With a skeptical look, she opened the screen door. "Come in."

I stepped into an entry hall that ran the length of the house. A staircase stood to the left. A marble top table was nestled below it on which perched an old-fashioned upright candlestick phone in beautiful black Bakelite. On the opposite wall, the pendulum of a clock ticked back and forth.

We crossed the hall to a parlor on the right. Faded and fussy wallpaper stretched up to a high ceiling. The wooden floor was scattered with mismatched pieces of furniture, tables covered with doilies, and a beat-up upright piano in one corner. In the middle of it all, an oval-shaped, braided rug valiantly attempted to pull everything together.

"Have a seat on the davenport," she said as she sat in an armchair next to a jukebox-sized console radio. "And take off that hat inside the house. What's your name?"

"Louis Columbo." Pulling off the fedora, I gazed around the room and shot her a smile. "Nice boarding house you have here."

The attempt at friendliness had no effect. She returned a stern look over the tops of her glasses and shook a bony finger at me. "It's not a boarding house. It's a rooming house."

"If you say so. What's the difference?"

"Meals. You're on your own for meals. Lord knows it's hard enough to cook for two with all this war rationing — sugar, meat, coffee, butter. I never seen the like." She shook her head with an expression of disgust. "The room is three dollars and fifty cents a week in advance. It has a sink and good ventilation. Don't be bringing in a hot plate or anything else like that. I'm afraid of fires. You can smoke down here but not in bed. Again, fires. You're free to use the radio here, but the selection is first come, first served. And if somebody tells you to turn it down, you turn it down."

"Yes, ma'am."

"No kids. No pets. And don't be bringing women back here. I'll have no truck with any of that."

I held up a hand. "It won't be a problem."

She narrowed her eyes. "Nor bunches of men for card playin' either."

"Fine by me. Is it okay if my dad stops by?"

"As long as he follows the rules too. Now after all that, are you still interested?"

"I am."

"You have the three fifty?"

"I have it." I patted my pocketful of change and tried another smile on her, which didn't work any better than the first one.

Mrs. Potter took a breath like I was putting her out. "Then I suppose you oughta see the room." She pushed on the chair arms to lift her thin frame. I followed her across the hall to the stairs.

The staircase had a dark glossy banister as wide as my hand. We went up several steps, then turned right and went up a few more. We emerged on the second floor with a long hallway running the length of the house. I counted five rooms that I could see.

I was gawking at this time capsule of a place, the high, plastered ceiling, the dark stained doors and tall baseboard, when Nellie called from down the hall. "Don't lollygag."

With floorboards creaking, we proceeded down the hall to where it made a ninety-degree turn to a short hallway on the right with two more doors and a back staircase.

"Bathroom's that way," she said, pointing down the short hall. Apparently, I would be sharing facilities with the other tenants. She opened a door opposite the turn in the hall. "You're room's this one."

It had two twin beds, a sink with exposed plumbing, and a narrow dresser beside another door. A single unshaded lightbulb was mounted on the ceiling. I wandered to the mystery door and opened it to find a minuscule closet.

"Looks great," I lied.

"Three fifty for the week in advance." This seemed to be Nell Potter's catch phrase.

I counted out the dimes on top of the thin bedspread. It wasn't a difficult calculation to work out that the rent amounted to a mere fifty cents a day. By Grabthar's Hammer, what a savings!

"Dimes? You're paying in dimes?"

I jangled my pocket. "You bet. And I have more where those came from." I had replicated way too many.

She glowered at me, scooped the dimes into her dress pocket, and left the room. I frisbeed my fedora onto one bed and stretched out on the other. For a few minutes I stared at the cracked plaster ceiling and collected my thoughts.

Nellie had been so prickly, it had put me off from asking about the murder. Prickly or not, I needed to figure out a way to do so. I also needed to talk with Muriel Marshall and Peter Ryan, who had accompanied Irene to the movie.

Maybe they were here now. No time like the present, I told myself. I jumped from the bed and headed down the hallway. I knocked on the first door to my right. No answer. Moving a few steps along, I knocked at the next door on the other side of the hall. I heard movement inside.

A moment later Muriel answered. She was dressed in business attire, or nearly so. She wore a white blouse with a brooch at the collar and a dark skirt ending below the knee. Below that she was barelegged and barefooted. She looked me up and down like she was picking out a cut of meat at the butcher shop. "Nice suit. Who are you?"

"I'm the new boarder. Louis Columbo."

She dropped her head and cast upturned eyes at me. "Hello, Louis Columbo. My name is Muriel, Muriel Marshall. No relation."

"No relation?"

She laughed. "To General George, silly. George Marshall?" She shot me a mischievous grin and wheeled around to pad across the room. A painted line ran up the back of each leg. This threw me until I realized that silk and nylon would have been needed for the war effort and thus hard to find. I guessed this was a way to give the appearance of seamed hosiery without actually having any. She slid into a pair of low heels and sat down in a chair to buckle the straps. Hey, how come her room got a chair, and mine didn't?

"Going somewhere?" I stayed in the doorway, knowing Mrs. Potter wouldn't approve of me stepping inside the room. I wondered if there was anything Mrs. Potter *would* approve of.

"To work. I have a job."

"That's too bad. I wanted to talk, get to know you."

A smile flickered across her face. Standing, she moved to the mirror above the sink and applied bright red lipstick. After blotting her lips, she faced me and locked eyes. "What do you think?"

"You'll do," I said with an approving nod. "How about I walk you to work? We can talk on the way. I'll buy you breakfast if you have time."

She grabbed a matching jacket from the bed and slipped it on. "It's all the way downtown. I take the bus."

"Then I'll ride with you. The offer of breakfast stands."

She walked to the doorway. Moving inside my personal space, she put a hand on my chest and patted. "You know, Lou, that's a whale of an idea."

We left the house and walked a couple of blocks to a bus stop on Prospect. A minute later a blue and yellow coach pulled up, and we boarded. As the bus pulled away, we swayed down the aisle, finding seats surrounded by other people going to work in office attire or skilled trade uniforms.

I asked, "Are you from Indianapolis originally?"

"No. I came here to find a job."

I waited for her to say more, but she didn't. I let it go and decided to bring up Irene. "You have your room all to yourself?"

Her gaze dropped to the floorboard of the bus. "I had a roommate. She died. Yesterday."

I tried to build as much shock into my voice as possible by pretending she had told me some awful news about a friend.

"That's terrible. What happened?"

For a minute she didn't answer. Then in a voice so low I could barely make it out over the rumble of the bus, she said, "She was stabbed during a movie."

"What?" I let my eyes grow larger. "I'm sorry." We were approaching downtown, and I decided to leave it at that for the time being.

The bus dropped us at the corner of Washington and Meridian. She looked up at the L.S. Ayers Building on the corner. At eight stories, the brick structure was as large as any in Indianapolis at that time. "This is me. Do you ever shop here?"

"I did as a kid." It was in the late 1980s, of course, forty-some years from now, before the department store went out of business. "Do you have time for breakfast?"

"I never have anything more than coffee, but according to the big clock on the side of the building, I have time for a quick cup."

She led me across Meridian and down the block to the cool art deco Woolworth's building. Inside the store, we veered to the side to a long lunch counter. We sat on stools and ordered two cups.

I asked, "What do you do at Ayers?"

"I type purchase orders until my fingers are black and blue, poor me."

She dribbled cream into her cup from a cow-shaped dispenser. The cow's tail circled around to form a handle, and the cream poured out from the cow's mouth. I was surprised no one else seemed to find that off-putting and glad I took my coffee black.

"Are you going to be a long-term tenant, Lou?" The way she said it, the way her eyes flashed, it came off like a come-on. I wondered if I should tell her I was engaged to someone several decades younger.

"I don't know. It seems like a nice place."

She looked at me sideways. "Maybe if you came from a Hooverville or the county poorhouse."

"You don't like it?"

She shrugged. "The house is okay. The landlords get on my nerves."

"How's that?"

"You'll see."

I took a sip. "What was your roommate's name?"

"Irene." She rubbed her forehead. "She didn't deserve to die like that."

"No. Of course not. You said it happened at a movie? Were you with her?"

"Right beside her."

"You didn't notice anything?"

"Not until I leaned over to offer her the rest of my popcorn, and I saw her head slumped forward. At first, I thought she was asleep, but then I saw the knife."

"What did you think happened? Did someone come down the row during the movie and stab her? Were people moving around?"

"Only like everybody. I was getting bumped so much I thought I was in a rodeo. But I'll tell you who did it," she said in a bitter voice. "A soldier was sitting behind us. He stabbed her."

"Are you sure?"

"Yes, I'm sure. The cops arrested the guy right there in the theater." Her eyes flashed at me. "I hope he fries." I must have winced because she said, "What?"

"I don't know. What if he didn't do it?"

"He did it, all right? He was sitting right behind her. His initials were on the knife. He asked her out on a couple of dates, but she refused to go with him. What more do you want?"

"Why wouldn't she date him?"

"What is this? What's with all the questions?"

"I don't know. It's some story, is all."

"What difference does it make why she wouldn't go out with him? That's her right, isn't it? Or it was."

"Sure, sure. Did they argue about it? Irene and the soldier, I mean. Did he get angry?"

She shook her head while gazing into her coffee. "No." She looked up. "But it had to be him … with the knife and all."

"I suppose. But he doesn't seem like the murdering type —"

"Who says he isn't the murdering type? How do you know what type he is?" Her eyes had switched from flirty to flinty.

"I … I mean, you said he wasn't angry when she wouldn't go out with him."

She frowned. "Doesn't mean he didn't do it."

"Do you know where they met?"

"Sure. I was there. Saturday night dancing at the Kit Kat Club."

The name of the club rang a bell. It was where the gangster Ray Noonan said he worked.

"When was that?"

"I don't know. A few weeks ago." The flirty flashed back into her eyes. "I could take you there this weekend. I bet you could cut a rug."

I figured I should definitely check out the place. Fortunately, I had recently taken a few lessons in the foxtrot and swing dancing in preparation for the wedding. I hoped that would get me by. I didn't know a rumba from a Roomba or a jitterbug from a June bug.

"Sounds fun," I said. "Did Irene go there often? Was she what you would call a party girl?"

Muriel laughed so loudly other customers along the lunch counter turned to look. "Hardly. Most times I had to drag her out kicking and screaming." She glanced at her watch and gulped the last of her coffee. "My typewriter is calling."

I stood with her and tossed dimes on the counter for the coffee and a tip. We walked back down the block to the Ayers building. "I guess I'll see you tonight then."

"Sure, Lou. You know where to find me. I'll be right down the hall."

She shot me a sultry wink and disappeared inside. I was going to have to watch my step with this one. I was a happily almost married man.

Chapter 13

One Across, Six Letters, To Kill

I had unfinished business back at the boarding house — excuse me, the rooming house — plenty of it. So far the morning had been a bust. No Lester. No Peter Ryan. Nellie wasn't helpful, and Muriel was dead set against Grandpa and more interested in flirting than finding the killer. My dreams of quickly solving the case were fading fast.

I made my way back to Olive Street and entered the parlor to find Lester Potter sitting in a chair, staring at a half-finished crossword puzzle in the newspaper. He wore bib overalls with rolled-up cuffs over a flannel shirt with the top button buttoned.

He looked up as I entered and locked narrow eyes on me. "Morning. Who are you?"

"I'm your new lodger. The name's Lou Columbo." I extended my hand.

"Lester Potter. This is my place." He shook my hand for about half a second, then dropped his gaze back to the paper. "Four-letter word for hazard." He glanced up with a grin. "All the four-letter words I know, they wouldn't dare put in the paper."

"How about risk?"

"That fits." He wrapped his tongue around a tooth and penciled in the word. "What are you doing this morning, Mr. Columbo?" he said, his eyes still on the puzzle. "Don't you have a job?"

"You bet I do. I'm in sales. I was just downtown at L.S. Ayers and spoke with someone in purchasing." It was the truth. "I have another appointment later." That was less truthful.

My mind raced to find an answer to what I anticipated would be his next question — sales of what? Housewares? Ladies' hats? Children's toys? I was painfully aware that I was standing there without a sample case or even a catalog of wares to back up my story. Fortunately, the puzzle seemed to distract him.

"Hmm. Seventeen down. The clue is title. Five letters, so mister doesn't fit."

"Queen?"

"Oh, those kinds of titles, huh? Not queen, though. It has an R in the middle."

"Baron."

"Barren? You mean like a desert?"

"No, baron like a duke or earl."

"Oh. Yeah, baron. That works."

Hoping I had bought enough goodwill with puzzle assistance to dive into an interview, I sat on the davenport. "I met Muriel on the bus. She told me about the death of Irene Giordano."

He fixed me with an empty stare. "What a shame. Such a waste."

"Nice girl?"

"She always paid the rent. Not like some people you have to nag and pester all the time." He fixed his eyes on me as if it were a warning.

"I understand you were at the theater at the time of her death." I hoped he and Muriel didn't compare notes or they would wonder where I got that information.

He answered with a grunt, his eyes darting back to the paper.

I said, "That must have been dreadful."

"Pardon?"

"I said it must have been dreadful, horrid. The murder."

Another grunt. He pulled a red bandana handkerchief from a pocket and blew his nose with a sound like a trombonist going for a high note. "Excuse me."

"Did you see anything?" I asked.

"Where?"

"At the theater."

"Yeah. We saw *Shadow of* ... something."

"I meant of the murder."

"What was there to see? It was dark."

"How about before or after? Was anyone acting suspiciously?"

"You're the one acting suspicious with all these questions. What are you, a reporter?" He raised the newspaper in front of his chest like a shield, an ironic defense against a supposed member of the press.

"No. No. I'm a … a crime novelist."

"A what?"

"I write detective mysteries. Have you heard of the … the Adrian Monk Mysteries? He's a private investigator with a troubled past and a fair number of personal problems."

Lester eyed me skeptically.

I said, "He solves crime with the help of his … his aunt … um … Jessica Fletcher." Boy, if that show existed, I would watch it for sure.

Lester hollered. "Nellie, get in here."

His wife pushed through a swinging door from the back of the house, wiping her hands on her apron. "I was in the middle of peeling potatoes, Lester."

"Fella here — your new tenant — is poking around about Irene's murder. Says he's a writer of some kind."

She wagged her index finger in my direction. "We don't want our personal business splashed all over the papers."

I held up my hands. "It won't be in the papers at all. I write books, not newspaper articles. And I'm only looking for general background information. I'll fictionalize the whole thing, set it in San Francisco. That's where Monk operates. It's just … a murder in a movie theater … that never happens. It would make a crackerjack novel."

"I don't want my sister reading some cheap, lurid book and finding me in it."

"She won't. First, I don't write cheap and lurid. Second, I'll change all the names. I'll change your identities. How about I make your characters — you and Lester — into a couple of young film stars, who are in Frisco to shoot a movie? And … and while you're screening the dailies, a production assistant is the one murdered."

Nellie fluffed her hair with one hand. "Hmm. Well … that's not so bad then. But if you're changing everything all around, why ask us questions about the real murder?"

"To capture your reactions, your emotions, and all the little details you noticed. Verisimilitude. That's what breathes life into a story."

Lester shook his head. "And here I thought writers used their imagination."

I smiled. "Do you have a few minutes now?"

Nellie frowned. "A few."

She sat in the chair on the other side of the radio from her husband, the same one from which she had interviewed me earlier. I figured those were probably their assigned seats, their "spots."

I pulled out my new notebook and pencil. "Did you see anyone in the theater acting unusual or suspicious?"

They shared a momentary glance before Nellie said, "Well, I thought it odd for Dr. Hatch to be taking in movies during the middle of the day. You'd think he surely had house calls he could be making."

"Okay," I said. "Anything else?"

"I didn't like those soldier boys either, laughing and carrying on like they were. They should have more respect for the uniform. I don't know what it is with young people these days. Those three acted just the same when they were here."

I said, "They were here? At this house."

"Yes, at this house. That's what the word *here* means, don't it?"

"Those same soldiers?"

"Yes, those same soldiers. I can tell one person from another, can't I? Even in uniform. Those three. Talking to the girls and making a ruckus and I don't know what all."

"Now, Nellie," Lester said, "they were just letting off steam." He shot me a knowing nod. "I know how soldiers are. I fought in Cuba."

"Cuba? Oh, you mean the Spanish-American war?"

"That's right. I fought with Teddy Roosevelt … though to hear him tell it later, you'd think he fought the whole dadgum war all by himself. Anyhow, we were a little rowdy ourselves when we made it back to Key West."

Nellie's lips tightened.

I asked, "When they came here, the soldiers, were they seeing both Irene and Muriel?"

"Oh yes." She shook her head in disapproval. "Those girls. Let me tell you, that Muriel is as man crazy as they come. I have to keep my eye on her. Irene at least was quiet and reserved, a nice girl." Nellie paused and sniffed with disdain. "Kind of nosey though."

"What do you mean?"

"I mean, she was always putting her oar in where it didn't belong."

"Like?"

"Like how you're doing right now."

"Sorry," I said, giving up. "Tell me about Peter Ryan."

"How do you know about him?" Nellie asked.

"Research. I know he's staying here."

Lester said, "He's all right."

Nellie said, "He's out all hours, day and night, hither and yon."

"He's a salesman, Nell. Door-to-door. Encyclopedias. And for a high-ticket item like that, you have to wait and talk with the man of the house. At least he's out working and not like those tramps and hobos hopping on and off the railroads. Or all those folks livin' off gov'ment jobs like the WPA and CCC and all that. I tell you, FDR has pretty near ruined this country."

I said, "Oh, I like to think our country's best years are ahead of us. Who knows? We might develop a vaccine for polio, invent amazing technology, put a man on the moon."

Lester scoffed. "Now I know you're a fiction writer if you're coming up with looney ideas like that.

"Fly to the moon," Nellie said, waving a dismissive hand. "I never heard the like. I don't know how you can talk about flying off to the moon when we have troubles enough here. We've just come out of a depression, and now we're plunged into another world war."

Lester said, "Let me tell you, son, the thirties weren't easy on anybody, especially me. I was a printer by trade. Worked for a community newspaper here in the square. Then the depression hit, and the stores all pulled their advertising. The news was so bad, nobody wanted to read it anyhow. First, they cut my wages. Then the paper went under completely. I tried to start a little weekly rag myself but couldn't make a go of it."

"Wow," I said.

"I had to scrounge to keep this house away from the bank. I picked up any odd job, any hustle I could find. I scavenged sticks to burn in the fireplace for heat. Walking around looking for sticks with a piece of cardboard stuck in my shoe to cover the holes. One time all we had to eat was bread and mustard. I ate mustard sandwiches for a month. Can't stand the sight of it now, mustard. People today are making big money with all this war industry. I worked for peanuts."

Nellie reached over and patted his leg. "We were talking about Mr. Ryan, Lester."

Lester nodded. "Oh, yeah. He's a real go-getter. Too bad he's 4-F. Bad ticker. Otherwise, the Army would have made him an officer probably." He looked at me. "Say, how come you're not in it?"

"The war?" I asked. "Wish I was. Flat feet."

He shot me a doubtful frown.

Nellie's eyes wandered toward the door she had come from. "I better be getting back to those potatoes."

"Right. Right," I said. "I have that appointment myself. I'll just dash upstairs first. Thanks for your time."

Lester said, "Wait. So which is it? Are you in sales or a writer?"

I stood and straightened my suit pants. "Both. Sales to feed myself while I'm trying to make it with short stories and novels."

He shook his head at me like I was batty.

I climbed the stairs and knocked on all the doors just in case Peter Ryan was around. Nobody answered. I returned to the ground floor and walked out the front door, headed for the *Shaymus*.

There I found Zastra in the office looking bored. "How's the case going, Gabe?"

"I've talked with three of the suspects so far. I wanted to confer with Oren … and you too. Oren?"

His face flashed on the view screen. "Hello, Gabriel."

"I thought I would report in. Have you been tapping into my translator bots?"

"No. I don't know Earthlings as you do. I will rely on your interpretation of them."

"Okay then." I sat down at my desk and gave them a rundown of my conversations with Muriel and the Potters. When I finished, I asked, "Do you see any clues?"

"Perhaps," Oren said. "I still want you to talk to this Peter Ryan."

"Me too. If I can catch him."

"These Potters seem odd … disapproving."

I waggled my head. "Oh, not too odd for old people of that generation … or any generation, come to think of it. As far as I know, that may be what comes from renting rooms to people."

Zastra asked, "Could the roommate have done it?"

"Murdered Irene? I don't see a motive."

"Are you kidding me? Two people sharing a room. That's a recipe for murder if I ever saw one."

Oren said, "There *is* something suspicious about her."

Zastra said, "You mean the fact that she seems interested in Gabe?"

"Ha ha," I said. "Let me remind you, Sarah is waiting for me at the altar. Or she will be in about eighty years."

"What I mean," Oren said, "is that for someone who was obviously making romantic advances toward you, it's odd she told you next to nothing about herself."

That was true. Most people try to impress a crush with talk of themselves. It's not like I didn't give her an opening. She didn't even tell me where she was from.

"I'll prod some more," I said. "Have you heard anything from Buad and Blan?"

"No. Let's check in with them. Buad, Blan?"

We heard Blan's voice in our ears. "Yeah, Chief."

"Did you find the military base?"

"We found it all right. That part was easy. But this is like a metropolis here. There are tens of thousands of soldiers. Finding those particular two will be like finding one seed in a feeder … or a hundred feeders."

Buad said, "We figured out the best time to identify them is at meals 'cause they enter in a line. We're working through them one mess hall at a time. That's what they call where they eat — a mess hall. Goofy name, huh?"

"Good luck," Oren said.

I left the office and walked down the steps in the central shaft to engineering. Jace had all the parts we had bought spread out on a table. He was wiring and soldering.

"How's it going?" I asked.

"I'm making progress, but I have a long way to go."

"Do you need anything else from the outside world?"

"Only parts that haven't yet been invented here, so no. I'm having to fabricate as I go along."

I left him and returned to the middle crew deck to whip up a snack in the galley. Quog was in there, eating another hamburger and reading from my phone. I replicated a banana for myself.

"What book did you pick?"

"*The Adventures of Sam Spade*. Short stories."

"Dashiell Hammett. Good choice." I took a bite of banana, chewed, and swallowed. "Do you want to tag along this afternoon? I'm planning to interview the doctor. That Ryan fellow too if I can catch him. These people are closer to your time than mine. I could use your insights."

Quog set down the phone and yawned. "Can we take the bus?"

"Sure."

He handed me back my phone. I like to think I'm not addicted, but it felt good having it back in my pocket, even though I was fifty years away from getting a signal.

Quog wiggled his eyebrows. "Do we need to replicate a few more simoleans' worth of dimes?"

"Simoleans? Simoleans? Quog, I think Sam Spade is rubbing off on you."

Chapter 14

What's Up, Doc?

A side door on the Fountain Square Theater Building led us into a small, tiled foyer with stairs, an elevator, and a directory sign that included the listing: *Dr. A Hatch 306*. We took the elevator, the car creaking and rumbling as it made its way up. The door opened on the third floor to linoleum in green and tan squares stretching down a long hallway. A line of dark wood doors topped by transoms stretched along both sides.

Number 306 opened to a small waiting room. Across the room, sitting in one of the chrome and Naugahyde chairs that rimmed the space, was a man in a disheveled suit with a cough like a seal in a circus act. He barked out about a dozen hacks nonstop, then pulled off his horn-rimmed glasses and wiped his eyes with a handkerchief.

Behind a window sat a woman in one of those old-timey white nurse uniforms, complete with cap. She sat at a tiny desk inside a cubbyhole surrounded by file cabinets.

We approached, doing our best to stay out of the coughing man's line of fire. "We'd like to see Dr. Hatch," I said.

"Names?" she asked, managing to add a patronizing tone to just that one word.

"Louis Columbo. This is my father, Doug."

"And what is your complaint?"

I shot her a smile. "Congress." The joke should have worked in any era.

However, Nurse Ratched, or so I now named her, was not amused. "Sir, this is a place of business. I advise you to take the comedy elsewhere."

I made my face serious and tried again. "We're investigating the death of Irene Giordano. She worked here."

The nurse looked me up and down. She presumably decided I wasn't joking this time because her expression switched from annoyance to concern. "Such a tragedy."

"Did you know her?"

"Not personally. I'm only here on loan until Doctor can find a replacement." She stood. "I'll tell him you're here." She disappeared into an inner chamber.

Quog whispered to me, "This reminds me of the office of the Earth doctor I used to go to as a child."

A minute later the door beside the nurse's window opened. Dr. Hatch, in shirt sleeves and tie with a stethoscope hanging around his neck, gave Quog and me a glimpse then said to the coughing man, "Mr. Brooks, would you give me a few minutes to talk to these gentlemen about a police matter?"

The man answered with three more coughs and a nod.

"Come this way, gentlemen."

He ushered us into a tile-floored examination room. A sink cabinet stood on one wall alongside one of those old glass-fronted, steel medicine cabinets. A wooden desk faced it from the other side of the room. In the middle, a stool on rollers sat near a cold metal examining table. We stood around the exam table like office mates meeting at a bar. I noticed Quog gazing fondly around at it all as if he were strolling down memory lane.

Hatch said, "I've already spoken with a detective ... Vukovich, I think."

"Yeah," I said. "We're with a different unit that's helping out. I'm Lieutenant Columbo and this is Sergeant Quog."

"Quog. That's an unusual name. I don't think I've ever heard it before."

"It's foreign," Quog said, which was the truth since it was his alien name.

I flicked open my notebook. "The victim, Irene Giordano, worked for you, correct?"

"Yes, she was employed here since ... since March of last year. I remember it because it was the day MacArthur left the Philippines."

"How was her work?"

"How is that relevant to her ... her death?"

"I'm just trying to get everything straight in my mind."

"Her work was fine ... most of the time. You know how Italians are."

What kind of ethnic prejudice was this? "Can't say that I do. How are they?"

He frowned. "Emotional. She yelled at a couple of unruly patients. And then there are those loud raucous families they have."

"She brought her family here to your office?"

"No, of course not. But they're close-knit, right? And the families have a lot of pull on them. Not always in the best way … or lawful way, if you know what I mean."

"What are you saying? Did she steal from you?"

"Well … I never had any proof of it. But once I had some supplies go missing. Whether she had taken them to stitch somebody up or … whatever, I never found out. And with Mussolini and the war …" He trailed off. "I think it might be significant that she was killed with a knife."

He strode over to the desk, pulled open a drawer, and came out with a cigarette, which he lit with a lighter from his pocket. That's the forties for you. Casual racism and doctors smoking, right in their offices no less.

I said, "So you think she was rubbed out by a knife-wielding fascist Italian mobster?"

"I don't know. They arrested that soldier."

"Right. Is it usual for you to go to the movies on a weekday afternoon?"

He returned to the exam table. "No, not at all. As it happened, I had no appointments, no walk-ins. I decided to let Irene go early. An hour or so later, when I was heading home, the movie poster caught my eye. I went in on a lark."

"You didn't know Irene was there also?"

"Not in the least. Not until after … when someone said her name."

"Were you planning on meeting anyone at the movie?"

The doctor's eyes flashed. "No. Did someone say I was?"

"I'm just asking. Do you know her roommate, Muriel?"

"We met once, but that's it. Pretty girl."

"Did you know any of the people who were identified at the theater? The Potters, for instance?"

"As it happens, they are patients of mine."

"What about Peter Ryan or Ray Noonan?"

He took a moment to puff on the cigarette before saying, "No."

"And I don't suppose you ever met the three soldiers, did you?"

He shook his head. "Look, Mr. Columbo, I might have given you the wrong impression earlier. True, Irene wasn't the best employee, but she was a good kid. I liked her. I believe I was something of a father figure to her since her father had passed. Terrible deal, some factory accident back during the Depression. She would sometimes confide in me when she had disagreements with her roommate or if her mom was having some problem or another."

"She had disagreements with Muriel? Anything major?"

He waved the cigarette. "Typical roommate issues. How much space they each got in the closet. Sharing clothes. Who's messy and who's neat."

"Which one was Irene, messy or neat?"

Hatch dismissed the question with a shake of the head. "I have no idea."

"Okay. Tell me this. She was stabbed in the back of the neck. As a doctor, what does that tell you?"

He felt for the stool and sat down. "I'm not a pathologist, but I know it's one of the most lethal spots on the body. The blade would sever the spinal cord, immediately rendering the person unable to move or speak, followed by virtually instant death. It's not an easy thing to do, though."

"You mean the killer would have to know what he or she was doing."

"Uh-huh. Again, a mobster … or a soldier."

"Or a doctor, right, Doc?" I threw it out with a chuckle but watched for his reaction. For a second, he looked like he was going to slug me. People did that sort of thing back in those days … or these days … at least in movies. I decided to move on. "What about blood splatter? None of the suspects had blood on them."

"Keep in mind I mostly deal with flu and accidental injuries. But I would think with a low-velocity weapon like a knife, there might not be much splatter. The back of the neck wouldn't gush like a slit throat."

After that unappetizing image, I wished I had a stool to sit on myself. I pulled off the fedora and waved it like a fan.

Hatch stood and stubbed out the cigarette in an amber glass ashtray on the desk. "Is there anything else? I have a patient waiting."

"No," I said. "Thank you for your time."

"You're welcome, Detective … Columbo, is it?" He walked us to a door that led directly from his examination room to the hallway.

I said, "You know, it's a funny thing. Irene didn't know when she came to work yesterday that you were going to let her off early, did she?"

"No. I didn't know myself."

"See, that's the funny thing. The killer couldn't have known either. This whole thing must have been a crime of convenience, an unfortunate coincidence."

"I suppose you're right, Detective. Strange how fate works."

"Yeah, well, I don't believe in coincidence."

Quog and I returned to the street where the day was growing warm. "Now where?" he asked.

I said, "I want to go back to the house and see if Peter Ryan is around."

"Well, after all that talk about blood, Gabriel, I wouldn't mind sitting a spell and getting something to drink."

Across the street the words *Pop's Diner* were painted on the big glass window of a storefront. "Let's go," I said.

It must have been close to noon because the place was bustling with people. We managed to find an empty booth and sat gazing dubiously at the chalkboard signs above the counter:

Pig's Knuckle 30¢

Knockwurst on Rye 20¢

Wheat Cakes 10¢

Pickled Egg 5¢

Really? This was like traveling to another culture. It was almost like being on an alien planet.

A waitress in an apron, cap, and a pin with *Betty* on it trotted over to the table. "What can I do you for?"

Quog said, "I'd like a Coke."

That sounded all right to me … and way better than pig's knuckles. "Same."

"No lunch? Our knockwurst will knock your socks off, and nobody has a beef with our brisket." She shot me a sideways smile, eyebrows raised in a question.

"Not for me. What about you … Dad?"

"Thanks, but no," Quog said. "I've eaten."

Betty jotted on her pad and moved off.

Quog took in the décor, which could be described simply as tile, linoleum, and shiny surfaces with signage about menu items. "There was a diner like this near home when I was growing up."

I said, "In my time, places like this are essentially gone. By and large, all we have are chain restaurants and fast food. Oh, you'll find a few reproductions of this kind of place here and there, retro nostalgia diners, but they aren't the same. They're all decorated with road signs and Elvis photos."

"That sounds like a loss. Ooh, a jukebox. How about you give me one of those dimes, Gabriel?"

I dug one out and pushed it across the table to him.

He came back swaying to the beat of *Chattanooga Choo Choo*. "My dad had this record," he said as he slid into the booth. "Glenn Miller. Too bad, rock and roll hasn't come around yet. I'd like to hear Chubby Checker."

"You know, in my time vinyl records are making a comeback," I said.

"Records went away? Good grief." Quog's face looked like a guy who just found out his mom had tossed out all his old comic books.

"Most everything is streamed nowadays."

"Then there's nothing you can hold in your hands. I remember buying the forty-five for *My Girl* by The Temptations. The thrill of walking home with it, setting it down on a record player, putting on the needle."

"Sorry. That's progress, I guess."

"Is it though? I found some of your music on your phone."

"What did you think?"

He shook his head.

"What? I have some of the best hits of the nineties — No Doubt, Green Day, Foo Fighters." If he didn't like that, what would he think of newer pop music?

"Whatever happened to Petula Clark? The Dave Clark Five?"

"Who?" I was whiplashing through the decades here.

The waitress showed up with the Cokes — in the old-style glass bottles, no less. "Do you two dreamboats need anything else? Pie? An order of fries?"

At that moment another waitress hollered out, "Paint a bowwow red and give it shoes."

A cook in the kitchen stuck his head through the window and yelled it back.

Betty must have seen the confused look on my face. "Hot dog with ketchup to go. Diner slang, get it? Moo juice is milk. Eve with a moldy lid is apple pie with cheese."

"Wow. Say, how about a different type of information? I just moved into a rooming house on Olive."

She eyed me suspiciously.

I said, "That's the place where the girl who was killed lived? Did you hear about that?"

"Yeah." She nodded solemnly.

"It's only around the corner from here and down the street. I was wondering if, by chance, you knew any of the people there."

"The old guy comes in here sometimes."

"Lester?"

"Yeah, that's him."

"What about Muriel Marshall or Peter Ryan?"

She flinched a little. "I know Pete Ryan. He's a real B. T. O."

"B. T. O?"

"Big time operator. A wolf. A guy on active duty."

"I didn't think he was in the service."

"Har har. Not that kind of active duty. You from the boondocks, mister? Get with the lingo."

Quog smirked. "You mean, he likes to go out on maneuvers."

"Now you're cooking with gas."

"He has a girl in every port."

"And then some. You ain't just whistling dixie."

Listening to the two of them go back and forth, I was glad I had watched a fair number of old movies. Otherwise, I would have been completely lost in the slang.

"What do you know about Muriel Marshall?" I asked.

"Bupkis. Never heard of her." The waitress's eyes shifted between Quog and me. "What's going on here? Are you guys like shamuses or something, gumshoes? Are you investigating the murder?"

I pushed the fedora back on my head with a thumb and propped an elbow on the back of the bench seat. "Something like that."

"I thought that soldier did it."

"We don't think so."

"Well, I hope you catch the guy who did. A girl can't feel safe walking around with a murderer on the loose."

Another patron called for her. She tore the check from her pad, placed it face down on the table, and scooted away.

I flipped over the bill. Two sodas, five cents each. I plopped down two dimes to cover the cokes, a tip, and the useful intel.

"I like her," Quog said, "That girl has moxie."

I blinked at him. "Quog, where are you getting all this slang?"

Chapter 15

Out in Left Field

Energized by the caffeine buzz, Quog and I walked the few blocks to the gray two-story on Olive Street. As we entered, a tinny *thwack* sounded from the parlor accompanied by excited crowd noises. We followed our ears and found Lester in the same chair he had been planted in earlier, leaning toward the radio with a hand behind one ear. The day had warmed, and with all the windows in the room shut, the parlor was growing stuffy. Yet Lester was still sitting there in long-sleeved flannel.

A voice on the set said, "The ball sails out to left field ... and Novikoff is there with the catch to close the inning. At the end of eight, the Cubs lead the Brooklyn Dodgers three to two. We'll be right back for the final inning after these messages."

The broadcast switched to a commercial of a child's voice complaining of an upset stomach and an authoritative male voice asserting that he had precisely the thing for it. Lester flicked a glance in our direction, then reached for the radio with a grimace of old-age pain and lowered the volume.

I said, "Mr. Potter, this is my father, Doug Columbo. Dad, this is Mr. Potter, my landlord."

Quog said, "Pleased to meet you. Homey place you have here." He patted the radio box, which Lester didn't appear to appreciate. "Is that the Cubs?"

"Yeah," Lester grunted.

"That reminds me of my childhood. My dad and I used to watch the Cubbies."

"You grew up in Chicago?"

"No, no." Quog waved a hand. "Tearho ... I mean, Terre Haute. Out US 40 by the state line."

94

"Yeah, I know where Terre Haute is, but it's sure a long way to haul up to Chicago from there just to see a game."

Quog stopped short and fixed me with a stare like a deer in the headlights. I saw the problem. Quog likely meant they had watched the games on TV, but that technology didn't yet exist in this period. I was afraid he would make it worse by saying he meant they listened to the games. But someone Quog's age in 1943 would have been a boy in the 1880s, long before the advent of radio.

I stepped up to pinch-hit for him. "Yeah, old Granddad was quite the Cubs fan. Rode the train up to Wrigley Field as often as he could." I hoped Wrigley Field was old enough for that statement to pass muster. I discovered later that it wasn't, but the error didn't seem to register with Lester. In any case, I thought it best to move the conversation along. "Is Peter Ryan in? I'd like to meet him."

Lester yelled out toward the back of the house. "Nellie, do you know if Ryan is in?"

She called back from another room. "I haven't seen him."

"What?" Lester bellowed. He pointed a thumb toward the back of the house. "She always mumbles."

Nellie shouted more loudly and slowly. "I don't know where he is."

I waved a hand. "Don't worry about it. We'll check upstairs. Which room is his?"

Lester hollered again. "Nellie, what room does Ryan have?"

"Number two."

"Did you say who? It's this Columbo guy who's asking. He wants to know." Lester shook his head in disgust.

"Not who ... number ... two."

"Two?"

"Yes, two. One, Two. Peter Ryan is in room number two. You know that, you old fool."

"How should I know?" he hollered. "I don't go up there. I can barely climb stairs anymore."

The game announcer came back on the radio. "We're back. And leading off in the ninth for the Cubs is Peanuts Lowrey."

Lester turned the volume up, nodding to us as if we were being dismissed. I tapped Quog on the arm, and we headed for the stairs.

"Heavens to Betsy," Quog said to me in a whisper as we crossed the hall. "That was a close one. I need to remember what decade I'm in. It's just their living room reminded me so much of my grandparents' house."

Which served to illustrate our generational differences. My grandparent's house was filled with 1980s shag carpeting and covered in paneling.

The door to room two was right across the hall from the top of the stairs. I knocked and heard, "Come in."

We pushed open the door and stepped through. Ryan was stretched out on the bed, his tie loose and his shoes off. He was smoking and staring at the ceiling. Did everybody in this era smoke?

I said, "Hi. I'm Lou Columbo. I moved in down the hall. This is my dad."

He nodded without moving from the bed. "Pete Ryan." He took another drag from the cigarette.

"I thought we weren't supposed to smoke up here."

He smirked. "What the old lady don't know won't hurt her. If it bothers you, I'll put it out."

"No, go right ahead." I cleared my throat and fought to hold back a cough. "You probably need it after all the excitement yesterday."

He twisted his neck to stare at me. "What excitement?"

"The murder."

"How do you know about that?"

"Muriel. I talked with her this morning."

He rolled his eyes. "Figures. She's probably told the whole city by now. We don't need newspapers with her around."

"Did you know Irene well?"

He flashed a gold tooth. "Not as well as I'd like to." The smile died quickly as he seemed to think better of the joke as soon as he said it. "Sorry. All I meant was she was kind of a cold fish."

"In what way?"

"I mean, she was shy. She didn't say much."

"Did you date her?"

"Let me give you a piece of rooming house advice, bub. It's not a good idea to date housemates. They live way too close. They see you coming and going. Before you know it, it's 'What were you doing out so late? Where were you?' I tell you, it's not healthy."

I hoped Muriel followed that rule because I was off the market.

"What was it like — the murder, I mean? Did you see anything?"

Ryan swept his legs around to bring himself to a sitting position. He hauled an empty coffee cup from the floor and flicked ashes into it. "Nah. The first I knew anything was when Muriel started screaming her head off."

"I hear they arrested some soldier. Do you think he did it?"

"Why not? The cops think he did. It was his knife, wasn't it?"

"But I heard he's just a simple farm boy."

"Farm boy, eh? Let me tell you, bub —"

"Lou."

"Lou, then. I grew up on a farm, and my old man was the orneriest cuss you'll ever run across. He'd get mad at the mule and beat it within an inch of its life. Scared the dickens out of me time and time again. So don't talk to me about simple, innocent farm boys."

"You and Muriel and Irene were sitting together in the theater. In what order?"

"Irene was in the middle. I was on her left."

"Was there any particular reason for that seating order?"

"What's with all the questions, Louie? Are you writing her life story?"

I put on a grin. "Something like that. I'm an author. This whole setup would make a great novel."

"You don't say? Well, if they make it into a movie, see if you can get Cary Grant to play me."

I laughed. "I'm not sure I have too much pull with casting. But as an author, I don't care much for the idea of the soldier stabbing her with his own knife. First, it isn't smart, and if you're writing a story, you want the antagonist to be smart. Second, it doesn't have enough intrigue."

"Intrigue? Okay, I'll bite. What *would* have intrigue?" He ground the cigarette into the cup and lit another.

"Oh, I don't know." I decided to throw out a couple of ideas to see how he reacted. "Love triangle with the roommate. Maybe some tie-in to gangsters."

Ryan chuckled. "I think you're barking up the wrong tree. Irene didn't know from gangsters. And she and Muriel didn't go for the same kind of men."

"Oh? What kind of men did Irene go for?"

"Beats me."

"How about a German spy? That would be an interesting angle for a story."

"Hardy har har. Why would the Nazis bother to kill a nurse? Buddy, you're way out in left field."

"Could be. Can you think of anyone who might have something against her?"

"Like I said, I didn't know her well."

"She didn't talk about having trouble with anybody?"

"Not to me."

It looked like the well was running dry. "What do you do for a living, Pete?"

"Encyclopedias. Door-to-door."

"That must entail a lot of walking."

He took a long drag on the cigarette. "Why do you think I'm back here in the middle of the day with my shoes off? Still, it's better than being out in the Pacific getting shot at. You meet a lot of lonely women going door-to-door."

What a sleazebag. "So as far as you know, Irene didn't have a boyfriend?"

"I don't think so. But one time I was with the girls at the Kit Kat Club, and I caught her making eyes at the bouncer. Can you imagine? I buy her a drink, and she puts peepers on somebody else. I tell ya, some dames."

"Wait. You mean Noonan? She was flirting with Ray Noonan? The guy who was at the movie?"

"You know him too, huh? Yeah, that guy."

"What do you think of him?"

"He's a cheap hood."

"Do you know if Noonan and Irene ever took it further than eye contact?"

"I wouldn't be in the know on anything like that."

"Right. What can you tell me about Irene's family?"

"Not much. What about 'em?"

"Where do they live?"

"Here in town. I think up in Fletcher Place. Oh, her dad's dead. Mama and the older kids are all working to support the little ones."

"So she didn't move far." I wondered if visiting the family would be helpful. "Why did she leave home?"

Ryan shrugged. "Beats me. Though now that you mention it, she made a few comments about her mom always telling her what to do and not do."

"I take it Irene didn't appreciate the maternal advice."

Ryan shot me a look that in my time would have been accompanied by, "Well, duh." I doubted Irene would have brought any of her problems to her mom.

"Yeah. Parents. Okay, Pete. Nice talk. See you around."

Quog and I returned to the hallway. I said, "C'mon, Dad. I'll show you my room."

We walked to the end of the corridor. I took a seat on one bed while Quog perched on the other. "What do you think?" I asked.

"About the room?" He bobbed his head around. "It's not bad."

"Yeah, all the discomforts of home. But I meant Ryan. Does he strike you as a murderer?"

Quog made a face. "He strikes me as a jerk. But, no, not a murderer. What's next?"

"I want to get a line on this Noonan character."

"How are you going to do that? Go to this Kit Kat Club?"

"Yeah, I think I will. And as it happens, Muriel wants me to take her."

"Interesting what Ryan said about Irene and Noonan. Perhaps you should ask the Potters about it. Maybe he came here."

"Good idea, Quog. You could be a detective. Let's go ask them about gentlemen callers."

We left my room and returned downstairs. The radio in the parlor was now switched off, and the room was empty.

"Mr. Potter?" I called. "Mrs. Potter?"

No answer. I pushed through the door Nellie had come from earlier and found a kitchen. Across a floor of cracked linoleum, a pot of something was stewing on an old cast iron cooking stove. The cooker was flanked on one side by a small white refrigerator with rounded edges and a worn and cluttered Hoosier cabinet on the other. A sink on skirted legs stood under a window beside a small wooden table and chairs. But no Nellie. I padded over to the back door and scanned the postage stamp yard. I saw a victory garden and a compost pile, but no people.

Another door led to the hallway from the front of the house, and another door led to a bedroom. I peeked in without stepping inside, not wanting to be caught in the Potters' private space.

In the corner of the kitchen, a set of back stairs led up. And next to that stood a fourth door — boy, this kitchen had a lot of doors. I thought I heard faint voices filtering through the door as if coming from a basement below. I grasped the handle and found the door locked.

I returned to the parlor to find Quog on the davenport flipping through the newspaper.

"Oh, what do you know?" Quog said. "*Alley Oop*, *Nancy*, *Li'l Abner*, *Blondie*. I remember reading these comics as a kid in the sixties." He chuckled. "Ah, that Dagwood." He flipped a few more pages. "The Cubs aren't doing great so far this season. I hope they ended up winning that game."

"Does it matter?" I asked. "It's ancient history in my time."

He flipped another page. "Oh my, Gabriel."

"What? War news?"

"No. Worse."

He folded the paper inside out and handed it to me. Staring at me was a mugshot of Grandpa Frank. The headline beside it read: *Soldier Confesses to Murder*.

Chapter 16

Through the Wringer

"No. No. That can't be right. Grandpa didn't do it. He told me he didn't. Why would he confess?"

"You know the cops. When they want a confession, they get a confession." Quog punched a fist into his palm as if to demonstrate the technique.

I scanned and rescanned the brief article, gripping the newspaper like I was trying to strangle the life out of it. "This says he confessed to police that he stabbed Irene Giordano. It quotes the police chief, saying the case is now closed." I took a step backward and dropped into Lester's chair. The cushion was lumpy in all the wrong places.

"What does this mean for your investigation, Gabriel?"

"It means we have to pick up the pace. I'm no lawyer, but I think he'll need to make an appearance in court to formally enter the plea. Then they'll proceed to sentencing in short order." I stared into space for a moment or two. "I need to talk to him. Now. Do you want to go to police headquarters with me?"

Quog nodded. We hurried out and caught a bus to take us downtown to the limestone-clad police building. With all the dimes nesting in my pocket, I was glad metal scanners weren't in use during this time.

Presenting ourselves at the front desk, I said, "Lou Columbo to see my client, Frank Lake."

The desk sergeant looked me over and then Quog. "Who's gramps here?"

I slapped on an offended expression, which wasn't too difficult given this guy's blatant ageism. "This just happens to be … um … Horace Rumpole, one of the foremost attorneys in Chicago, an expert in bloodstains. I've brought him in to advise on the case."

The sergeant heaved a sigh and said, "All right. Follow me."

He led us to the same dreary interview room I had visited the evening before. Quog stared at the gray cinder block walls. He squinted at the glaring light over our heads. "My, my. This place would make a guy confess if for no other reason than to get out of here."

"Maybe that's what happened," I said in a gloomy tone.

An officer escorted Grandpa Frank into the room. One lip was swollen. A bruise spread across his cheek. The cop pushed him down into a chair and stood behind him.

I leaned in. "Frank, what's all this about confessing? You told me you were innocent."

He shook his head. "I am innocent. But they kept talking about how strong their case against me was. They said if I confessed, they'd take the death penalty off the table. I figured as long as I'm alive, there would be hope of proving my innocence … someday."

"Yeah. But pleading guilty."

"You don't know what it was like, Mr. Columbo." His eyes darted around the room. "They kept me in here for hours, hot lights, nothing to eat or drink, grilling me over and over. I thought the brass knuckle routine only existed in the movies." He shifted his jaw gingerly left and right. "It doesn't. They ran me through the wringer."

With a pounding in my head, I felt like I'd been through a spin cycle myself.

The bruise on his cheek was a nasty yellow. I wanted to document it and the fat lip in case we later needed to challenge the confession. But how? I needed to risk using the Android.

I slipped my phone out of my pocket and tapped it against the side of my hand as if it were some kind of high-tech black plastic cigarette case. When no super thin cigarette popped out, I shrugged and kept on talking.

"We can still fight this, Frank." I held the phone in front of my chest like a thing that just happened to still be in my hand. With a few swipes of my thumb, I brought up the camera and snapped a subtle picture, coughing to cover the electronic *click*. The harsh overhead light at least made for a clear shot. I slid the phone back into my pocket. "Do you have a lawyer, Frank?"

He looked confused. "I thought you were my lawyer, Mr. Columbo."

"Yeah. About that." I pushed the fedora back and rubbed my forehead. "I'm actually an investigator. Saying I was a lawyer was the only way I could get in to see you." I glanced up at the cop, whose face was now growing red. "You're going to need a real lawyer before you enter your plea in court. But I'm going to try to prove your innocence before it comes to that."

His brows wrinkled. "Who … who hired you to investigate?"

Obviously, I couldn't tell this teenager the client was his grandson. Or a team of space alien detectives. "The victim's family," I said.

"You mean they don't believe I did it? Everyone believes I did it. The Army brass was here. They even think I'm guilty. They're talking about a dishonorable discharge." He hung his head.

"The family wants to know for sure. They don't want the real killer to get away with it."

Frank looked at me with tired eyes and drew in a breath. "And can you? Can you find the person who killed Irene?" His eyes flicked between me and Quog.

I said, "By the way, this is Mr. Rumpole. He's helping us with the case."

"Glad to hear it. Many hands make light work."

I nearly laughed … and cried. I don't know how many times Grandpa had said that to me in my childhood — probably every time we had to clear the table after a family meal.

Frank asked, "Are you getting anywhere?"

"We may be. Irene's employer, Dr. Hatch, thinks she might have been involved with the mob somehow."

He shook his head. "I don't believe it."

"Okay, well, he may be lying, which would make him a suspect. And the guy who was at the movies with Irene and Muriel, Peter Ryan. He seems sketchy."

Frank rubbed the back of his neck, no easy feat while wearing handcuffs. "It doesn't sound like much, but keep at it, I guess."

"We will. Do you know when you have to make your plea in court?"

"Not 'til Monday."

"Good. That gives us a little bit of time. Have you been talking to your parents?"

"They call every day."

"Next time, tell them to hire an attorney."

"They don't have much money."

Quog said, "We can help."

I didn't know what Quog meant by that. Was he thinking we could replicate a fifty-pound feed sack full of dimes for a retainer? Was he planning on contributing a diamond to the cause? In any case, the offer brought a weak smile to Frank's face.

"Thanks."

He stood, wincing as he pulled himself from the chair. "I feel about eighty-five."

"I'll call you Grandpa then." I was smiling and biting my lip at the same time.

We watched the guard lead him out. I pressed fingers to my forehead, trying to rub away the pain. "C'mon. We need to talk with Oren."

We caught a bus to Garfield Park where the beauty of the spring day was completely lost on me. We entered the *Shaymus* and climbed to the office.

Zastra was sitting at her desk staring into a device. She glanced up. "I hope you're here because you solved the case. I'm about to go nuts stuck on this backward planet. I can't leave the ship. And trapped in the past, I can't even send messages to anyone alive in my time. The only vids I can stream are ones from a hundred years ago. Thank Gort these stone age people here can't detect wormhole streaming."

"Don't start," I said.

Quog said, "Here they go to the movies instead of streaming vids to themselves. Frames on a reel, not bits in a download."

Zastra said, "Sounds inconvenient."

Quog raised his chin. "Oh, I don't know. I think it makes for a sociable experience."

"Yeah, you two witnessed a murder. I bet that was a fantastic social experience."

I said, "Can we talk about the case? We've got problems. I need Oren."

The face of Dwayne Johnson popped up on the screen. I told Oren about the confession and walked him through the situation given my limited detective-novel understanding of the American justice system.

Quog said, "This whole thing is cock-eyed. It's a bunch of malarky. Anyone can see Frank Lake is not a murderer."

Oren said, "At least we still have time to prove his innocence."

"Sure," I said. "I guess if he's not facing the electric chair, we have years to do it."

"Not years. The timeline is more fragile than that. How would spending years, even months, in prison change your grandfather? And when he got out, assuming he does, would your grandmother marry an ex-con, even if we exonerate him?

Besides, we can't stay in this time period forever … or on Earth for that matter. We are people from the future, remember? And most of us are from other planets."

"Then leave me here if you have to. Listen, I'm not giving up. I'll work on the case myself. If what you said about the splinter timeline is true, then I don't have any choice but to stay. All you need to do is check on me from time to time in the present … my present, that is. If I show up there, then it means I've gotten the timeline fixed, right?"

"No. You wouldn't show up there. You'd still be here in the 1940s regardless of your grandfather's circumstances."

"Then check back with me in the forties."

"Time travel is strictly prohibited."

"Like that's ever stopped you. You continually break the Earth quarantine to pick me up for cases."

"Time travel is different. It is exceedingly dangerous."

"I think I've figured that much out already with the whole destroying my family thing."

"No doubt. But let's postpone this discussion. For the time being, we can stay, and we can try to solve this murder. Now, let's talk through what you've learned."

Still reeling from the specter of being left behind, I gave him a report on my interviews with Dr. Hatch and Peter Ryan. "What do you think?" I asked.

"The question is what do you think? You are the expert on Earthlings."

"My impression is they're all hiding something. But I don't know what."

"Concerning what the doctor said about Irene's family possibly having criminal connections, do you put any credence in that?"

"Not much. Grandpa doesn't think so, and he knew her."

"Not as well as the doctor did."

"No, that's true. But what you need to realize is in this time period, seeing people in terms of ethnic stereotypes is … well, it's kind of a given. It's the basis for a huge part of their humor. The fighting Irishman. The cheap Scotsman. French people in berets and white shirts with horizontal stripes. Plenty of people besides Italians were involved in crime. If we're looking for gangsters here, I would focus on Noonan."

Oren said, "Then pass on her family for now and check out Ray Noonan."

"Will do. Any progress with Buad and Blan?"

"Let me check. Buad, Blan? Have you been able to find the soldiers?"

Buad's voice sounded in our ears. "Yeah, yeah, Chief. We located the guys. Took us long enough, but we found them. This place is nuts. All these guys are shooting guns and climbing walls and crawling under barbed wire and running up and down hills."

Blan joined in. "Hey, get this. Today they dug these holes — called 'em foxholes, except it would have to be a crazy big fox to need a hole that size. Anyway, everybody had to hunker down in their hole while somebody flew over in an airplane and dropped sacks of flour out. If the soldiers got splattered with flour, it meant their hole wasn't good enough and they had to do it over again."

Buad said, "That's not where our two guys were, though. If they were, they might have talked while they dug, and we could have heard something. Instead, they were sitting in a classroom all day, listening to some guy yammer on about radio communications. They didn't have much time for talking. But we've followed them to their nests."

"Barracks," I said.

"Yeah, whatever. We'll listen in tonight as things calm down."

"Satisfactory," Oren said. "Keep us posted."

I gazed up through the skylight in the ceiling of the *Shaymus*. The sky had softened, a sign that evening was coming on. "I should probably return to the house to talk with Muriel about going to the Kit Kat Club."

Quog said, "I'll stay here. You don't want me tagging along on your date."

"It's not a date. I'm engaged, almost married. All I'm doing is interviewing a suspect."

"In any case, I'm tuckered out, and I'd like to get back to those swell books on your phone."

I handed over the device and left the ship once more.

Chapter 17

The Kit Kat Club

Night had fallen by the time I reached the Potters' house. I climbed the stairs and knocked on Muriel's door. She cracked it open for a peek and then opened it wider when she saw it was me.

"Hey there, Lou." She leaned against the doorframe, a playful grin on her face.

I waggled my eyebrows. "It's Friday night. How about the Kit Kat Club?"

"You read my mind. Give me two shakes to powder my nose. I'm starving. Can we eat there?"

"Why not?"

She winked and disappeared behind the door.

Eating at the club sounded expensive. I went to my room, shut the door, and counted out my dimes on the bedspread. Five bucks and change. The diner had advertised knockwurst on rye for twenty cents. My Coke was a nickel. I figured, double that, quadruple it even. Make it a buck or so for each of us. I should be fine.

I peeled off the suit and washed up in the sink in my room. A noticeable five o'clock shadow had taken up residence on my face. Since this was before the era of fashionable stubble, I gave myself a touch up. Thankfully, I had remembered my shaving kit from the *Shaymus*.

As I was slipping on my jacket, I heard a knock. It was my date. No, not a date, I reminded myself — merely someone getting me into the Kit Kat Club. But when I opened the door, she sure was dressed for a date. She wore a ribbon in her hair, a string of pearls around her neck, and a long sleeveless dress, white with red polka dots.

"Polka dots," I said. "Are we going to polka?"

"Not if I have anything to say about it."

I escorted her down the stairs and out into a warm evening. The way she was dressed up, it seemed wrong to take the bus. We walked to Fountain Square and hailed a cab. Muriel gave the address, and we rode downtown.

"Terty-five cents," the cabbie said as he pulled up outside the club.

I slipped him four dimes and mentally deducted it from cash on hand.

The club was housed on the ground floor of a three-story office building, nondescript except for a red awning with an artful line drawing of a cat. Underneath stood two brass stanchions with a velvet rope barring the way. Ray Noonan was standing behind it.

Noonan bobbed his head at Muriel like he recognized her and let us enter. We passed through a small lobby with coat check and other necessary facilities into a large room, lined with floor-to-ceiling curtains. White tablecloth tables surrounded a wooden dance floor.

At the back of the room stood a stage, currently unpopulated by musicians, but with a piano, drum set, and about a dozen of those big band music stands with the fronts on them. Block letters KKC were printed across the stand fronts. I was relieved somebody hadn't decided to be cute and spell club with a K.

We found a table and rubbernecked around at the other patrons. Couples were eating, drinking, laughing. Some of the men were in uniform. A middle-aged couple at the table behind us was having a more serious, fretful conversation about a son in the Marines.

At a corner booth sat an older guy beside two floozies who could have been his granddaughters except for the way they were laughing at everything he said. In his tuxedo with his gray hair and well-trimmed beard, he looked well preserved for whatever his age might be — anywhere between sixty and seventy-five.

"Who's that?" I asked, nodding in the man's direction.

"Boss McKinney," Muriel said. "He owns the joint."

A waiter came and handed us menus. Knockwurst sandwiches weren't on the bill of fare. Everything was way fancier and cost three or four bucks.

Muriel said, "Lamb chop, please."

I went with the scallops while I considered how I was going to pay for it all.

"Wine?" the waiter asked.

"Sure," I said. What did it matter? I was already in the hole.

As the waiter left, Muriel said, "Pete says you're a writer and you want to use Irene's death as research for a book."

I held up a hand. "Excuse me a minute. I need to see a man about a horse."

I slipped back to the lobby and dashed into the gents. Fortunately, the place was empty. "Zastra," I said through my translator bots, "I need your help."

I heard her raspy voice in my ear. "Let me guess, Gabe. You're pinned down in a blaster battle and need me to come save you."

"Ha. Shows what you know. They don't even have blasters on Earth. I need more dimes replicated. Can you make them and send Quog out in a cab to me?"

"What am I — your personal assistant?"

"Hey, you said you were bored. I need some money fast."

"Fine. How many do you need?"

"I'm currently about two bucks short. But Muriel may not be done drinking. Make it fifty dimes. No, wait. Quog will need cab fare. Make it sixty. Oh, just make it seventy."

"Seventy dimes. Is that what you're going with? Are you sure?"

"Yes. I'm at the Kit Kat Club downtown. The cabbie should know the place."

I returned to our table. "Sorry."

"So about you being an author?" She leaned toward me across the table.

I decided to change the story to follow up on the espionage angle. I gave her a crooked grin. "That's just what I told Pete and the Potters. Actually, I'm a spy."

She bit her lip playfully. "Is that so? For which side?"

"Oh, the good guys definitely."

Her mischievous smile faded. "Is that why you're asking questions about Irene? Why would a nurse at a general practitioner's office be in the know on allied war plans?"

"Well, when you say it that way, I admit it doesn't sound likely."

"Although, she did have a secret."

I sat up straighter. "What secret?"

"She wouldn't tell me. I could tell something was bothering her, and I asked, but her lips were sealed."

"When was this?"

"Tuesday night? Wednesday night? One of those."

"Right before she was killed."

"Yeah."

"Why didn't you mention this sooner?"

"I just thought of it. Why didn't you tell me you were a spy sooner?"

"I wasn't sure I could trust you."

"And now you think you can?"

"So much so that I have a confession. I was at the movie yesterday when Irene was killed."

"You were?" Muriel asked it slowly, suspiciously.

"Pure coincidence, but I saw her with you. I have to say, you two could have passed for sisters."

"People said that sometimes."

"My point is … in the dark … could the killer have gotten you mixed up?"

Her eyes grew larger. "You mean Lake might have been trying to kill me?"

"Not him. Forget him. But somebody."

"No, Frank Lake killed her 'cause she wouldn't go out with him."

I let it go and changed the subject. "What do you know about Irene's job?"

"She worked for that bossy old doctor. He was always calling her into work at all hours of the day and night."

"He had patients come in at night?"

"No, but he'd be there all hours doing paperwork. And sometimes he insisted she stay."

"Do you think he was … you know, making a play for her?"

She made a face and raised her eyebrows. "I wondered as much myself, but she never said anything like that."

"How long did you room with her?"

"Almost a year. She moved in after she got the job."

"Pete said her family didn't live far away. Why did she move out?"

"The noise. She had six or seven little siblings."

Our food arrived, and we dug in. I steered the conversation toward asking questions about her. Muriel had lived at the rooming house for two years. Her former roommate was a girl named Peggy, who married a rich guy and moved into a mansion up on Meridian. Before the war, all the other rooms had been filled with men, but one by one they had left to go into the service, all except Peter Ryan.

The conversation drifted into popular music, a topic I could keep up with only because of my turn in the swing band in high school. I had just gotten myself in a fix by mixing up Tommy Dorsey and Jimmy Dorsey when the waiter bailed me out by coming to the table.

"Mr. Columbo?"

"Yes."

"There's a gentleman here to see you."

"Be right back," I told Muriel.

I found Quog by the front door. I held out my hands, and he began scooping dimes from his pocket. A few fell to the floor, and Quog jumped after them, wincing in old-guy discomfort as he straightened. The coat check girl watched us doubtfully while blowing and popping bubblegum bubbles.

"Mercy me," Quog said when he completed the funds transfer. "Oh. The meter in the cab is at forty-three cents, and I still have the return trip."

I thumbed ten dimes back into his hand. "Give him a tip. And thanks."

I returned to the table, my pocket bulging enough to have a gerbil inside. Muriel had finished eating. She pulled a cigarette from her purse and held it unlit between her fingers. "Do you have a light for a lady?"

Ah, yes. In the old movies, guys were always lighting women's cigarettes. It was a whole thing and something I was unprepared to participate in. "Sorry. No lighter. I don't smoke." I signaled to a waiter, and he came over and did the deed.

Musicians began drifting onto the stage, tuning up, playing a few licks, joking with each other. As I downed my last scallop, an announcer mounted the platform, stepped behind one of those old fist-sized microphones, and said, "And now, ladies and gentlemen, for your dancing and listening pleasure, the Kit Kat Club presents Larry Star and the Starliners."

The band burst into a dreamy ballad. The waiter brought the check for dinner, which came to seven dollars and twenty cents. I stacked up the dimes on the table, glad to get them out of my pocket.

Muriel snickered at me. "You paid for the cab with dimes too. I'm gonna start calling you Dimes. Yeah, Dimes Columbo. Well, Dimes, are you going to sit there or ask me to dance?"

I stood and led her to the floor. As we swayed to the music she leaned into me, her head on my chest. Now, lest you think I was two-timing Sarah, let me be clear. Romance was the furthest thing from my mind, especially with a woman who was born in the same decade as my grandmother.

All I was doing was playing a role. I needed information about the murder, and the price was a little harmless flirting and dancing. Not that it wasn't enjoyable. Not that I wasn't flattered by her attention. But I was engaged to be married, and nothing was going to happen here. That was my intention, even before all the facts came out.

A question had been nagging at me. "Lester said the soldiers came to the house to see Irene."

"Yeah. Irene and me. I told you Frank Lake asked her out a couple of times. One time was that night here. And then he came around and asked her again. He wouldn't quit pestering her."

"What I don't understand is how he knew where she lived. Did she tell him?"

"I don't think so, but he knew me from high school. When he went off to basic training, his mom got my address from my mom. Then we ran into him and his buddies here."

I stopped dancing. "You went to high school with him? In Clinton?"

"How do you know about Clinton?"

"I ... I've been investigating."

"Frank was two years behind me in school. My little sister thinks he's a dreamboat. Wait 'til she hears he's a murderer."

The ballroom was warm with bodies, but I felt a cold chill. "What's your sister's name?"

"Lois."

I stopped dancing. "Not Lois Jordan? Your name is Marshall."

She dropped her head. "I guess I have a confession to make too. It's time I let you in on my deep, dark secret. I'm divorced, Dimes. Jordan was my maiden name."

Muriel. This was Great-Aunt Muriel. I vaguely recalled her from the few times she visited. She hung out with Nana and didn't engage with us kids. What I mainly remembered was her blue hair set in a rigid perm. She chain-smoked and talked about her ex-husbands, of which she had apparently had several. Here I was slow dancing with Aunt Muriel. Eww. I mean, eww. Reflexively, I pulled back.

"What's the matter, Dimes? Are you too Sunday School to be interested in a divorcee?"

I swallowed. "No. No. I'm just surprised. You grew up with Frank, huh?" I took her hand again and resumed dancing, though she had to feel a new stiffness in my body.

"How do you know Lois?" she asked.

"I ... um ... spoke with Frank, and he mentioned her."

She sneered. "That thug better leave my little sis alone."

"Listen, I don't think he did it."

This time she was the one to pull back. "How do you figure?" It came out as more of an accusation than a question.

"As I said, I talked to him. He said he didn't do it, and I believe him."

"Oh," she said with exaggerated sarcasm. "Well, if he says he didn't do it. I'm sure a murderer would never lie. You're trying to get him off. You're trying to free that meatball who killed my friend."

"Muriel, you want the right guy to go to prison, don't you?"

She shook out of my arms and spoke in words like rifle shots. "I need a drink. Pull out some dimes, Dimes, and buy me a drink."

We returned to the table. I waved toward the waiter. He slalomed through the room toward us and took our order. When he left, we sat in silence.

I said, "Look, if Frank did it, he did it, and I'll accept that. But I don't think he did it."

She scowled at me. "So that's why the twenty questions. Everything about Irene and Pete and me. Am I a suspect?"

"I can't see a motive for you."

"But you've been looking for one."

"I'm investigating."

"As a spy or an author or what?"

"As me. I want to know the truth."

"What's it to you, Dimes?"

"More than you know."

Muriel glared at me. "You're something else, you know that?"

The drinks came. She downed hers in one gulp and stood. She held a palm out toward me. "Cab fare. I'm going home. Alone."

I dropped some dimes in her hand and watched her go. I sat there nursing my drink. Ray Noonan came in and made his way to Boss McKinney's table, leaning over to exchange words. Noonan was who I had come to see. Since my date had bolted, this looked like the ideal time.

Noonan nodded to McKinney and walked off. I stood and followed him. I caught up to him in the lobby where he was chatting up the coat check girl.

I called out with a wave of my hand as if I had spotted a long-lost friend. "Well, if it isn't Ray Noonan as I live and breathe."

I was trying hard to be nonchalant about it all, but I wasn't. I had faced off with hoodlums before — alien hoodlums, in fact — Thomians as huge as gorillas and nearly as smart. But in those cases, I had generally had Zastra there for backup. I wasn't enthusiastic about facing a gangster — and maybe his gangster pals too — all alone.

Chapter 18

Paper Moon

Ray Noonan pulled his eyes away from the coat check girl and regarded me with a cocky smirk. "Do I know you?"

I leaned against the wall, trying to summon an equal level of bravado. "Maybe you should. We have the same taste in movies. And we're both familiar with Irene Giordano."

"Who's she?" He glanced at the coat check girl as if to make sure this mention of another woman's name wasn't sabotaging his chances with her. The girl blew a bubble and popped it.

"C'mon, Noonan," I said. "Yesterday at the movies. She was the person somebody stabbed. And I understand she was previously in here and made eyes at you. She was a looker. Don't tell me you didn't notice her."

He ran thumbs down the backs of his jacket lapels. "What do you want me to say? I'm a sharp dresser. Dames pick up on that. Doesn't mean I chase 'em. Excuse me, I didn't catch your name."

"Lou Columbo. I'm a private investigator."

"You are? No offense, but you must not be that big 'cause I never heard of you."

"I normally work out of town." Way, way out of town, I thought. "I'm looking into Irene's murder."

"I wish you luck. I hate to see a doll treated in such a way."

"So you did know her."

He gave a flick to one shoulder. "I saw the body at the theater."

"Do you know what she was involved in? Any idea who might have killed her, or why?"

"Sorry. Like I said, I didn't know her."

"Do you know Muriel Marshall?"

"I don't believe so. Who is she?"

"The woman I came in with tonight."

"She's a looker too if I remember right. But no, we haven't met."

"What about Peter Ryan? Or Dr. Arthur Hatch? Or Lester and Nellie Potter?"

"Are they patrons of the Kit Kat Club?"

"Some of them, yes."

"Funny. None of those names ring a bell."

"Do you know the Giordano family?"

"The way you say it, you make it sound like a crime family. What are you implying, Columbo?"

"I'm not implying. I'm asking."

"Then no. I don't know them. I keep my head down and do my job."

"What is your job exactly?"

"I keep the riffraff out." He looked me up and down. "Supposed to anyway. Could be I was falling down on the job tonight. Or if tensions rise between any of the patrons, I intervene before anything untoward happens. I almost had to intercede earlier between you and your girl. That was a doozy of a fight you two had. What was it all about?"

"Turns out we root for different baseball teams. Cardinals, Cubs. You know how it is."

"Me, I'm a Reds fan. By the way, I haven't had a chance to get back to the picture show. Do you know how the movie ends? Did he get away with it or not?"

"Do bad guys *ever* win in the final reel?"

He smiled. "They don't in the movies, but you might be surprised what happens in real life."

"Not if I can help it, Noonan."

"Oh, you're that kind of shamus, eh? Truth and justice and all that. Well, take my advice, Columbo, watch your step."

I wanted to get in the last word, but I couldn't think of anything, so I merely swept past him toward the door. Outside, the night air was cool. I decided to walk back to Fountain Square to clear my head and think things over. Noonan hadn't been helpful. I suppose I shouldn't have expected him to be.

In some of the cases I've worked, everybody has a motive. In this one, it seemed nobody had a reason to want Irene dead. I wondered if we should widen our suspect pool. There had been lots of other patrons at the movie. The trouble was, I had no way of knowing who they were. Even if I could identify them, it would take days or weeks to interview them all by myself. Grandpa Frank didn't have that kind of time.

What did we know about Irene? She was a shy girl who didn't date much but was interested in guys, possibly the wrong kind of guys. She had a good job as a nurse. She may not have gotten along so well with her family. And something was bothering her in the days leading up to her death, something she didn't want to discuss with Muriel, or so Muriel said.

I walked along Virginia Avenue under a daffodil moon hanging in the sky, the kind of moon somebody would draw for a prom decoration or for a backdrop in a play. I had been in 1943 for two days, yet everything seemed to have an unreal quality. Thousands of movies had been made about this era — the war in Europe, in the Pacific, here at home. It would be easy enough to imagine all these people simply as actors dressed in period suits, the neighborhoods all Hollywood sets.

I think what most made it seem unreal was Sarah, or rather her absence. When I was on other planets, I could gaze up at the sky and know that she was out there on a world orbiting one of those specks of light, and I could return to her. Now I was in a place where she wasn't even born yet. And if I didn't fix the timeline, I would never see her again. It was like a bad dream.

And yet all this was deadly real. A young woman had been murdered. My grandfather was arrested. The moon above me was real as well, though yet untouched by astronaut boots or rover tires.

This was 1943. Somewhere in this world young men were shooting and being shot at, fighting and dying. Somewhere bombs were falling. Somewhere in camps with names such as Auschwitz and Buchenwald, names none of these people here yet knew, the Nazis were applying their final solution to six million innocent people. Here in Indy and across the country, people were going without sugar, gasoline, nylon, and rubber for the sake of the war effort.

And on a farm outside Clinton, Indiana, my great-grandmother was probably praying for her son, wondering what would happen to him. Millions of fathers and mothers all over the country were praying for sons and daughters in the service and far from home.

In the club, on buses, everywhere I went, I had overheard snatches of conversation about the war. It was on everybody's mind. They all were going about their daily lives, but at any moment concern about the war or the future or loved ones in danger would come bubbling up to the surface.

With the abrupt clatter of a glass bottle skittering across concrete half a block behind me, my thoughts snapped back to the here and now. I fought the urge to glance back, to pick up my pace. It might only be somebody else walking home. It might be somebody tossing something from a passing car. But Noonan's words were echoing in my mind. "Watch your step." I intended to.

I turned right at the corner, a risky move since the side streets were darker than Virginia Avenue, but I wanted to make sure I wasn't being followed. I walked that block, then took another right. I paused and strained to listen in the darkness. I heard nothing except a dog barking somewhere in the distance blocks away. I walked on and hung a third right and a fourth. Back on Virginia again, I ducked into a doorway and waited. I hummed the *Jeopardy* theme song in my head six times to count off three minutes.

Footsteps sounded from up the street. I pressed myself against the door and froze in place. They came nearer, nearer. It sounded like two sets of steps. I heard low voices, a giggle. Two young women passed in front of me. One of them saw me out of the corner of her eye and jumped with a sharp intake of breath.

I said, "Sorry. Didn't mean to scare you. Can I walk with you? For your safety?"

She nearly shouted the no at me. They picked up their pace and hurried on. To keep from creeping them out any more than I already had, I waited another two minutes before I stepped back out and resumed my walk. To be on the safe side, I followed a roundabout route to the rooming house on Olive Street.

As I passed Muriel's door, I stopped and knocked with the shave-and-a-haircut rhythm.

She called from inside with a tired voice. "Who is it?"

"Lou."

"Go away, Dimes."

"I wanted to make sure you got home safely."

"Go away. I can take care of myself."

I moved on to my room, hung up my suit, and slid between the sheets. I was starting to nod off when I heard Buad's voice in my ear coming through my translator bots.

"Hey, guys, we got something."

I sat up in bed.

Oren's voice said, "What is it, Buad?"

"We were perched in one of the windows in their barracks. The one soldier, that Dean Costa fella, just said to the other one, 'Red, I haven't heard nothing about Frank. I'm worried.' Then the other one said, 'We can't talk here. Let's go outside.' Blan followed them. You can listen in."

The next voice I heard was a man's. "Red, I'm feeling guilty about this whole thing. Frank's gonna take the rap for this. We gotta do something."

Another voice answered in an accusing tone. "What do propose we do, Dean?"

"I think we should tell the truth."

"And drop ourselves in the soup along with Frank? We already lied to the cops. If they find out, they'll throw the book at us, not to mention what the Army will do to us. Lookit, Frank didn't do it. The cops will figure it out."

"Man, what kind of hayseed are you? You think innocent people don't get convicted of crimes? You think a jury is gonna see past all the evidence in front of them into his innocent soul? It don't work that way, Red. Ask my cousin who's doing time for a crime he never did. We can't let Frank take the rap."

The voices fell silent. After half a minute, I said, "What are they doing?"

Blan answered in a whisper. "Nothing much. They're pacing around and sucking on those burning tube things. What are those doohickies good for?"

"Not much. That's what people back in this era did to help them think."

"Yeah? Maybe you should try it, bonehead."

"No thanks. I have coffee. Those things can kill you."

"Shush. Red's walking back over to Dean."

We heard Red say, "To tell you the truth, I can't even remember what happened exactly."

"Yeah? Well, I do. You asked Frank for his knife 'cause you couldn't open that box of candy with your hands all sore from rope climbing. What did you do with it?"

"I don't think I did anything with it. Right then, I got the box open. I don't think I ever touched the knife. Did Frank even hand it to me?"

"He placed it on the counter."

"I thought he picked it back up, Dean."

"You didn't pick it up?"

"Between you, me, and the man in the moon, I don't know. I don't think so."

"And you ain't just saying that, Red?"

"No. What do you mean? You think I would make something up to save my skin and throw Frank to the wolves?"

"All I'm saying is if you don't do something to help Frank out, then I will."

"Are you gonna squeal? Dean, you'll get us all booted out of the Army."

"I don't know what I'm gonna do, but I can't let Frank take the fall. Wait. I saw a movie once where two people confessed to a crime. Each confession created what they called reasonable doubt for the other one, and both guys got off the hook."

"You're going to confess to killing her? Now who's being naïve? They'll find a way to convict one of you for murder and the other for obstructing the investigation or whatever they call it … and me for lying to the cops in the first place."

"Well, I gotta do something."

"What you gotta do, Dean, is shut up. That's what you gotta do. And I gotta catch some sleep. Reveille comes around awful early."

"You think about this, Red."

"I'll think about it. I'll think about it. Now, let's catch some winks."

Blan said, "Red walked back inside. I think that's it."

Oren asked, "Did the other one, Dean Costa, go inside?"

"No. He's burning another of those tubes."

"Gabriel, any questions or comments?" Oren asked.

I said, "Blan, would you say these guys are acting guilty?"

"Yeah. Didn't you pick up on that, knothead?"

"I'm looking for confirmation from non-verbal cues, all right?"

Zastra's voice hissed. "Do you think either of them will do anything following this conversation?"

"It's hard to tell," Blan said. "Earthlings are weird."

I couldn't disagree with the statement.

Oren said, "Then stay there and keep an eye on them."

"Will do. But let me tell you, this isn't the safest place here with all these guns. Buad was almost shot out of the sky today by an artillery shell ten times his size."

"If those two have any more information, I want it. But be careful. Leave if you must."

The conversation ended. I rolled over and tried to go to sleep. This time it took a while.

Chapter 19

Not Before I've Had My Coffee

I must have fallen asleep sometime because I awoke with the sun shining in my window. That and a question on my mind, a question Quog had brought up the day before. Noonan had said he hadn't had any contact with Irene, but did he? Based on the way Noonan had been with the coat check girl, I didn't think having a pretty woman flirt with him was something he would ignore. I wondered what the Potters had to say about that. I wondered what Muriel would say. Assuming she was willing to talk to me.

I sat on the edge of the bed for a minute and rubbed the sleep from my eyes, thinking about coffee. I wanted to be home in my bungalow where I had a coffee maker only a few steps away. I yearned to be on the *Shaymus* with a replicator in the galley to make me a cup. But I wasn't in any of those places. I would need to get dressed and walk to the diner to rustle up my morning infusion of brain fuel. And yet first, I needed to find the answer to my question.

I pulled myself from the bed and trudged down the hallway to wash and shave and perform other essential tasks. Sadly, the bathroom was locked. I rapped on the door.

The voice from inside was Peter Ryan's. "Occupied."

Living alone, I wasn't used to waiting for bathrooms. You could look at this as good practice for married life, but in that moment, I wasn't quite so philosophical. "How long do you think you'll be?"

"Hey, it's like the monkey who got his tail caught in a fan."

"What?"

"It won't be as long as it was."

Which was less than helpful. I went back to my room and washed and shaved in my sink to take my mind off other biological necessities. By the time I pulled up the knot on my tie, I heard the bathroom door groan open. I slipped in to use the facilities.

When I came out, Muriel was there holding a towel and tapping her foot impatiently. "Dimes," she said icily.

"Can I ask you a question, Muriel? Um … did Irene ever date Ray Noonan, the bouncer at the club?"

She shook her head in tight motions. "Not that I ever knew. And I doubt it. Guys like him want a girl a little less straightlaced than Irene."

"So you know Noonan?"

"I know his type. Now, if you don't mind …" She stepped toward the door.

"Listen, I … I keep thinking about how the killer might have gotten Irene confused with you."

"Frank Lake, you mean?" Her eyes bored holes into me.

"Whatever." I struggled to get my foggy brain to compose the sentences in a way that wouldn't make her mad. "Frank or one of the other soldiers. There's a question as to which one was actually in possession of the knife. Anyway, did any of them have anything against you."

She made a face. "No."

"What about your ex? Where's he?"

"Hold your voice down. Nellie wouldn't approve of my checkered past. Last I heard, he was on a ship out in the Pacific."

"Can you think of anybody who would want to hurt you? It's important, Muriel, because if they were after you, then they might try again."

Her hard eyes softened a little. In a not totally sarcastic voice, she said, "Aw, Dimes, you really do care."

"Well, sure. I don't want to see you get murdered." She was family and all.

Muriel patted my cheek. "You're sweet … and dumb. Frank Lake did it, and he meant to kill Irene. She wouldn't go out with him, and he didn't like it." She swept past me into the bathroom and closed the door.

I descended the stairs to look for Lester and Nellie. The parlor was empty, but I could hear noises coming from the kitchen. I pushed the door open a crack and saw Nellie standing at the oven with her back to me.

"Mrs. Potter?"

She shrieked and whirled around. "Mr. Columbo. You scared the living daylights out of me."

"Sorry. Maybe I should have knocked."

"Maybe you should have."

"I had a question about Irene."

She huffed out a sigh and turned back to whatever she was stirring on the stovetop. I chose to interpret it as permission to continue.

"You told me about the soldiers visiting. Did she see any other men? Did she ever go out on dates or have any men over to visit."

Without turning, she said, "I don't allow visitors up in the rooms. You know that, don't you?"

"Yes ma'am. Visiting on the porch, I mean. Or dates."

She glanced at me over her shoulder. "You'd need to ask Lester. He's the one who sits in the parlor all day and keeps an eye on everybody's comings and goings. I spend my time back here in the kitchen working my fingers to the bone."

"Thanks. I'll ask him. Do you know where he is?"

She answered quickly. "He's not here."

"Oh?" I let the question hang in the air. I've found if you do that, most people are uncomfortable enough with silence that they'll keep talking.

Five seconds later she said, "He went to see Dr. Hatch."

"I hope he's not sick."

"Not that I know of, but nobody tells me anything. The doctor called to see him … out of the blue."

"Lester hadn't been to see him recently or had tests?"

She glared at me without answering.

"Okay, thanks." I pushed open the swinging kitchen door to leave, then stopped as a thought struck me. Maybe it was my brain running in slow motion without benefit of my morning coffee. Or maybe using Columbo as an alias was starting to rub off on me. "Oh, Mrs. Potter, I almost forgot. Muriel said Irene seemed troubled by something in the days right before she died. You wouldn't happen to know what that was about, would you?"

"We were not confidants, Mr. Columbo. I'm sure I wouldn't know."

"No, I suppose not. Thanks anyway."

I swept through the parlor and into the hall, noting the time on the pendulum clock on the wall as nine-thirteen. Now, what would Lester Potter be talking to Arthur Hatch about on a Saturday morning if he weren't sick? Stepping through the front door, I crossed the porch and set out up the street, determined to find out.

I powerwalked up Olive, then along Prospect to the big Fountain Square Theater building. I eyed Pop's Diner across the street. A cup of joe was calling my name, but this mysterious meeting was more of a priority. I slipped in the side door of the theater building and took the stairs two at a time as quietly as I could to the third floor.

I passed Hatch's office door to the next one down the hall, the one that led directly to his examination room, the one Quog and I had exited through the day before. If a conversation was going on inside, I hoped to be able to listen in from there. The room, however, seemed as quiet as a morgue.

I moved back to the office door. I knew I wouldn't be able to hear anything from there unless they were talking in the waiting room. But if it were unlocked, I might be able to sneak in and hear something from the nurse's cubby. Unfortunately, the office door was locked.

I returned to the exam room door. Still no sounds. I had a kooky idea of storming in and confronting them, but when I tried the knob, I found it locked as well.

I went back to the office door one more time. I knocked, even though that would blow any element of surprise. No one answered. I didn't even hear hushed voices or sounds of people moving around in reaction to my knock.

I had assumed they would meet here since the doctor's office would be empty early on a Saturday morning. Where else could they be? Did I miss them? Less concerned now with being as quiet as a mouse, I clomped down the stairs, my footsteps echoing up the stairwell.

What to do next? The answer came to me as I stepped out onto the street and spied the diner. A caffeine fix was exactly what I needed to help me think things through and come up with a plan of action.

As I entered, I spotted Lester at the counter. He wore a jacket zipped up to his neck. I dropped onto the stool next to him.

"Good morning, Mr. Potter."

He looked up with a startled expression and took a moment to recognize me. "Morning."

"Having breakfast out?"

"The wife won't make anything like this." He nodded toward his plate filled with biscuits and gravy. "With her it's always egg egg egg."

I noticed Peter Ryan sitting in a booth, digging into a stack of flapjacks. We made eye contact and nodded to each other, more of an acknowledgment than a cheerful howdy.

"I was talking to your wife," I said to Lester. "She said you had to go see the doctor. Hope it isn't anything serious." Judging from his order, clogged arteries weren't beyond the realm of reason ... or of any concern to him.

Lester fixed me with a doubtful stare. "I don't know what he wanted. I was supposed to meet him here, but he didn't show." He forked in another bite. "How's your book research coming?"

"Hmm?" I smiled stupidly at him, trying to think, without the benefit of coffee, what book he meant. That's the trouble with making up stories, boys and girls. "Oh, the book on Irene, you mean ... well, not on Irene exactly but inspired by her story. See, I'm working on a couple of book ideas at the same time. That's why I didn't ... at first ... Yeah, I've been retracing her steps, talking to friends. It's coming along. Thanks for asking."

Lester stared at me without responding.

The waitress came over. "What ya need, sugar?"

"Coffee. Black," I said. "And keep it topped up."

She pulled a cup and saucer from under the counter and filled it. I closed my eyes and breathed in the aroma.

"Anything else?"

I opened my eyes. "Um ... sure. I could eat." I scanned the menu on the wall. "I'll have a fried egg and toast."

"Coming up, lover." She called out, "Chicken on a raft."

From the kitchen, the short-order cook repeated it back.

"Love the diner slang, don't you?" I asked Lester.

He grunted in answer as he forked in another bite.

After a few sips of caffeine, I felt enough like a coherent human being to ask Lester, "Have you ever heard of a guy named Ray Noonan?"

"Who?" Lester asked. I couldn't read any disingenuousness in his face.

"He's a guy whose name came up in asking about Irene. I was curious if he ever came around to visit her."

Lester chomped down on a bite of biscuit and shook his head. "Far as I know, she didn't date anybody. She'd go out on the town with Muriel sometimes, but I never saw her leave the house with a man in tow."

There went another promising lead crashing and burning before my eyes. I needed a break in this case, though not necessarily the one that was about to happen.

As I was sopping up the last of the egg yolk with a corner of my toast, sounds of a commotion came from outside. Everyone in the diner turned to gawk. I spun around on the stool to see a woman in white at the side door of the theater building. She was leaning with one arm on the open door, head down, taking in gasps of air. A small crowd was gathering around her, making a fuss.

I glanced at the green paper under my plate detailing what I owed and threw down enough dimes to cover it plus a generous tip. I downed the last sip of coffee and rushed out across the street.

The people in the crowd were straining their necks to see the woman. They were talking, both to her and to each other.

"That's terrible."

"Somebody, get her some water."

"Has anybody called the police?"

I asked a man at the back of the pack, "What's going on?"

His answer made me wish I had a second cup of coffee inside me. "There's a stiff up in one of the offices — some doctor."

Chapter 20

Like a Hole in the Head

I recognized the woman in white. She was Dr. Hatch's temporary nurse, the disapproving one I had christened Nurse Ratched the day before. She wasn't looking so haughty this morning.

Lester's voice shouted behind me. "Who is it? Who's dead?"

The nurse looked up, wide eyes darting from one person to the next. "It's … it's Dr. Hatch. Dr. Arthur Hatch."

Sirens were approaching. I wanted to see the body and check for clues before the cops took over. I shouldered my way through the crowd and into the open door. I raced up the stairs, this time finding the door to number 306 standing open. I glanced around the waiting room and then hurried through to the exam room.

He was spread across the floor, face down, a gash on the back of his head, a dark pool spreading across the black-and-white tile floor. A baby scale, metal pan on a heavy cast iron base, sat on the exam table. Blood stained one of the feet.

I crouched beside him and ventured placing two fingers on the side of his neck. No carotid pulse.

A rim had dried around the outside of the blood pool. I pulled the pencil out of my pocket and poked at the skin that had formed across the surface. Underneath, the blood was still liquid. He hadn't been dead long.

In his hand, the doctor clutched a prescription pad where he had scrawled a few chicken scratches. Seriously, it looked more like a child's drawing of a mountain range than words. Maybe he was trying to write the name of his killer but was losing motor control even as he wrote it. Or it could just be the indecipherable handwriting of a doctor. A pharmacist might be able to read it. I couldn't make heads or tails of it.

Earlier I had tried both doors unsuccessfully, making this the old dead body in a locked room trope. This one, however, wasn't so hard to explain. The answer was on the floor a foot in front of the door to the hallway — a ring of keys that the killer had either slid under the door or pitched through the transom after locking up.

I stood and turned three hundred sixty degrees, trying to compare everything with what I had seen there the day before like in one of those find-the-differences puzzles they always had in doctors' waiting rooms when I was a kid. To the best of my recollection, everything looked the same except for the scale and the body on the floor.

"Oren," I said through the translator bot connection. "We have another death in paradox."

"Who, Gabriel?"

"Dr. Hatch." I described the scene. "It's definitely not an accident. He didn't slip and bang his head on the scale, not with the bloody leg of the murder weapon resting on the table rather than pointing up. It can't be suicide either. People don't bludgeon themselves to death. This was murder."

Oren said, "With a blow to the back of the head, the killer had to be someone Hatch trusted or at least didn't expect to attack him. Or possibly the murderer stole behind him unawares."

"One thing is certain. Somebody is deadly serious about something. First, they kill Irene and then Dr. Hatch. And here I am asking everybody I run into about Irene and standing over Hatch's body. I'm willing to bet whoever killed them isn't too pleased with me. You know, getting murdered here would mess up my timeline for sure."

"Correct. I suggest you leave there at once."

"I will. Right after I take a quick peek at the murder weapon."

Without touching it, I scrutinized the baby scale. I wasn't looking for fingerprints. Without powder or a magnifying glass, there wasn't much chance of me lifting prints. And without a police department at my disposal, I couldn't do anything with them in any case. But I hoped to find something, and I did. I spotted something gooey and brown on one of the other legs. I had moved in for a closer look when footsteps sounded behind me. I looked up to see Detective Vukovich entering, followed by two uniformed officers.

"You again," Vukovich said. "What are you doing here? It's Columbo, right?"

I shoved the pencil in a pants pocket, hoping that would wipe away any traces of blood they could identify with 1940s technology. "Hi, Detective. I was in the neighborhood when I heard all the hubbub."

From the hard expression on his face, I don't think he believed me. "And you thought what — you'd, stroll up and interfere with the crime scene?"

"I had to. You remember the Army business I *didn't* tell you about?"

Vukovich grunted.

I flipped up a hand. "Well, Hatch was also involved. I needed to take a gander at the body."

"How do I know you didn't kill him?"

"Because everybody downstairs told you I ran up after the body was discovered."

He eyeballed me while pulling the Tums can from his pocket and popping a tablet in his mouth. "What have you touched here?"

"Nothing, Detective. Well, except for the artery in his neck to confirm he was dead."

He crunched the Tums. "I'm going to want to talk to you … downtown."

"I'd rather not. I have things to do. Besides, there's not much I can tell you. War secrets, you know."

"Yeah. Well, I don't necessarily buy into all that hokum. The nurse just told me a cop named Columbo was here yesterday. You know, it's illegal to impersonate a police officer."

"I never said I was with the cops. It's not my fault she jumped to conclusions."

"What's your interest in all this?"

"I … Like I said, Hatch was involved in my business with the Army. And when his nurse gets killed, you know, it raises security questions."

"Hmm. I'll need to verify all that. Who's your contact?"

"My contact … in the Army? I'm afraid that's classified."

"Nice try. Give me a name, Columbo."

"Okay. But if you get chewed out, it isn't my fault."

I had stalled as long as I could. I had to give him a name. Then I would need to find a way for his call to this fictional person to be intercepted and routed to a friend. Fortunately, the *Shaymus* had an AI named WALT, an acronym for Wormhole Atomic Long-Range Telecommunications. WALT was a miracle worker when it came to information exchange. He — I thought of the software as a he — could do anything from interface with my cell phone to open pin-sized wormholes in space to send nearly instantaneous messages across the galaxy.

I said, "My contact is Colonel WALT … ers … Colonel Walters … at Camp Atterbury. Satisfied? Will you let me go about my business now?"

"We still need to talk." Vukovich nodded to one of the uniforms. "Give this gentleman a ride downtown courtesy of the city." To the other he said, "Go back down and take witness statements. I want to know when Mr. Columbo showed up."

The cop assigned to me asked, "Is he arrested?"

"Not at this time," Vukovich said.

The cop took me downstairs. The police cruiser was a big old Chevy that reminded me of the sheriff in Pixar's *Cars*, though I kind of think Sheriff was a Mercury. The siren on top was shaped like a jet engine, only smaller. The steering wheel was big enough for a toddler to use as a hula hoop. Not that the cop let me steer or run the siren. I had to sit in the back seat.

"Awesome car," I said to the patrolman. The compliment drew zero response.

The cop drove leisurely through the streets to a back entrance of the police headquarters and parked in a lot beside other patrol cars. He got me out and led me inside through a maze of hallways, dropping me off in one of the interrogation rooms. The door clicked behind him, and I was left alone. Which was good since I had work to do.

"WALT," I said over the translator bot connection.

"Hey, Gabriel. How ya doing?" For reasons never explained to me, WALT sounded exactly like the actor Owen Wilson.

"WALT, I need you to do something."

"Whoa. Whoa. No 'Hi, WALT. How have you been WALT?' You know, just because I'm software doesn't mean I don't have feelings. Well, I guess I don't have feelings per se, but I do appreciate the social conventions of friendship."

"WALT, I'd love to catch up with you and shoot the breeze, but I'm in police custody, and I need you to do a thing before one of them makes a phone call."

"Okay. Okay. Honestly. What do you need?"

"Somebody from the police headquarters is going to telephone a Colonel Walters at a place called Camp Atterbury. I need it intercepted and routed to someone who will tell them I'm working with the Army. Oh, and for purposes of the call, my name is Lou Tenant Columbo."

"Sure, Gabriel. I can hack into the Earth mobile telephone system, easy."

"I bet you can. However, cell phone service hasn't been invented yet, WALT."

"It hasn't? Then what do they use? Are the conversations broadcast over radio frequencies? I've been monitoring them. Hey, have you ever heard of Red Skelton? He's hilarious."

I didn't have time to be sucked into a discussion of the golden age of radio. "In this era, phone conversations are carried over dedicated copper wires."

"Wow! You mean it's a closed system? That's going to be harder."

"Can you do it?"

"Can I do it? C'mon. What are you talking about? I have an idea already. I'll need some help from a biological, though." He meant someone with a body. "Do you know how the signal is encoded?"

The door cracked open, and a cop stuck in his head to give the place the rubberneck treatment. "Who are you talking to?"

"No one," I said.

I heard WALT in my ear. "Oh, like I'm nobody? Unbelievable."

"While I'm waiting, I'm working on lines for a community theater play I'm in. We're doing *Our Town*. You ought to come see it."

The cop scowled and shut the door.

"WALT, I'm not sure about the encoding. I'm not sure there is much encoding. I think it uses a membrane or something to pick up sound vibrations and convert them to electrical pulses … somehow."

"If you can't be precise, what we'll do is use a universal line decoder. I'll ask Zastra to slap it on the line where it exits the police building there. I can communicate with it remotely and monitor the calls."

"Don't send Zastra. She'd scare the children … and the adults. Send Quog."

"All right. What is this Camp Atterbury place?"

"A military base. Somebody can find the number in the phone book."

"A book? You're telling me they keep communications information in a book? That's kind of low-tech, don't you think? And not the most engrossing reading I would imagine."

"Wait. I just remembered. I looked for it yesterday, and it isn't in the phone book. Quog can call the operator."

"The who?"

"And when the call comes in, have Oren take it. Colonel Walters should sound authoritative, not like a surfer dude."

"What's that supposed to mean, Gabriel?"

"Do you have all that? Do I need to repeat anything?"

"C'mon. I'm an AI, Gabriel. It's all recorded. Unbelievable."

The connection to WALT fell silent. Now all I had to do was wait and hope Quog got the device connected in time. It wasn't long before boredom set in along with a bit of claustrophobia. There was nothing to do in this dingy, dinky room — no TV to watch, no books to read, no Internet to surf. I tried to sleep, but my cup of coffee from the diner prevented that from happening.

To keep my mind occupied, I went back over the facts of the case. The murder of Hatch cast the inquiry in a new light. Irene had worked for Hatch, which made it likely the murders were connected. Did the same person kill them both? Or did Hatch kill Irene, and someone then killed him in revenge? Oren had once told me to always assume a single killer.

Did Lester Potter meet Hatch in his office and kill him there before casually strolling across the street to eat breakfast? Or had someone else done it, preventing Hatch from keeping his appointment with Lester at the diner? Peter Ryan had also been in the diner right across the street from the murder. Could he have had something to do with Hatch's death?

And what was going to happen to me here? If they arrested me, would they give me a cell next to Grandpa Frank's? It would give me a chance to quiz him more about family stories, but it sure wouldn't move the case along.

After going over everything multiple times, I wondered if Quog had gotten the phone line fixed yet. "Quog," I said. No answer. Maybe he hadn't been added to our translator bot network since he wasn't part of the Galactic Detective Agency team. I contacted WALT instead.

"Hey, Gabriel," WALT said in his familiar drawl.

"Did Quog install the decoder ring thingy?"

"It's called a universal line decoder, Gabriel. Yes, it came online a few minutes ago. Quog had to replicate some Earth money so he could ride in a taxi. Weird all the ways you biologicals move from place to place."

"Yeah, WALT, physical space is a funny thing."

"So do you have time to talk now? How's Sarah?"

"She's fine. Matter of fact, WALT, if we get out of this mess and I can find my way back to my own time, we're going to —"

I stopped as I heard a click at the door.

"Going to do what, Gabriel?" WALT asked. "What are you doing?"

I said in a whisper. "Can't talk now, WALT. Someone's coming."

"Honestly? Unbelievable."

The door opened and Detective Vukovich walked in. He gave me a nod. "Well, Columbo, your story checks out with Colonel Walters."

I fought hard to suppress the smirk that wanted to crawl across my face. "Does that mean I'm free to go?"

"Not quite yet. I have a few questions for you."

Chapter 21

A Friendly Chat with Vukovich

"Sure, Detective," I said like an eager eight-year-old. "What can I answer for you?"

Vukovich didn't sit. He pulled out one of the metal chairs from the other side of the table and leaned a foot on the seat, his thick eyebrows tented. "You think you're cute, don't you, Columbo?"

"That's what my fiancée says." I enjoyed making the joke, though it pained me a little to think about Sarah. I needed to get out of here. I needed to fix this mess.

"Earlier you told me you were passing by when you heard the commotion outside Hatch's office."

"In a manner of speaking. I was eating breakfast at the diner across the street."

He gave me a hard stare. "See, I know that's a lie. A witness said she saw a man about your height and weight in a blue suit enter the building and exit again a few minutes before the body was discovered."

Which made me a suspect for murder. A flock of butterflies took flight inside my stomach on a tour of my upper gastrointestinal tract. I had a decision to make and make fast. Either I denied it, claiming it must have been some other guy in a blue suit, a stance that might not hold up if I were put in a lineup, or else I come clean.

It was hard to say which answer would land me in deeper trouble and which one would get me released. And since I was the only operative of the Galactic Detective Agency who could walk around Indianapolis and investigate this case, I badly needed to be released.

Vukovich was staring at me with penetrating eyes but a basically kind, honest face. For once, I decided to go with the advice Nana Lois always gave me, to tell the truth.

"Yeah. Okay, I've been investigating Irene Giordano's murder. I heard about a meeting Lester Potter and Dr. Hatch were having, and that got me interested. I assumed they were meeting in Hatch's office, but when I arrived, the doors were locked, and I couldn't hear anything. That's when I went across the street."

"Yeah, we're going to talk about your little investigation because I don't find your name in the state listing of private investigators. Working with the Army doesn't exempt you from obeying the law. Also, I can't find you in the phone book as an attorney." I started to make an excuse, but he held up a hand to stop me. "But let's deal with this morning first. You say you went up to his office, but no one was there."

"As far as I could tell. That's why, when I heard there was a murder, I ran back up. Think about it. Why would I go there a second time if I had seen it all already when I killed the guy."

"Oh, I don't know. Maybe the second trip up was to provide a cover story for why we would find your fingerprints there."

That was an excellent point. Vukovich was good.

"Except by now, you know my fingerprints weren't there. Well, they might be on a doorknob or something, but that's 'cause I was there the day before. The nurse will confirm that. Today I didn't touch the murder weapon or anything except the doc's neck to see if he was still alive. Isn't that what the lab told you?"

Vukovich gave a halfhearted shrug. "The full lab report hasn't come in yet. What do you think this is — some radio drama? But your prints probably aren't on it. It didn't look like there were any prints on the baby scale other than the doc's, which we checked at the scene. The killer must have wiped them or worn gloves."

"No fingerprints other than the owner's. Just like the knife in Irene Giordano's neck."

"You still contend the soldier didn't do it?"

"Doesn't this second murder prove it?"

"You've been watching too many gangster movies, Columbo. We have murders every week. Doesn't mean they're connected. Besides, he confessed already."

If I wore glasses, I would have pulled them down and glared at him over them like a reproachful mother. "He confessed all right ... with some not-so-subtle persuasion from your boys."

Vukovich made a sour face and dug in his side jacket pocket for a Tums. "Okay, wisenheimer, tell me what you've learned in your … investigation." He said the word with the inflection of air quotes.

"The Potters said Irene tended to nose into things."

"Yeah, I knew that."

"Hatch thought she might be mobbed up."

"That ain't news either."

"Okay. How about this? Peter Ryan caught her making eyes at Ray Noonan at the Kit Kat Club."

His head cocked. "Now, that I didn't know. Noonan, huh? He's mixed up in this somehow. I'd bet my pension on it."

"What do you think of Peter Ryan?"

Vukovich grimaced. "I'm asking the questions here."

"Sorry. I thought we had a kind of collaboration thing going there for a minute."

"Dream on, Columbo. But I figure Ryan's all right … if you like that kind of bird. Do you have anything else interesting?"

I ran my hands through my hair. "The day of the murder — Irene's murder — Carl Beck, the theater manager, walked into the auditorium moments after an usher went to fetch him. Beck first told me he was upstairs in his office, but when I confronted him about how he couldn't have gotten down that fast, he changed his story to say he was checking receipts at the ticket booth."

"I didn't know that either, but I wouldn't make book on it. It's not unreasonable to be confused about such a minor detail."

"If you say so. Here's another tidbit. I spoke to Noonan at the club last night. Of course, he says he knows nothing about Irene's murder. But I'm almost positive somebody tailed me on the way back to the rooming house."

Vukovich rubbed a hand across his jowls. "Might be something. Might not. But you need to be careful. You're playing with fire. What rooming house, by the way?"

"The Potters' place."

"You're staying there? Where the dead girl lived? You just had to be where the action is, didn't you? I gotta tell you, Columbo, you need to leave the investigating to us. People are getting murdered, and the next one could be you."

"Believe me, Detective, the thought has crossed my mind." On the other hand, I had survived people and even bots trying to kill me on a bunch of alien worlds. This wasn't anything new.

He hoisted his leg off the seat and spun the chair around to sit on it front to back. "What do you know about this supposed meeting between Hatch and Potter?"

"I was talking to Mrs. Potter this morning. She said Hatch called up Lester and asked to meet."

"Old guy like that, it could have been related to Potter's health."

"Unlikely. She said Lester hadn't been to the doctor recently. Well, she implied it anyway." Now that I thought about it, she had mainly answered me in glares and left the interpretation up to me.

Vukovich threw me a dismissive scowl. "Likely as not, he'd seen the doctor without telling his wife about it. Didn't want to worry the missus."

"I suppose."

"And you say they were to meet at Hatch's office?"

"Well, that's what I assumed. But when I saw Lester at Pop's and asked him about it, he said they were supposed to meet there … there as in at the diner. But does that make sense when the doc had a private office right across the street?"

Vukovich waggled a hand back and forth. "Depends on the meeting agenda. If it's something private like money or Lester's health —"

"Or murder," I said.

"That too. Those kinds of things they would want to talk about in the office. But what if the doc was on a committee for some event, the Fourth of July celebration or some such, and he was hitting Lester up for help? That kind of meeting you might do in a restaurant."

"You know, Detective, for someone who chews Tums like they're M&Ms, you sure do expect the best of people." I was almost certain M&Ms were invented by this time. What I wasn't quite as certain about was whether *invented* was the right word to use for candy.

"You're cracking me up, Columbo," he said in a deadpan. "You should be on the stage. How about we leave all this behind, you and I? We could be the next Abbot and Costello."

"Gee, do you think so? Guess what? I can sing too."

"You're gonna be singing. You gonna tell me everything I want to know."

"I have been, Detective. Honest. I've been unloading it like a hay wagon."

He stood again and paced a few steps. "Or maybe the meeting was about Mrs. Potter's health. Could be Lester had called him earlier in the week with concerns about her losing her hearing or something."

"Her hearing seems fine to me."

"I said, or something."

"We could ask Lester that."

"I will ask Lester that. You can butt out."

"You're ignoring what a terrific resource I can be. I'm right there in the rooming house, undercover, so to speak."

"Thanks, but no thanks. You don't have a P.I. license, and I'm not using amateurs."

I was hardly an amateur. I may not have worked as many cases as he had, but I had experience on way more planets. Something else popped into my head. "I saw some gunk stuck to the baby scale."

Vukovich shrugged. "Yeah. It was slime or mucus or something."

"From the killer?"

"Who knows? Could be from a baby."

Too bad they didn't have DNA analysis in the forties. "A baby who's a killer. That'd be something, huh, Detective."

"You're wearing me out, Columbo. The question is if the two murders are linked, then what connects them?"

"Are you asking for my opinion, Detective?"

He scowled at me for a moment before answering. "Why not? You're a smart guy. Too smart for your own good."

"It would have to be something both victims knew, something somehow related to the practice since I don't think they traveled in the same circles otherwise. Perhaps a patient with a grudge or a secret to bury. Or maybe they both saw something dodgy going on in the building one day."

For several seconds Vukovich said nothing. "Makes sense. I'll have some uniforms talk to all the other tenants. They might catch some of them this afternoon, but we won't get much 'til Monday."

"Frank Lake has a deadline on Monday when he has to enter a plea in court."

"What do you want me to do, roust people out of bed on the weekend?"

"Why not? It's a murder investigation."

"Yeah? Well, I can only ruffle so many feathers, and some of the tenants are powerful people."

"What about the prescription pad?"

"I haven't found anybody who can read it. The doc's brain was probably in the process of shutting down while he was writing." He rubbed the back of his neck and sighed. "All right, Columbo. I'm gonna let you go, but you better not make a monkey out of me. If I find out you've been withholding information …" He let the threat hang in the air.

Withholding information. I was holding back so much information. I was concealing how I came from the twenty-first century. How I knew where he could find a whole spaceship full of extraterrestrials. How my very existence was riding on the outcome of this case. All of that I had to keep to myself. But in terms of clues to the murders, I had dumped everything right in his lap. More power to him if he solved the case before I did. Probably it would be better for the timeline anyway. Instead, in answer I shot him my winningest smile.

"You know, Columbo, there's something fishy about you, something I can't put my finger on. But it doesn't add up, and I don't like it." He stood and knocked at the door. An officer opened it. The detective signaled with his head for me to vamoose.

As I passed him in the doorway, Vukovich put a fatherly hand on my arm. "Hey, remember, stay out of this."

Chapter 22

I Don't Stay Out of This, and Neither Does Zastra

I hailed a cab to hurry back to Garfield Park and the *Shaymus* where I briefed Oren and Zastra on my evening at the Kit Kat Club and the second murder.

"I don't like it," Oren said with as stern a digital face as I had ever seen on him. "We may have made things worse for the timeline. For all we know it may have been Gabriel's investigation of the murder that caused the doctor to be killed."

"Wait. What?" I said. "You think I'm somehow mangling the timeline even more just by asking questions?"

"Sounds about right," Zastra said.

I shot her a look. "But if Hatch's death is connected to Irene's, then surely it would have happened regardless."

Oren said, "That is possible but not at all certain. In any case, it is a certainty now. Assuming we can still recreate a timeline with you in it, that future will now not include Doctor Arthur Hatch."

"Can we search old newspaper accounts to find out how it would have been?"

"They will have all changed. We will never know for sure how this would have played out without your presence. And the longer we stay here, the more you may warp the future. Jace, how long before the chrono drive is repaired?"

Jace's voice came over a speaker. "I need at least another day, Oren."

"All right. Keep me posted."

I was confused. "What are you saying, Oren? You want to give up? You want to leave me here?"

"At least you would be safe, as will history as previously written … more or less."

"No. There's no way I'm going to let my grandfather go to prison for a crime he didn't commit. For his sake even if not for mine, we have to solve this."

Oren was silent for a moment, longer than you would think for someone who processed thoughts at the speed of computer chips. "There are four possibilities."

"For what?" I asked.

"For the murders, Gabriel." In those few seconds, he had sifted through all the data and reduced the solution of the case down to only a quartet of scenarios. "The first is that they are related to the medical practice."

"Okay. What are the others?"

Oren shook his head. "Let's deal with them one at a time. I want you and Zastra to break into the doctor's office."

Zastra said, "It's about time we got a grownup involved."

"Break in tonight?" I asked.

"Today, if possible," Oren said.

"You want me to stroll down the street in broad daylight with a lizard warrior princess?"

"Not a princess," Zastra said with a growl.

Oren said, "The longer we are here, the more dangerous it becomes."

"You wanna see dangerous? Wait 'til the general public gets a load of Zastra. Besides, the police are probably still crawling over the place."

"I will leave the details to you. You know Earth. Break in and go through patient files and anything else you can find. Look for any connections to anyone related to Irene Giordano's murder. Send me images of anything relevant via your translator bots. Zastra, I want you to perform a psionic spectral analysis."

She nodded her scaly head. "Got it."

I said, "Are you good with this, Zastra?"

"I'm done sitting around here, that's for sure."

I didn't like our odds of walking a mile and a half without being spotted by someone, and public transportation was out of the question. But it was better than being grounded on the ship doing nothing until they flew off and stranded me here. Zastra and I walked down the steps from the office to the crew deck.

She said, "Open ramp."

As the ramp began to lower, I said, "Belay that order." I had picked up that cool phrase from watching *Star Trek*. The *Shaymus*, however, didn't seem to understand the word *belay*, which I admit is kind of niche. Instead, it just kept opening the front door. "Stop. Raise ramp."

The drawbridge reversed course, and Zastra glowered at me. "What now?"

"You can't go out looking like —"

"Like what?"

I wiggled a hand at her general appearance.

"This is the way I look."

"Don't I know it? And trust me, if Godzilla had been filmed already, we could just say you were his kid sister. But we need to try to make you less conspicuous. Let's go replicate something."

Glaring in annoyance, she followed me around to the galley. I stepped to the counter and asked the machine, "What do you have on file in the way of a straw hat?"

The replicator buzzed and a flat-topped boater hat appeared. It would work great if we were forming a barbershop quartet, but it wasn't much of a disguise.

"Nope," I said. "What else do you have on tap?"

This time a hat appeared that would be appropriate for hoeing the garden. Zastra growled at the headgear. "I'm not going out looking like a ratooshi farmer."

I said, "Let's see if we can make it a bit more stylish to the times. Replicator, revise straw hat. Make it yellow and wrap a wide black cloth band around it."

The replicator buzzed again, and the result was more like something you might see on the street on a spring day in the 1940s.

I handed it to Zastra. "Try this on."

She didn't like it much, but she complied. The effect wasn't bad. However, I could still make out the green scales on her chin.

I turned back to the replicator. "Make the brim larger."

"Please specify the amount of increase."

This was no time for half measures. "Twice as big. And make it so the brim curves down."

That one did the trick. I said, "Wow! You look like Ingrid Bergman in *Casablanca*."

She didn't, of course. She looked closer to Kermit the Frog in a sombrero. But I figured it would pass. It was still a weird look — a lady's fashion hat over a leather duster, leggings, and combat boots — but at least it wouldn't start people screaming.

She said, "If you ever breathe a word of this to anyone, so help me Gort …"

"I won't," I said while trying to figure out how I could snap a picture. Regrettably, Quog still had my phone. "Keep your hands in your pockets while we're walking. And your head down."

We set out for the doc's office, keeping to the side streets, collecting only a few curious stares along the way. We did have one incident. Passing a bus stop, a guy called out at the yellow bonnet, "Hey, cutie pie, c'mon over here. I like 'em tall like you."

Zastra froze in her tracks, lifted her green scaly head toward the jerk, and snarled. The color drained from the guy's face. He dashed headlong across the street, nearly getting hit by a Studebaker in his rush to beat feet.

"Are you sure that was wise?" I asked.

"Nobody calls me cutie pie."

We walked on to Fountain Square. Fortunately, the police had cleared out of Dr. Hatch's office, and the rest of the floor was empty on a Saturday afternoon.

"Can I take my hands out now?" she asked in a disgruntled tone.

"Be my guest."

Zastra pulled out a palm-sized case, extracted a slender sliver strip, and inserted it into the lock. I had seen this soft key tech before. When the strip touched the metal inside the lock, a chemical reaction began, causing the strip to expand to fit the tumblers. This was why alien worlds don't use the same kind of locks we do.

A moment later Zastra opened the door. She relocked it behind us and dropped the straw hat on a waiting room chair. We hurried through the door leading to the back rooms.

Zastra thumbed a claw toward the nurse's cubby. "You start looking at patient records. I want to examine the crime scene with galaxy-class tech."

I sat and rifled through the files, scanning for names of people associated with the case. It was a good thing the HIPAA law for medical privacy wouldn't be passed for several decades.

I started with the Potters. I found no recent notes or lab results for either of them, making it unlikely Hatch wanted to talk to Lester about anything medical. Back in 1940, the chart noted that Lester had limited range of motion. I could have guessed that from how slow and halting his movements were.

I found nothing at all on Ray Noonan or Peter Ryan or Muriel Marshall. They must not have been patients. Neither was Irene Giordano.

I did find a chart on Carl Beck, the theater manager, which was suspicious because Beck hadn't mentioned being a patient when I had asked him how he knew Hatch. There were notes on a minor skin cancer issue and also chronic eye infections attributed to mustard gas from the first world war. I wondered on which side Beck had fought.

I checked for Frank Lake, Dean Costa, and any Fraser I could find since I didn't know Red's real first name. All I found was a Ralph Fraser, who was sixty-two and obviously not the right one.

I was striking out in the patient records unless you count the fact that coming up with no results was itself a result that might tell us something. I decided to look for employee records. They weren't in the file. More likely, they were kept in the doctor's desk in the exam room.

I moved in there and found Zastra running some electronic doodad that swept a green laser line around the room. "Find anything?" I asked.

"Nothing and too much. There have been hundreds of people through here. Show me where the body was."

The blood pool was still there but not the corpse, and the cops hadn't drawn a helpful chalk outline. I had to orient myself to remember how it had been. I pointed to a spot beside the exam table.

She ran the laser line over the area. "Uh-huh. That gives me a reference point. Here, look at this. I'll play it through your translator bots." She pressed a button on the device, and my vision filled with a jumble of colored outlines of human footprints.

"What is all this?"

"Residue of movements over the last nineteen hours. What you're seeing first is the cumulative view. Now, I'll play it chronologically."

"You can do that?"

She gave me the kind of cold look reptiles are famous for. "This will be sped up faster than real time."

Over my field of vision, I now saw a pristine tile floor. Then playing like an animated GIF, the outline of red footprints walked into the room, over to the desk for a moment, then out of the room again. They returned along with a set of blue footsteps. The two sets of prints stood in the middle of the room facing each other. When the red footprints spun away from the blue ones, the blue tracks stepped to the side of the room, then came up close behind the red ones. The red footprints disappeared.

Zastra said, "That must have been when he was struck down."

The blue steps left through the hallway door. We saw nothing until a set of purple footprints with narrow heels came in and left again, which must have been the nurse, and then green footprints, which had to be me. They were followed by a whole crayon box of colors moving around everywhere.

"Those are the cops," I said.

"Right. We only care about the blue ones. Those belong to the killer. Can you tell anything from their shape?"

"Most likely a man. It's the shape of a man's shoe and larger than Hatch's."

"Or a woman wearing a man's shoes?"

"Doubtful. That would look weird in this time period. And what would be the point? The killer wouldn't know you had this awesome gadget."

"All right. I think we're done then. The police have taken away the murder weapon, so I can't examine it for DNA."

"I need to check the desk."

I moved to it and began pulling out drawers. I found a checkbook, which I flipped through without anything unusual jumping out. I found the pack of cigarettes Hatch had used the day before, a stack of medical journals, more prescription pads, and a spiral notebook. I leafed through the notebook pages finding handwritten scrawls. I could interpret a few of them — sore throats, arthritis, and other ailments. This must have been where he took notes during appointments before transferring them to patient charts.

The last two pages in the notebook were different. One had a single number written on it: *872*. Whether that referred to dollars or the number of people he had treated or some kind of dosage, I didn't know. The other page had two words printed in block letters: *RATION COUPONS*. Unlike the message on the prescription pad, this was completely legible. He should have been so precise in writing the name of his killer, but I suppose he had been in a rush, seeing as how he was dying and all.

The only thing I found related to Irene was an accounting book with entries showing her pay. She made a paltry $40 a week. Though with rent at $3.50 a week split with a roommate, I guess it wasn't bad.

I was checking for hidden compartments in the desk when muffled voices came from the hall. Zastra and I exchanged glances. The voices stopped outside the office, and the outside door rattled. Somebody seemed to have the same idea we had of going through the place.

I rushed out and crossed the waiting room as quickly and quietly as I could. Through the frosted glass door, I saw two vague shapes. They could have been men or women or polar bears for all I could tell. Wondering if they could see me as easily, I dropped to the floor and put my back against the door, watching the handle wiggle left and right.

A voice said, "Locked."

It was a man's voice, though the one word didn't give me enough to identify who it was. A minute later the handle quit turning, and footsteps echoed away.

Zastra slipped to the doorway and asked with only a glance if they were gone. I answered yes with another glance.

"We ought to skedaddle ourselves," I said. "I'm not sure we learned much. The killer was probably a man and someone Hatch trusted enough to turn his back to. And Lester didn't have any recent diagnoses that would warrant a talk. That's the crop."

Zastra shrugged. "I had fun anyway … well, except for the hat. It beats sitting around doing nothing. Besides Oren may be able to deduce something from all this. Especially our unexpected visitors."

I held out the crook of my arm. "Well, m'lady, don your bonnet, and I shall escort you home."

The glare she gave me could have peeled wallpaper.

Chapter 23

Stormy Weather

Lightning cracked as we descended the stairs from Hatch's office. By the time we reached the door to the street, the sky had opened and was pouring it out by the bucketful. Zastra pulled the hood of her duster over her head and stuffed the wide-brimmed straw hat into a garbage can, apparently not worried about people taking a close look at her in the deluge.

I pulled my fedora down as far as it would go and flipped up my jacket collar. Taking a bus or a cab would have been nice for staying dry, but I couldn't risk it with my Srathan companion. We ran through the rain, dodging from doorway to tree all the way back to Garfield Park.

We splashed into the *Shaymus* and sloshed around the crew deck to our quarters. Cleaning bots appeared in the hallway behind us to sop up the puddles. I stepped into cabin eight, shed the jacket and pants, and hung them in the pressing cabinet on the wall. When it beeped a minute later, the suit was dry and freshly pressed. I did the same for shirt, socks, and underwear, while I hopped into the sonic shower, which dried as well as cleaned. I redressed and went up to the office. Zastra was already there, and we gave Oren our reports.

I said, "Earlier you mentioned four possibilities. I'm guessing the connection to the doctor's office didn't exactly pan out. What's the next alternative?"

Oren said, "First of all, the examination of the doctor's office was not a complete loss."

"You learned something from all that? What?"

He smiled without answering. "As to investigating the next theory of the crime, I am hesitant. It could be dangerous for you. Two people have been killed already."

"Look, Oren, my life is on the line anyway."

He jiggled his finger. "Only life as you have known it, not your physical existence."

"That's the same thing as far as I'm concerned. I'm willing to take the chance to put things right for my grandpa and myself."

"All right then. I want you to return to the Kit Kat Club and talk to this Ray Noonan about Dr. Hatch's murder."

"You think Noonan might already know about it?"

"It is possible based on the clues."

Zastra said, "Do you want some backup?"

"Are you gonna slip on a jitterbug dress and come dancing with me?"

She made a face. "On second thought, you'll probably be fine. Call me if you need me."

"I have a few hours yet. I think I'll replicate some lunch and check in on Jace. I might have a lie-down. I've had quite the day so far with murders and police interrogations and break-ins and all. Have Buad and Blan come up with anything else?"

"No, I've told them to return," Oren said. "I believe we have gotten all we can from those two soldiers."

"I've been thinking about the conversation we overheard. Red asked to borrow Frank's knife but may or may not have actually picked it up. This means the knife might have been in Frank's possession or Red's or maybe even left on the concession counter where anyone could have picked it up. There's also my little test that suggests it could have fallen from a pocket."

"Correct. What do you think, Gabriel? Would it help Frank's defense if those facts were known?"

I pulled off the fedora and ran a hand through my hair. "I doubt it. None of it conclusively puts the murder weapon in anyone else's hands. I suppose, if we can't find the killer, then we can tell Frank's lawyer about it ... his real lawyer."

"I would much prefer to identify the real killer."

"Me too. But how?"

Oren said, "A woman unexpectedly goes to a theater. A knife falls from a pocket or is left on a counter. No one could plan for such things. This appears to be a crime of opportunity."

"You mean the killer saw Irene and the knife and said, 'Well, I wasn't intending to kill her today, but what the heck?' Is that the idea?"

He shot me a glare of irritation. "Something along those lines. What I mean is it speaks more of passion than of planning, of desperation more than design."

"Well, tonight I guess I'll see how desperate Noonan acts."

"That's what worries me."

I found Quog in the galley with a paperback in his hands. The cover matched a Nero Wolfe e-book I had on my phone.

"Where did you find that?" I asked.

He closed the book over his thumb and looked up. "Guess what? The replicator already had the recipe for old-style paper books. I only had to have WALT pull the text and cover art from your phone."

"Wow. Talk about print on demand."

"Holding an actual book in my hands sure takes me back. As a kid, I read *Charlotte's Web*, *A Wrinkle in Time*, all the Narnia books." He pulled my phone from his pocket and handed it over. "You can have this now."

I tucked it away. "Replicator, two slices of pizza. How are things going, Quog?"

"Swell."

"Swell? Quog, I'm thinking you need to lay off the old detective stories and read something contemporary. You'll need different lingo to fit into the twenty-first century."

"You think I'll sound like a fuddy-duddy?"

"See, there you go again." I wished I could steer him toward something more modern, but the selections on my Kindle tended toward the classics in detective fiction and sci-fi. "You should try *Ender's Game*. At least that would move you into the eighties."

"Oh, I think I'll stick with Nero Wolfe. Speaking of murder mysteries, how is yours coming?"

I sat down with my pizza. "I think we're closing in. Tonight, I'm going to try to match wits with a gangster, which is way cool."

He looked at me skeptically. "And extremely dangerous."

"I'll be careful, Dad."

After eating, I returned to cabin eight to attempt a nap. I thought I might be up late that night and could use the rest. Little did I know how right I was.

I awoke sometime later. The question was what time was it? Was I late for the club or still early? I knew Kah-Rehn wouldn't know, but I had another idea.

"WALT."

"Hey, Gabriel. What's up?"

"I have a question. You said you've been monitoring the radio waves going through the air, right?"

"Sure thing. I love some of this music. Do you know Duke Ellington?" WALT started singing *It Don't Mean a Thing if it Ain't Got That Swing*, though not as on-key as you might expect an AI to be.

Why would he even sing? Couldn't he just play back the recording? I didn't want to take the time to ask.

"WALT. WALT."

"Hmm? What, Gabriel?"

"The radio also broadcasts the local time periodically. Can you pick that up?"

"Oh yeah. You bet I can. I'll scan the dial." He was gone for a minute or two. "Here, Gabriel. Listen to this."

A deep voice came over the speakers. "It's thirty-eight minutes past eight o'clock, and you're listening to the sounds of WFBM, twelve sixty on your radio dial."

"Thanks, WALT. That's exactly what I needed."

"If you want some Duke Ellington pumped into your ears, let me know."

"Um ... right."

When I left the *Shaymus*, I found the rainy day had transitioned into a dark, drizzly night. I walked up Shelby with my hat pulled low until I could flag down a cab.

"Where to, mister?" The cabbie was a small guy with a hooked nose.

"Kit Kat Club. Do you know it?"

"Sure. I know it. But if you don't mind me saying, most guys go there with a dame. You're not looking to steal one off somebody, are you?"

I laughed. "Do you think I could?"

"Not if you're smart. Not in that place."

It probably wasn't a place where a fella ought to go around accusing people of murder either. As I stepped out of the cab, I spotted Noonan at his post at the front door. I approached, and he smirked at me. "Columbo, right?"

"Yeah," I said, stepping under the red awning out of the mist. "Lou."

He nodded. "So, Lou — can I call you Lou?"

"Why not? Since we're on a first-name basis, should I call you Ray?"

"It's Noonan to you. So this makes two nights in a row for you here. You're becoming a regular. I hope you aren't coming around with more questions about those girls I don't know?" He pulled out a cigarette and dug in a pocket for a lighter.

I paused before answering as a couple ran past us into the club.

"No, this time I'm asking about the late Arthur Hatch."

The lighter flame flickered in his hand. "Hatch is dead?"

"You knew him, Noonan?"

"Yeah, I knew the doc … by sight at least."

"He came here dancing?"

No answer.

"Or did he have business with the boss?"

Still no answer, but his face told me I'd struck gold.

"What kind of business?"

"Not yours, that's for sure. You want to know more, you should ask the boss."

"I'm asking you, Noonan."

"What? You gonna get tough with me?"

Another couple darting into the club prevented me from answering. Which was fine since I didn't have much of an answer. Obviously, I wasn't planning to challenge him here on his home turf. As a rule, I prefer using my wits rather than my fists anyway. But he didn't need to know that. I crossed my arms and tried my best to look hard-boiled.

"Amscray, Columbo. Mind your own beeswax."

I couldn't help myself. I laughed out loud. Beeswax? And Pig Latin? I hadn't heard anything like that since fourth grade. I think he interpreted the guffaw as me calling his bluff, and it threw him off his game. His eyes shifted left and right.

"Okay, Columbo. Between you and me, Hatch owed the boss some lettuce."

Off in the distance, thunder rolled.

"How much?"

"Like I should tell you." He paused, then relented. "A few centuries."

I wondered if a few hundred dollars was a lot for a doctor in the forties. Was it enough for murder?

"What was the debt for?"

He flicked some ash into the brass smoking stand beside him. "Let's just say the late doc was not proficient at picking boxers."

On a hunch, I asked, "Did you meet him at the theater Thursday?"

Noonan appeared impressed. "How'd you know?"

I grinned. So that *was* Hatch, but he wasn't waiting for a date.

Noonan said, "He called and said he had something to tell us. But all he had to say was he would pay up soon, which didn't much impress me. The boss wants greenbacks, not promises."

"Did McKinney have him killed?"

Noonan's face grew as dark as the night beyond the awning. "Hold your voice down. Are you loopy or what? First of all, it's Mr. McKinney to you. Second, what would be the sense in having the doc killed? In case you haven't noticed, dead men don't pay off their debts."

He had a point, but I was unconvinced. They might knock off one deadbeat as a warning to the others. It was motive at least for Hatch's murder, if not Irene's. The nagging thought in my mind was that, assuming they *were* willing to kill someone over a gambling debt, they probably wouldn't hesitate to kill somebody like me who was poking around into it. I needed to tread carefully.

"Okay, Noonan. Thanks for the info. Don't worry. My lips are sealed." I hoped that was reassuring to him.

He stubbed out the cigarette. "Listen, Columbo, I got a piece of advice for you. You're messing with something a whole lot bigger than you, and if you don't back off, it's gonna stomp you like a bug. Now, either go inside the club or take a hike. Your ugly mug is scaring off the customers."

No need to get nasty, I thought. I scowled at him and walked in. I didn't have much on the agenda other than rattling Noonan's chain, but I figured it wouldn't hurt to see what was happening.

The place had a sizeable crowd, but few were dancing, and the band was starting to look demoralized. At his regular table, Boss McKinney was conferring with a redheaded beauty.

I spotted Peter Ryan sitting with a blonde, a martini glass in front of each of them. It wouldn't hurt to check up on him since he suspiciously kept popping up everywhere. I wandered toward the table.

"Ryan," I said.

He looked up from his date like he couldn't place my face. Then it came to him. "Oh, Columbus, right?"

"Columbo."

"Right. Right."

"Are you going to introduce me?"

He gave me the evil eye. "This is Evelyn."

"Hello, Evelyn."

"Pleased to meet you, I'm sure." She was wearing a wedding band, not Ryan's unless I had missed an important plot point. Her eyes met mine for only an instant before dropping to the tablecloth.

"Do you want to join us?" Ryan asked. His tone was inviting, but his face warned me off.

"Nah, I'm just seeing what's going on here."

He didn't say anything. He wanted me to move on.

I said, "That was sure something this morning."

"What was?"

"Across the street from the diner. You were there. Dr. Hatch."

Evelyn glanced up. "What about Dr. Hatch?"

I said, "He was murdered in his office."

She gasped. "He's ... he's dead? My doctor? He's dead?" She jumped up and ran off toward the ladies' room.

Ryan flew from the chair, glaring savagely. "Are you nuts, talking like that around a dame? They don't want to hear about murders."

"By the way," I asked, "did you know Hatch?"

He made a grab for my shirt. I stepped back to evade him, bumping into a man sitting at another table. The guy stood and glowered at us wordlessly. I thought both of them were going to take a swing at me or even at each other. A waiter showed up and soothed things over.

"Sorry," I said to everyone in the vicinity.

Ryan straightened his jacket. "Who's this Dr. Hatch?"

"Nobody. Sorry." I walked away as people gawked.

Chapter 24

A Tail as Old as Time

I breezed past the coat check station toward the door of the Kit Kat Club. Noonan was gone from out front, replaced by a guy in a massive amount of brown tweed who could have made two of me. With that kind of backup around, I was glad I hadn't tried getting tough earlier. Stepping past the giant to the sidewalk, I shot him a friendly nod. He returned a steely glare. Some people, huh? You try to bring a little friendliness and humanity into the world, and what do you get?

The rain had finally stopped, leaving the streets as shiny as a new marble. There were no cabs at the curb, which was okay by me. I wanted to think over my conversation with Noonan. I set off walking toward Virginia Avenue.

Had he given me any clues? The gambling debt made a possible motive for Hatch's murder. But Noonan was right about how the doctor's death would mean they wouldn't be paid. And how could it possibly tie to Irene's death? Why would they kill her for Hatch's debt?

It worried me a little that Noonan had been so candid about discussing it. Weren't gangsters supposed to be tight lipped and not say nuttin' about nuttin'? Was Noonan merely mouthing off? Was he trying to set up Boss McKinney to take the fall? Or was he setting me up for something? Maybe he didn't mind telling me because he was planning on knocking me off, an idea that didn't appeal to me in the least.

I was passing a shoe repair shop when I thought I heard footsteps behind me, giving me the same sense of being followed as I had had the night before. I glanced around at my surroundings — shops closed for the night, an auto mechanic's garage silent at this hour, an apartment building where you probably needed to be buzzed up. I would have settled for any bungalow with a light on in the window, but I couldn't find any.

My heart racing, I thought through my options. If somebody was tailing me, then I didn't dare lead them back to the *Shaymus*. I wouldn't want to lead them to the house on Olive Street where I was staying either. I figured the trick I had pulled last night of darting around a block probably wouldn't work again. They would be ready for it and head me off.

I wondered if pizza delivery existed in this era and if hitting a buzzer at an apartment building and saying I had a delivery would open a door. I dismissed the idea as too risky since it would mean standing on the stoop for at least a couple of minutes.

I needed another idea. If the Internet existed, I could have googled, "fun ways to lose a tail." I scanned the street for a passing cab. Nothing.

In the next block, I spotted a café on the other side of the street. Warm, reassuring light beamed through plate glass windows out into the night. I angled across and went in, grabbing a table in the back where I could face the door.

A waitress came over, pulling a pad from a pocket and a pencil from behind her ear. "What can I bring you, sweetie?"

"Coffee." My nerves were already jittery, but I needed to order something, and eating wasn't remotely possible.

She left and came back with a white ceramic mug full of joe. "I haven't seen you in here before, darlin'. Are you from out of town?"

I took a sip and a calming breath. "You could say that."

"Where do you call home?"

How was I supposed to answer that? Indianapolis of the future? Outer space? "Let's just say you can get there from here, but it takes a long time."

"Um … sure … if you say so." She put the check down on the table and walked away.

I sat and sipped the coffee, thinking over the situation. I figured if I waited long enough, whoever was tailing me would give up … maybe. At least I hoped they would. On the other hand, here I was fenced in like a cow in a barnyard. If they were still out front somewhere, all they had to do was wait. Eventually, the place would close, and I would have to leave. I needed to get out before that happened. I figured there was a back door I could slip out, but at the moment, a dark alley didn't sound appealing at all, not compared to the security of a well-lit café with witnesses.

Through the door came a specimen in a green suit, size extra-large. He looked smart enough to screw in a lightbulb, assuming you gave him adequate instructions and were on hand to provide hints. He plopped down on a stool at the counter near the front and ordered a glass of milk. While waiting for it to be poured, he spun around on the stool, eyeing all the patrons with a suspicious stare. His eyes lingered on me, and he gave me a little salute with his meaty hand. Now what was I going to do?

A cab pulled up at the front. This was my chance. I dropped two dimes beside the cup and raced toward the door.

The ox in green spun on his stool and stuck out a leg to trip me, but his timing was off. I saw it early enough to hurtle over it, thankful that the stools in the joint weren't any taller. I sailed through the door and to the cab, nearly knocking aside the passenger who was taking his time getting out of the back.

"Watch it, mac," he said.

"Sorry." I swept into the seat, slammed the door, and sang out, "Drive."

With a start, I saw movement from the corner of my eye. Another guy was sharing the backseat with me — or more accurately, I with him — a little guy in a bowler hat, who had been short-changed in the chin department. He most definitely was not with the gang. He pressed his back against the other door and blinked at me repeatedly.

"Sorry, mister," the cabbie said, thumbing toward the little guy. "I'm already engaged."

"What a coincidence. I am too. Lovely girl." The mountain in the green suit barreled out of the café door toward the cab. I put all the insistence I could muster into my voice. "But this is a matter of life and death. Drive! Go! Go!"

The cabbie pulled away with a screech of tires.

The little guy beside me said, "But ... but."

"Where to?" the driver asked.

"For now, straight ahead. I'll tell you when to turn."

The guy in the bowler, his voice tremulous, said, "I need to go to north Capital."

We were heading in the opposite direction. "Sorry," I said. "I'll get out as soon as I can."

"But ..."

The cabbie was a kid, even younger than Grandpa Frank. I pegged him at sixteen or seventeen. Our eyes met in the rearview mirror, and in them I saw both thrill and alarm. "Gee, mister, are you in trouble?

"I can't tell yet."

"Wow! This is like in the movies."

"Just what I was thinking, kid. Exciting, huh?"

I watched the street signs as we passed them. Delaware. Alabama. While the cityscape had changed considerably in the last eighty years, the street grid was much the same. "Turn north on East Street."

He did.

I said, "When you come to Washington, turn east."

The guy in the bowler said, "Couldn't you turn west? Toward Capital?"

"You'll get your turn," I said.

"This should be my turn." He was less nervous now, more irate.

The cabbie asked, "You aren't running from the cops, are you, mister? My folks would kill me if I got arrested."

"My heavens," said the bowler hat guy. "Are you a hoodlum?"

"Take it easy," I said. "Getting arrested is the least of our problems. Hey, kid, can you tell if anybody is following us?"

His eyes shot to the rearview mirror. "I … I don't know. What would it look like?"

I twisted in the seat. A few headlights trailed behind us, but they were a block or more away and didn't seem insistent on keeping up. I said, "Turn south again when you can."

"Where?"

"Anywhere. The quieter the street, the better." We turned into a neighborhood. "Good. Pull to the curb away from a streetlamp and switch off your lights."

He did. "What now?"

"Wait a minute or two. I'll tell you."

The bowler hat guy heaved an offended huff. "I really must insist —"

"Eh, put a sock in it," the cabbie said.

Bowler hat guy crossed his arms and leaned back in the seat. We waited. No cars rolled past us.

A minute later, I said, "Right. I think we lost them. Drive on up the street. Take it easy. Which way is Shelby from here?"

"A few blocks east."

"Good. Take it south."

My seatmate huffed again. "Are you going to make us drive all over town?"

"Nah. I was thinking of going to Bloomington. How's that sound?"

"Mister," the cabbie said. "I don't want any trouble. Where can I let you out?"

"Raymond Street." I figured I wouldn't have him take me all the way to the park in case somebody later got to him or to my unwilling rideshare companion.

We reached Raymond, and the cab pulled up to the curb. I paid extra for the service and hopped out. As the taxi sped off, I set out on foot for the park, breathing a sigh of relief.

Then a pair of headlights swept around the corner along the line of houses, catching me in their beams. The car stopped in the street, and two guys jumped out, running up the sidewalk after me.

How had they managed to follow me after all my precautions? Who were these guys? I felt like Butch Cassidy running from the Pinkertons in that awesome movie Hollywood would make in another twenty-some years.

I took off as fast as I could, managing to pant out the word, "Oren."

"Yes, Gabriel," came the voice in my ear.

"There are ... guys ... after me."

"Where are you?"

"On the street ... north ... of the park."

"I'll send Zastra. Do you know who they are?"

"Well ... I just came from ... pulling Noonan's chain ... so let's do the math."

I ran along Raymond, unwilling to dart onto a side street with the cavalry on the way. I put on as much speed as I could muster, but the men were gaining on me, and I wasn't sure how much longer I could keep up the pace.

Finally, a block ahead under a streetlamp I saw a figure in a hooded duster that I recognized. After all these days of keeping Zastra under wraps, I hoped she would throw back her hood and give the hoods behind me the fright of their lives. She didn't get the chance.

Zastra dashed toward me, yelling, "Run, Gabe."

Helpful tip. Why hadn't I thought of that? I was already sprinting like Scooby-Doo racing away from a ghost.

She raised a green hand grasping a blaster. But at that moment I felt hands on my arms and the muzzle of a gun in my back. A car squealed up to the curb as a suffocating burlap bag came down over my head. Something — probably the grip of another gun — thumped my head. It didn't knock me out, but boy did it hurt.

Rough hands bum-rushed me onto the street and into the car. The door slammed shut, and the car jerked away. As it turned up an alley, one more sound came to me — an explosion of asphalt and gravel. My guess was Zastra had taken a blaster shot at the fleeing auto, missing it and giving the Indy streets one more pothole to deal with.

Chapter 25

Sorry, I'm a Bit Tied Up Right Now

"See if he's packing," a familiar voice said.

"Is that you, Noonan?" I asked. "Funny meeting you here. How are you doing? I almost didn't recognize you with this bag over my head."

Hands dug inside my jacket. Other hands pushed me forward in the car seat and felt around at the back of my belt.

"Watch it," I said. "I'm ticklish."

"He's clean," came another voice.

"Tie him up," Noonan said.

Somebody yanked my hands behind my back and looped a rope around them. They cinched it tight, and I rode like that for several minutes, which let me tell you, was far from the most comfortable car ride of my life. When we stopped, they pulled me out and walked me over rough ground into a building. From the sound of our footsteps treading across concrete and echoing, it must have been a large structure.

"Where are we?" I said it in full voice, trying to gauge the size of the place from the sound.

"Can it," Noonan said.

We walked for a minute or so. Then hinges creaked open, and, judging from the changing sounds, we moved into a much smaller space. I heard the *squeak* of metal legs pulled across linoleum and was pushed down into a chair. The bag was snatched off my head, and I blinked into fluorescent lights.

Noonan and two other guys were grinning at me with the most disturbing smirks I've ever seen in my life. One of the henchmen was the bulky milk drinker from the café. The other one, short and thin, I hadn't seen before. But I couldn't help but notice how he was pointing a snub-nosed revolver at my chest.

Now, in my day job as a software developer, I've never had a gun pulled on me. I like to think it's because I do a good job for my clients. But working for the Galactic Detective Agency, I've stared down the wrong end of gun barrels and blasters time and time again. It's never an enjoyable experience. I'd give it a one-star rating at best — would not recommend.

I found myself in a small, dingy office, a square room constructed of flimsy plywood walls. If the building was a warehouse — and from what I could see through the open doorway, it probably was — then this must be the foreman's office. It had one metal desk, one rolling metal armchair with torn padding behind the desk, one uncomfortable metal straight chair where I was sitting, a file cabinet in a corner, and an out-of-date 1941 calendar on the wall showing a drawing of a woman in surprisingly short overalls next to a giant-sized monkey wrench. It was the kind of drawing they used to say would motivate our fighting men. More like distract them, I thought. Everything was covered by a layer of dust thick enough to date back to the Hoover administration.

The short guy, the one who was new to me said, "I tell you, mac, we had a time with you. Jumping in the taxi like that was a first-class move. 'Specially how you slipped past Darrell there." He waved the revolver in the direction of the big guy.

Wait. The milk drinker's name was Darrell? What kind of gangster name was Darrell? Shouldn't it be Mugsy or Jimmy or Moose?

"Thanks," I said. "What are you going to do with me?"

"We're gonna have a nice chat." Noonan held out a length of rope to the little guy. "Tie his ankles, Weasel."

Weasel. There you go. Weasel sounded more like a proper name for a henchman.

The little guy holstered his piece and tied my ankles together. Now I was bound hand and foot.

I said, "You know, we could have talked at the club."

Noonan said, "I thought the situation called for a more private conversation."

"Okay, shoot," I said, immediately regretting my choice of words.

"I'm not the one who'll be asking the questions."

"Who then?"

"Keep your shirt on."

161

"Yeah. I don't suppose I could take it off given the restraints. Mind if I grab a quick nap? I've had quite the day."

Noonan's only answer was a cold stare.

Darrell said, "We could play cards while we wait. Hey, Columbo, do you know how to play pinochle?"

"Afraid not. Euchre's my game."

"That'll work. There's four of us."

Noonan sneered. "We're not playing cards. One of you would have to take him as a partner, and then you wouldn't want to rough him up once we get the word."

Darrell shrugged. "Depends on what kind of a partner he was."

Noonan wiggled a come-here finger at the other two. They stepped outside the office and closed the door. I could hear them talking in hushed tones. I wanted to listen in, but this was my chance to call for help.

"Oren," I whispered.

"Yes, Gabriel." I heard his voice in my ear. "Zastra said they apprehended you. Where are you now?"

"I haven't a clue. That's what I wanted to ask about. Remember that time you said you couldn't track someone's location through translator bots?"

"Of course, I remember. My memory is stored digitally with a sophisticated search algorithm."

"Right. Anyway, is that still the case?"

"Yes."

"Nuts."

The door opened and Darrell re-entered.

"Where are the others?" I asked.

He didn't answer. He sat down and put his feet up on the desk. We eyed each other in awkward silence.

What I said earlier about people not being comfortable with quiet applies to me as well, especially in this instance with the prospect of receiving a beating looming in my near future.

I said, "So who do you like for the race this year?" I figured since this was May, things would be heating up at the speedway on the other side of town.

"What race?"

"*The* race. The Indianapolis 500. The thing Indy is famous for."

"What are you talking about? There's no race this year … or last year even."

"There isn't?" Was I in some weird parallel universe? "Why not?"

Darrell shook his head at me like I was flunking kindergarten. "'Cause of the war. You've heard of the war, right? And gas rationing? Where have you been?"

"Oh, right. Sorry. I guess this kidnapping has me stressed." I lowered my voice. "You guys aren't going to kill me, are you?"

"Not my call."

I didn't find that at all reassuring.

"Gabriel." Oren was back in my ear. "What can you tell me about where you are and your circumstances?"

Unfortunately, I couldn't answer him directly with Darrell six feet away from me. I said, "Boy, Darrell, that Weasel guy did a good job tying me up. He knows his knots. Here I am stuck in … in …" I bobbed my head around. "What kind of place is this? A warehouse? A factory? It sure looks like a huge place."

Darrell blinked at me without answering.

Oren said, "I'll send Buad and Blan out to try to locate the building. What else can you tell us?"

I said, "We all came here in one car. I suppose it's still out front. But Noonan said someone else is coming in a second car, right?"

Darrell said, "What are you flapping your lips about?"

Oren said, "Any idea how far you might be from the park?"

I said, "You know, Darrell, it sure didn't take us long to get here, did it? Five minutes or so at twenty miles an hour. Maybe a mile and a half or two miles from Raymond Street."

Darrell scowled. "Drive it in the hanger, would you?"

I didn't know that one. "Pardon?"

"Shut up." Darrell pulled his feet from the desk and sat forward in the chair with a scowl like he was threatening to come over and give me what for.

I nodded and showed him how tightly I could press my lips together. In my ear Oren said, "I'll stay connected to see what else I can learn."

Outside the office, footsteps echoed across the concrete. Boss McKinney strode into the little room with Noonan and Weasel on his heels. Darrell popped to his feet.

McKinney leaned back against the desk, his ankles and arms casually crossed. He scrutinized me with steel eyes. I felt like a gazelle being appraised by a lion. Finally, he gestured to Weasel. "I need a cup of coffee."

Weasel hurried out.

For Oren's benefit I said, "Oh, is there a coffee shop or diner or drug store nearby? If it's not too much trouble, I'd take a milkshake."

Oren said, "Did you hear that, Blan?"

"Sure thing," Blan said. "Warehouse or factory with a couple of cars near a coffee shop or something. We're circling out from the park. Zastra's following on foot. So far, all we've seen are a bunch of houses."

Boss McKinney went back to staring at me. If his plan was to unnerve me, it was working.

I said, "This is about the murders, right? Irene Giordano and Arthur Hatch?"

"Hatch is really dead?"

"I saw his body."

The boss indicated his displeasure with a choice word or two. Unless he was putting on an act for my benefit, he wasn't pleased with the plot twist.

"To answer your question, Mr. Columbo, no, this isn't about murders. I hear you've been asking questions about my business. You've been in my club twice in as many nights and keep causing disturbances. I don't know anything about murders, but I know when I'm being harassed."

I couldn't decide if I believed him or not, but clearly, my best chance for getting out of this alive would be if he honestly had nothing to do with the homicides. "Look, Mr. McKinney, I don't care about your business. I've only been investigating these deaths."

"Is that so? Well, to me this seems like part of a larger pattern of pressure from the DA's office. I think you're in cahoots with the cops, Columbo."

"Hardly. The cops arrested my gra ... my ... my great friend."

"And now you're trying to pin it on me, so they'll drop the charges on him."

"No. Listen, I'm only trying to find out who did it."

"What's it to you?"

"I have ... a personal interest in the case."

"Because of your friend? Or because of this Irene person?"

"Both."

"No wonder Noonan doesn't like you."

So maybe something *was* going on between Noonan and Irene.

"What are you, Columbo, some kind of gumshoe?"

"I prefer private eye." I tried sounding tough.

"Do you work by yourself?"

I definitely didn't want to tell them I worked alone, which would leave them with no reason not to bump me off then and there. What else could I say? I figured, what the heck?

"I'm part of the Galactic Detective Agency."

"Galactic?"

"It's a team of extraterrestrial crime fighters. Our chief is a disembodied consciousness who exists inside a computer."

"A funny guy, huh?" McKinney looked around at the others. "We got a regular Jack Benny here. You work with little green men, do you?"

"No. Well, Zastra is green, but she's female … and not so little."

Weasel came back in with coffee steaming in a waxed cup. The boss blew across the top of it and took a sip.

"You're not helping me here, Mr. Columbo."

"What can I do for you?"

"Convince me you're not trying to take me down, and I might let you off with a warning from Darrell."

Darrell flexed his fingers and made a fist. Just what I needed — showing up to my wedding with a black eye and a bloody lip. Still, it would be better than not showing up at all.

"Honest, Mr. McKinney. My only goal is to solve the murders."

He shot me a sideways look. "Right. Or at least get your friend out of trouble."

"Sure, but —"

"What if I told you Darrell here committed those crimes?"

Darrell's face clouded with confusion. "Boss?"

"Did he?" I asked.

McKinney waved a hand. "I have no idea. As I said, I know nothing about the murders. However, Darrell has committed crimes in the past. Of course, he's like a son to me. I would hate to see him in a jam with the law. But then a lot of people have lost sons in this war. It's a sacrifice any of us may be called on to make for the greater good."

Darrell said, "Boss?"

I shook my head. "It won't do. He wasn't at the theater when Irene Giordano was stabbed. Believe me, I would remember him. You know, I can't simply throw somebody to the cops. They need proof."

"You might be surprised what the police will settle for. But if that's the way you feel, then no, Darrell didn't do it." He shot the big guy a wink. "Don't fret, Darrell. I was only feeling him out."

I wanted to point out that Noonan was at the theater, and the cops would easily buy his guilt in the crimes. But I didn't think the suggestion would win me any popularity contests … other than with Darrell maybe.

I heard Buad's voice in my ear. "Hey, knucklehead, we may have found the place, a long metal building with two cars out front. We'll give Zastra a few minutes to get here."

"I may not have a few minutes," I said.

McKinney studied me. "What's that supposed to mean?"

I said, "Um … What I mean is time is ticking. I need to free my friend before he enters a guilty plea in court Monday morning."

McKinney rolled his eyes like I had told a pun he didn't find funny. "You know, Mr. Columbo, you should worry less about Monday and more about tonight. Let me tell you something —"

But he never got the chance to tell me because at that moment an explosion thundered from somewhere in the building, and everyone jumped.

"What was that?" Boss McKinney asked, his eyes wild.

I said, "Gee, I don't know. Sounded like a ray gun to me. Hey, you don't suppose it's those little green men, do you?"

Chapter 26

Let 'em Have it

The stomping of boots echoed from somewhere in the warehouse. A flash of yellow fluttered through the air outside the office door as a beam of blue light shot into the little room and burned a hole through the top of the desk.

Weasel squealed and hit the deck. I rolled off the chair, thankful that though I was tied, I wasn't tied to it. Boss McKinney dashed to the other side of Darrell, who ducked behind the remains of the desk, both of them with eyes the size of golf balls.

Noonan pulled a pistol from under his arm, moved to the doorway, and fired two shots into the darkness. He glanced back into the office, his eyes filled with grim determination. "Darrell, run the boss out of here."

Darrell stared back at him, color draining from the big man's face. "What, now? How? We can't go out there. We'll get zapped. We'll be vaporized." He gazed in horror as another blaster shot tore into the desk chair, sending up a spray of bits of vinyl and stuffing.

The footfalls were coming closer, Zastra's plan of action obviously being not stealth but striking terror. It seemed to be succeeding.

"Well, the boss can't stay in here," Noonan said. "We'll give you cover. You get him out to his car."

Darrell shot a questioning glance at McKinney and drew a nod. Then to Noonan, "Which door should I use?"

"I don't know. Whichever one where you don't hear stomping or see whatever it is that's flying around. Get him to the car and tell the driver to take him to the club pronto."

"Not the club," Boss McKinney said. "We don't know who this is or what else they're planning. I'll go to the safe house."

"Fine," Noonan said. "Then, Darrell, you come back in and help us. Get a move on."

Darrell threw an arm around McKinney and rushed him out of the office. I saw a couple of flashes of blaster shots. I heard gunshots in answer but no screams of pain, so I assumed they made it out.

Noonan took a long moment to glare at me, shaking his gun in my direction. Again, not a fan. "What's out there?"

I shrugged. "I'm guessing it's somebody who doesn't like you — probably a big somebody from the sound of those boots. And they must be flying a radio-controlled plane. Have you seen those things? They're the bees' knees."

"It won't be after I pour some lead into it. Get up, Weasel. C'mon."

Weasel gave me a dirty look as he rose from the floor. Rods in hand, the two hoods burst through the doorway. They ducked for cover behind crates and began returning fire.

There I was with my ankles tied together and my wrists bound behind me. I rolled to my knees and pushed myself to my feet, nearly falling in the process and having to take a dozen micro-steps back to keep my balance.

I baby-stepped toward the door to try to see what was going on. After thirty seconds, during which I moved a total of about six inches, I gave up the shuffling and took a hop. On the second hop, I reached the doorframe and managed to steady myself against it.

The warehouse was shrouded in shadows. The only light came through a line of windows just below the high roofline where the moon shone from a sky at last cleared of clouds. Noonan and Weasel sheltered behind wooden crates some twenty feet apart, taking occasional shots at movement in the other end of the long building.

From that direction came blue shafts of laser fire cutting through the darkness, drilling holes through crates, and exploding pallets to smithereens. Some blasts originated from floor level. Others came wheeling through the air like *Star Wars* fighter ships on a strafing run.

On an earlier case, I had seen Buad and Blan strap tiny blasters to their taloned feet so they could perform such acrobatics. Trust me, it looked as adorable as it sounds. But that wasn't something you wanted to mention to them, at least not while they were armed.

A blaster shot hit the crate where Noonan was sheltering, blowing a blackened hole through the side of it a foot above his head. He yelped in surprise. Another shot hit a stack of small boxes, obliterating one of them into scraps of cardboard and sending the others billowing into the air. Meanwhile, bullets were flying, striking metal beams overhead and careening off with the *boing* of ricochets toward who knew where.

Over my translator bot connection I said, "Guys, be careful of those bullets."

Blan's voice answered. "Bullets? You're kidding me. I thought those were gumdrops. Thanks for the tip, numskull, but I think we recognize old-style projectile weapons when we see them."

"Stop it. I'm only trying to help."

"You can help by telling us where those guys are."

"There are two of them. They're straight out from the office door spaced evenly across the width of the place. They're crouching behind crates.

"Thanks … dummy."

Always with the insults. The way Buad and Blan treated me, would you even call it friendly fire if I ended up getting hit by a stray laser shot?

Zastra bounded to the top of a tall container, her lizard face gleaming in the moonlight. She squeezed off a shot before vaulting off into the darkness.

Noonan yelled, "Did you see that? What was that thing?"

Weasel fired and called back. "I don't know. They got … It looks like they got a dinosaur."

"And flamethrowers. Where's Darrell when we need him?"

"You really expected him to come back, Noonan? He's probably halfway to Chicago by now."

A blue streak of light tore a hole in the office wall, obliterating the pinup calendar and passing within inches of my head. Okay, within a few feet of my head maybe, but way too close for comfort. I figured I had performed my reconnaissance duty. I hopped back across the office and threw myself behind the desk, hunkering down and praying that no stray shot, either lead or laser, would take me out.

A minute later I peeked over the desk and spotted Zastra crouching on top of a stack of crates, firing blaster shots down at Weasel. What she didn't see was Noonan huddled behind a wooden barrel near the office door. He raised his gun and centered her in his sights.

There was no time to yell out a warning. I wheeled my shoulders across the top of the desk, landed on my feet, and bounded out through the door like a trussed-up kangaroo. Noonan turned in time to see me but fortunately not in time to shoot me. I slammed into him, knocking the gun from his hand and sending us both sprawling across the floor. I rolled like a pencil into the darkness behind a crate before he could regain his pistol.

As I lay panting in the darkness, Weasel yelled. "Ow! They got me. Ouch, that smarts."

I gazed out through the dim light and saw him on the floor propped against a crate, clutching a black spot on his arm. Now all they had to do was take out Noonan. One of the Avanians streaked overhead, firing down at him. The beam struck a cardboard box at Noonan's feet, causing it to erupt into flames and light up his position. Noonan dived behind a forklift.

I wished I had a blaster. More specifically, I wished somebody would come and untie my hands and then hand me a blaster. "Guys, I'm tied up over in the corner, by the way."

Buad said, "That's terrific, dumbbell. Awesome. Tell you what, we'll ignore this guy shooting at us and come untie you. We wouldn't want your wrists getting chafed or nothing."

"The thing is … I can help. I have a direct line of sight."

"Don't worry. We'll get him."

Over the sounds of gunfire, sirens wailed in the distance, growing louder. I said, "Zastra, the cops are coming. You need to make a break for it. If they catch you, you'll end up in the circus. Let Buad and Blan finish up. They won't draw suspicion."

She replied, "Yeah, you're right. You guys have this?"

Blan said, "Of course, we do." He made another dive for the target. His blast struck a tire of the forklift, blowing it out with a *bang*. Noonan took off into the darkness.

The sirens continued growing louder and closer. Finally, the wailing stopped, replaced by the *thump* of car doors slamming somewhere outside the building.

The muffled sound of a voice coming through a megaphone said, "This is the police. Come out with your hands up."

Weasel shouted in a stage whisper, "Hey, Noonan, where are you? Help me up before the coppers bust in here. We need to scram."

But Noonan didn't answer. He had already scrammed. Outside I heard an unfamiliar voice call out, "Hold it there, pal." Apparently, Noonan hadn't scrammed far.

I caterpillar-crawled back into the office to the side of the desk where I could be seen but was at least partially protected in case somebody started blazing away. I sat on the floor with my fettered feet stretched out in front, hoping a cop with a calm head found me.

Weasel presumably had much the same idea because I heard him yell, "I give up. I give up. I'm wounded here and can't come out. I've tossed my gun."

A clatter of footsteps approached.

Someone said, "Over there."

"I'm unarmed. I'm unarmed," Weasel said.

"Get your hands up."

"I can't. I've been shot."

"All right, on your feet."

"Ow. Watch it. I'm hurt here."

"You'll live. Get him outa here, boys."

The footsteps moved off. A uniformed cop stepped to the office doorway, gun in hand. He gazed at me with a puzzled expression, then grinned and used the barrel of his piece to push his peaked cap back on his head. I highly doubted that was an approved procedure. "What's your story, bub?"

I said, "I'm the captive."

"Are you the one who called it in?"

I strained to lift my bound hands an inch or two behind my back, which was all I could muster. "Does it look like I could use a phone?"

"Must have been one of the neighbors then. Who was doing all the shooting?"

"The gangsters you caught."

"Yeah. Tell me something I don't already know … like who they were shooting at."

"I couldn't see anything from in here. What are the gangsters saying?"

"They aren't making any sense. One of them said something about birds with ray guns."

I gave that a hearty, dismissive laugh. "Well, that's quite the story."

"Which side were you —" The cop was interrupted by Buad and Blan swarming around his head.

Blan said, "We'll get rid of this guy, Gabe, and then you can come with us." Of course, without translator bots, the cop would have heard it merely as chirps. They pecked at his ear. They knocked his cap off. He swatted at them with an arm.

The officer yelled, "Hey, hey! Somebody, find a broom and shoo them birds outta here."

The scene would have been hilarious if the cop hadn't raised his service revolver. I needed to intervene before he blew Buad and Blan to feathers. "Hey, you two, clear out. Scram. I'll be okay in police hands." Which was only the latest in a long line of misjudgments I've made. The Avanians flew off.

"Who were you talking to?" the cop asked, re-hatting himself.

"The birds."

"What? Are you like Snow White chatting with the birdies?"

I said, "Someday my prince will come. I guess that's you."

He sneered at me. "So which side were you on?"

"Neither. I was nabbed by Noonan and Weasel. Then these other guys — I don't know who — burst in. Anyway, if you can untie me, Officer, I'll be on my way."

"I'll untie you, but you ain't going anywhere, brother, except to police headquarters where we can straighten this whole thing out."

Chapter 27

Trampling my Carmen Miranda Rights

"Lou Columbo." Detective Vukovich looked up from the papers on his desk as I was escorted into his office. "You keep turning up at crime scenes like a bad penny."

"I know, Detective," I said. "I'm getting as tired of it as you are."

The plainclothes detective holding my arm led me to a chair. I sat. He hovered.

Vukovich's office was nothing fancy, a small room with one large window framed in dark stained trim. I supposed I was there instead of in an interrogation room in recognition of the fact that this time I clearly was the victim.

Though that didn't stop them from trying to pull a power move on me. Vukovich got up, walked around the desk, and leaned against it, forcing me to look up at him. The other guy switched on the desk lamp and tilted it up into my face.

"Why don't you tell me what happened," Vukovich said. His suit was beyond wrinkled. If he hadn't slept in it, he had certainly worn it for hours on end. I glanced down at my suit. It wasn't looking much better.

"Simple. I was walking down the street when Noonan and two goons jumped out and shoved me into a car and took me to the place where your guys found me."

"Only that's not the whole story, is it? We were called in by a neighbor who heard shots. Who was shooting at who?"

"Whom," I said. "Who was shooting at whom. Whom is the objective case, and —"

"Just answer the question, wise guy."

"Hey, I was tied up in the office. I couldn't see a thing. I'm guessing a rival gang?"

"We didn't find a rival gang. We didn't even find both of Noonan's goons. You said there were two, right? We arrested one. What happened to the other thug?"

I was hesitant to drag Boss McKinney into it. He didn't seem like the kind of guy you would want to rat on. "I guess he slipped out. Say, could you move that light out of my eyes? It's giving me a headache."

"Nah, I wanna see when you lie." Vukovich wore a smug look on his face. "My guys saw scorch marks and burned stuff everywhere, and this Weasel character said something about ray guns. What do you know about that?"

I laughed. "Ray guns. That's a good one. Maybe the Martians are invading. You better get on the horn to Flash Gordon."

"Don't be such a wisenheimer, Columbo."

The detective looming over me stretched his hand like he was itching to give me a pop.

"What about ..." Vukovich paused to make a face and shake a Tums from his handy container, "... an alligator man?"

"I don't think it was a man."

"What was it then?"

I twirled a finger around the side of my head in the old gesture for calling someone nuts. "I'm guessing an overactive imagination."

Vukovich made a low growling sound. "All right. Let's back up. Why did they grab you?"

"You have Noonan. Why don't you ask him his motivation?"

"We are asking him. I'm asking you too."

"Well, you probably won't like this, Detective, but I visited the Kit Kat Club to ask Noonan about Dr. Hatch's murder."

Vukovich rubbed his eyes. He chased the first Tums with a second. "Are you an idiot? Talk about walking into the lion's den. What did I tell you, Columbo? What did I tell you? You know, we oughta throw you in the can for going around pretending to be an investigator. But we'll skip it for now. Well, let's hear it. In your professional opinion, did Noonan do the murders?"

I scratched my forehead. "I'd like to say yes, but I don't think so, Detective. I got the impression those guys were mainly irked about me poking around their ... various business enterprises."

Vukovich started to reach for the Tums canister a third time but let it go. "Sounds right. You're lucky to still be alive."

"Which is more than Irene Giordano and Arthur Hatch can say."

"So, Columbo, have you discovered who *did* kill them?"

"Beats me. I'm running out of suspects. The roommate? The theater manager?"

"Maybe you," Vukovich said.

I waved a refuting hand. "I don't have a motive."

"None we know of ... yet. What happened to the other goon who kidnapped you?"

"I already told you. I don't know."

"You know what I think? I think this is bigger than Noonan. I think his boss or his boss's boss came in to grill you, and the missing goon got him out when the shooting started. We found tire tracks from a second car."

"Or were those from the other guys who were shooting at Noonan and his gang?"

"No. The shooting was still going on when my guys pulled up, and there was no car there."

"Oh. Okay."

"Who were those guys?"

"I didn't see them."

"I've about had it with you, Columbo. Spill it. Talk, or I'll make you talk."

I gave him a cold stare.

"Mike," Vukovich said.

The other guy stepped up and slapped me on the cheek. Hard.

"How you like them apples?" Mike said.

"Hey," I snapped. "What's that all about? What about my Miranda rights?" Between getting kidnapped by thugs and beaten up by the cops, being a 1940s detective was starting to lose its allure.

"What are you talking about?" Vukovich said. "You mean like Carmen Miranda?"

I was about two decades too early for Miranda, the famous Supreme Court ruling that became incorporated into the dialogue of every cop show since the sixties. That's why Vukovich hadn't caught my reference. But I understood his. Carmen Miranda was a singer best known — if you can believe it — for dancing in a hat made out of fruit and more or less immortalized in the Chiquita banana logo.

"Are you gonna talk?" Vukovich asked.

"I've talked already."

"That does it. Columbo, we're charging you with impeding a police investigation and withholding information."

"I'm sorry, what?"

"Stick him in the tank, Mike."

Mike grabbed my arm and pulled me to my feet.

"I was the victim. I was kidnapped. Wait, don't I get a phone call?"

Mike paused.

Vukovich said, "Yeah. Give him his call."

Mike led me out to a wooden phone nook built into a hallway wall. I lifted the heavy black receiver and goggled at the dial. I had a vague recollection of using one in my childhood. Then again, it might have been a Fisher-Price play phone. I seem to remember it having two eyes and a happy mouth.

If you've never had the pleasure, here's how a phone dial works. There's a hole in it for each number one through nine with a zero down past the nine. You stick your finger in the appropriate hole, drag it clockwise until it stops, and then lift your finger and let it rotate back. Dialing a one or a two was quick. Dialing a nine or a zero would take a second. And, of course, you had to know the number or look it up in the phone book since it didn't store your contacts. Crazy, huh?

With the cop watching, I dialed a number, starting with the local exchange printed in the center of the dial, then picking the last four digits at random. My finger hopped from hole to hole, the dial whirring back and forth. The line began to ring. After the second ring, somebody answered.

"Hello," said a voice on the other end.

I said, "Oren, I've been arrested."

The voice on the phone said, "You got the wrong number, pal. There's no Oren here."

Meanwhile, Oren's voice in my ear said, "What do we need to do, Gabriel?"

I said, "Send Quog to the police station with money to arrange bail."

The voice on the line said, "What? Who are you? Who's this Coag?"

Oren said, "All right. Sit tight."

The voice said, "Is this the Burgess kid? You think you can bother decent people with prank calls? I'm gonna have a talk with your father, you little —"

I hung up the phone.

The cop led me to a communal cell filled with drunks and punks. The place looked filthy and smelled worse. Various, mismatched inmates paced, slept, or stared off into space. On a concrete bench along the wall, Weasel was snoring, his arm snuggled tight in a sling. Noonan leaned against the wall near him smoking a cigarette. I sat down on a bench in the middle of the cell facing the bars at the front. I rubbed my eyes with both hands. When I opened them again, Noonan had plopped down beside me.

"What did you tell them?" he asked.

"I told them you grabbed me off the street, but I didn't mention anyone else."

"Smart move. I told them you picked a fight with Weasel, that you acted like you were on some kind of dope."

I rolled my eyes. "Thanks. Appreciate it."

"Hey, I gotta know. Back at the warehouse, who or what was shooting at us? I saw this lizard face and two little birdies. And those laser guns. It was like something out of a comic book."

"To quote you, Noonan, you're messing with something a whole lot bigger than you."

He rubbed his hands back and forth on his pant legs.

I said, "You really didn't have anything to do with the murders, did you?"

"I've been trying to tell you that, Columbo. Scout's honor."

"You were a boy scout, Noonan?"

He shrugged. "As a kid, I was a lookout for guys running gin. That's a scout, ain't it?"

I had to laugh. "So any ideas about who killed Irene Giordano and Arthur Hatch? Just between you and me."

"Look at it this way. Hatch owed some gambling debts, and, as I understand it, the people he owed were putting pressure on him." Noonan shot me a wink. "Which means he was desperate for money. There are always ways a doctor can come by cash, capeesh?"

"Drugs?"

Noonan shrugged. "Sometimes a prescription pad goes missing. It happens. Or if not that, a guy can do off-the-books surgeries for somebody who needs to be stitched up on the quiet. Either way, this doctor is dealing with not the nicest sort of people. So I figure somebody knocked him off to hush him up. And maybe the nurse too for good measure."

"Nah," I said. "It doesn't work. Why kill the nurse first if taking her out was only cleaning up loose ends?"

"Maybe that's not what it was. Maybe she was the go-between. Or it could be that hitting her was a warning."

I shuddered at the thought. "Noonan, you have a devious mind."

"Thank you. I find it comes in handy." He pushed himself up from the bench and walked to the other side of the cell.

I sat there thinking about what he had said. My mind drifted, and for a while I went down a rabbit hole imagining a TV series about a crook like Noonan who solves crimes by thinking like other crooks. The premise was interesting, though it probably didn't have the legs to work on a broadcast network where they would need to squeeze out fifteen or twenty episodes. Possibly an eight-episode season on a streaming service.

I forced my thoughts back to the thornier problems of the case at hand. If Hatch didn't kill Irene, and McKinney's boys didn't kill either of them, then who did? And why? I hoped Oren had an idea because I sure didn't.

And here it was, the wee hours of Sunday morning if not later. In not much more than twenty-four hours, Grandpa Frank would be pleading guilty in court, a move that would change the trajectory of his life and probably mean my life would never happen. If we couldn't somehow solve the case, then I couldn't go home. There would be no home waiting for me in the twenty-first century.

Chapter 28

Gabriel Lake, Nazi Hunter

I must have dozed off because the rattle of a key in the cell door roused me. Opening my eyes, I felt my cheek against something scratchy with the smell of stale beer. I jerked upright to see a drunk in a dirty wool overcoat sitting next to me, shooting me a toothless smile.

A uniformed cop standing at the cell door said, "Columbo, you made bail."

I pulled myself to my feet and stepped toward the door.

"Bye," the drunk told me.

I waved cautiously and quickly followed the cop out of the cell. He led me to the front of the building, where I was met by Quog and a man in a checked suit and pork pie hat.

The man pointed a cigar in my direction and asked Quog, "This your guy?"

"Sure is. How are you, Gabriel … I mean, Lou?"

I nodded.

The guy poked my lapel with a stubby finger. "All right then. Your court date is Tuesday, June first. If you don't show, I come looking for you. Got it?"

"Yeah." I wasn't too worried about it. If everything went well, I would never see June 1943. Let the bail bondsman try to find me then.

The man turned back to Quog. "And next time, for the love of Pete, bring some folding money. Sheesh!"

The sun was coming up as Quog and I left the police building and headed down the block toward a bus stop. His bulging pants pockets jangled with each step.

"I had no idea how much your bail would be," he said. "Do you want some of these?"

"No thanks. I need to travel light. But I truly appreciate being bailed out."

"You're welcome. It's nice to be out and about on a morning like this. I haven't been doing much."

"Just reading, huh?"

"Well, that and answering questions about Earth for Oren."

"What kind of questions?"

The bus pulled up, leaving my Q without an A. Quog paid our fare along with the fares for everybody else at the stop. We found seats. I leaned my face against the cool side window and drifted off to sleep again. Quog had to nudge me when we reached Garfield Park.

"You should get some breakfast in you, Gabriel, and then hit your bunk."

"No way," I said with a yawn. "Time is running out on this case. With this catnap and enough caffeine, I'll be fine." I'm not sure I truly believed that, and from the skeptical smirk on his face, I don't think Quog did either.

We stepped aboard the *Shaymus*, where I first visited the galley to replicate an extra-large coffee. Then I climbed to the office and said, "Oren."

Buad and Blan were in their habitat, snoozing on the perch. Buad opened one eye and squawked, "Hey, knucklehead, couldn't this wait? We're sleeping here. It's bad enough we had to risk life and wing rescuing you … again. Now you're waking us up at the crack of dawn?"

"I need to talk to Oren. If you don't like it, go fly somewhere else. Use my cabin if you want, I'm not going to."

Oren's face came on the view screen. "Hello, Gabriel. It is good to see you out of jail."

"Yeah, I couldn't accomplish anything on the case from behind bars. Though, maybe I did. I'm convinced Noonan didn't do it. The question is what now?"

"What did you learn at the club?"

"Not much." I told him about seeing Ryan at the Kit Kat and about what Noonan and McKinney had said about the murders, including Noonan's jailhouse theory of the crime.

"Do you think that scenario is likely?" Oren asked.

"Not terribly. When I spoke with Hatch he seemed straight as an arrow. I don't think a guy like that would turn to crime even in a pinch."

"Then again, he might have fooled you," said Blan. "You ain't exactly the quickest ship at the spaceport."

"Go back to sleep," I said.

"How can I with all your caterwauling?"

Oren said, "This war that is going on, is espionage a possibility?"

"It could be. I mean, there was plenty of spying — codes and double agents and so forth. This was the biggest war Earth ever had … or so far, at least. But whether any intelligence activity was conducted in Indianapolis, who knows? Indy has always had a large German community. Matter of fact, the oldest restaurant in town is The Rathskeller. You can get schnitzel there and brats and sauerkraut and the works."

"Those are foods, I take it?"

"Yeah. German foods. I thought about having the wedding rehearsal dinner there just so I could say for better or wurst."

"Are you finished, Gabriel?"

"Yes, sir. I am now."

"See what you can learn about Mr. Beck and his war sympathies. If it is espionage, he is the most likely culprit. Can you come up with a ruse to flush him out?"

I bobbed my head. "I'll give it a shot. I'm not going to hold back. We're running out of time. What if he doesn't pan out?"

"Then go to the rooming house."

"For what purpose?"

"There's no need to discuss it until after you check out Beck."

"If you say so. He probably isn't at the theater yet. Anything else you want me to do first?"

"Sleep?"

"No way. I'll grab a donut for sustenance and energy and be on my way."

In the galley, I replicated the donut along with a few other items I thought might come in handy. I wondered what time Beck would reach the theater to open for a Sunday matinee. For that matter, I wondered what time it was right now.

"Hey, WALT."

The AI drawl came back to me. "Hey, Gabriel."

"WALT, would you check the time from the radio for me."

"Sure thing."

I munched a donut while I waited for him to scan the AM frequency band. He was back sooner than I expected.

"It's eight-twenty, Gabriel."

"Thanks."

I ran through the numbers in my head. The Sunday matinee might not start until one o'clock. Beck and his staff surely wouldn't come in before ten-thirty. That meant I had more than two hours for a walk of about thirty minutes. Quog and Oren were right. I needed a nap.

"WALT, would you keep monitoring the time and wake me at nine-thirty?"

"Sure thing, Gabriel."

I shuffled to my cabin, took off my jacket, hung it in the pressing cabinet to freshen it up, and dropped on the bunk. I wondered if I could fall asleep quickly enough to make a nap worthwhile. Turns out I could because my next conscious thought was of WALT calling me. I got up, sonic showered, dressed, and set off for Fountain Square, using the time to think up an approach to take with Beck.

The Sunday morning was soft and warm. Clouds floated across a blue sky. I passed families walking to church, the men and boys in suits, the women and little girls in dresses, hats, and patent leather shoes. Behind a white picket fence, a boy tossed a stick for a golden retriever over and over. The scene was peaceful, idyllic. Or it would have been were I not sleep deprived, stressed out, and trying to catch a murderer.

I reached Fountain Square and ducked into Hook's Drugs. The pay phones were at the back. I found the number I wanted from the book, stuck in a nickel from my change, and dialed. This would only work if Beck had something to hide. If he didn't take the bait, then it would probably eliminate him, and I could move on to the rooming house right away.

A voice answered. "Fountain Square Theater. Now showing: *Shadow of a Doubt* starring Teresa Wright and Joseph Cotton."

"I'd like to speak with Carl Beck, please."

"May I ask who's calling?"

"A friend."

"Um … does this friend have a name?"

"Sure. But I'm betting Mr. Beck doesn't want me to give it to you. It might not be good for your career."

The line was silent for a moment. "I'll get him."

I waited a minute, two minutes, maybe three. The longer it took, the more I expected to be told that Beck wasn't coming. But it was his voice I heard next.

"This is Carl Beck. May I help you?"

"I can help you. I know what you did, and it's only going to take a few hundred to keep me quiet."

"What's this about? Who is this?"

"Not over the phone, Beck. Meet me at the Corner Drugstore up on Virginia. Ten minutes."

"I can't be there in ten minutes."

"Ten minutes. Come alone and bring cash."

I hung up and walked out of Hook's to a streetlamp where I could watch the front of the theater. I leaned against the pole with my head down, glancing up periodically.

Five minutes later, Beck strolled out the door, crossed Shelby, and marched up Virginia. One could assume he felt guilty about something. Now I just had to find out what.

No one was at the ticket booth. I moved on to the door and found it locked. I needed to get in while Beck was gone. I pounded on the glass.

Billy the usher came over and opened it. "We're not open yet, mister."

"Hi, Billy. Remember me? I was here investigating the murder."

"Yes sir, I recollect you."

"I need to go back and examine the floor around where the young woman was sitting."

"Mister, the place has been cleaned since then."

"Has it?"

He hung his head. "Well, it was supposed to be."

"Just let me take a look-see."

Billy let me in. I walked toward the auditorium. Just as I reached the door, I looked over my shoulder and saw that no one was watching me. I veered off to the side and slipped through the door to the stairway.

I moved up the stairs as quietly as I could, knowing they went right past the projection booth. When I hit a bad squeak halfway up, I froze and counted off thirty seconds before proceeding.

As I suspected, the office door at the top of the stairs was locked, which was why I had replicated some soft key strips before I left the ship. I pushed one in and waited a few seconds for the metal to expand to fit the lock. I gave it a twist and entered Beck's sanctum, my eyes nearly watering from the nicotine in the air.

I tried the file cabinets first, but nothing was there except employee records, tax statements, and oddly, a cat food bowl. Next, I set to work on the desk, pulling out drawers and thumbing through papers. I found ledger books for the theater, yellow notepads, pencils, an ink bottle, safety pins, a box of paper clips, and three buttons. One drawer contained nothing but a carton of cigarettes, half a bottle of whiskey, and a dirty glass.

I found flyers from the studios for upcoming features. I thought if I slipped a few of those in my pocket, I could clean up on eBay back in the twenty-first century. But I let it go since it was more important to me to make sure I, in fact, returned to the twenty-first century. I didn't find any notes about troop strength or industrial output, or any of the details and statistics spies in novels are always interested in.

At the back of the lap drawer, I came across a small leather journal. Embossed on the front were the letters LGA. What might that be? The Ladies Golf Association? The Legion of Gentlemen Adventurers? I slid the built-in elastic strap off the cover and opened it to the title page. Loyal Germans of America. Yikes! This guy really was an undercover agent.

I flipped the pages and found a recipe for potato pancakes, plans for a small Oktoberfest party, and a note that the club's bank balance stood at $27.52, clearly not enough to topple the U.S. government. The book also contained multiple scribbled comments about how Hitler was ruining Germany and how celebrating German heritage did not mean they agreed with German politics. It turned out the LGA weren't Nazi sympathizers or spies. They were anti-Hitler German Americans.

Of course, that didn't mean Beck wasn't a murderer for some other reason. Something had caused him to walk up the street toward a meeting with an unknown blackmailer. But that could be anything.

I put the journal back and rifled through the ledger books trying to spot either payments or income that looked suspicious. But with a theater bringing in tons of cash — all of it in change — it wouldn't be difficult to disguise funds.

I flipped through the notepads and dug around for loose papers, looking for any reference to Irene Giordano or Arthur Hatch. Nothing.

I decided I had time to check in with the chief. "Oren, it doesn't look like Beck is a Nazi, and I can't find any connection to either of our victims. But he's feeling guilty enough about something to fall for the old meet-me-if-you-know-what's-good-for-you scheme. He could be back soon. Is there anything else you want me to check before I duck out?"

"No. People have many secrets and feel guilty about any number of past behaviors. That, in itself, does not make them murderers or spies. Proceed to the rooming house. The answer has to be there."

I slipped out of the office and relocked it. At the bottom of the stairs, I cracked open the door and peered out before stepping into the lobby.

Someone behind me cleared their throat. "Excuse me, sir."

"Hmm?" I spun around to see Billy the usher. I tried to look innocent. "Hi, Billy. Sorry, I'm lost. Can you point me in the direction of the little boys' room?"

Chapter 29

The Search for Schlock

As I stepped from the sidewalk to the brick path leading to the rooming house, I muttered, "Oren, I'm at the Potter's place."

"Excellent, Gabriel. Proceed."

"With what? What am I looking for exactly?"

"A motive for murder."

"And you think it's here?"

"You haven't found it anywhere else."

"Well, maybe I didn't look in the right places. Maybe I didn't ask the right questions."

"It does no good to second-guess yourself, Gabriel. Focus on what is ahead, not what is behind."

I crossed the porch and went inside. From beyond the hall came sounds of a tinny shouting voice. I found Nellie in the parlor listening to somebody on the radio preaching about Hell. Lester was missing in action.

Her eyes flicked up. "Where were *you* last night?"

Where hadn't I been? Clubbing, getting clubbed, being an innocent bystander at a shootout, napping in the county lockup. Not that I was going to tell her about any of it. "I was visiting my sick mother."

She responded with a look bordering on sympathy … or within a mile or two of the border anyway. I returned to the stairs and climbed.

I stopped and knocked on Muriel's door, thinking she might be able to help me. That is, if she were *willing* to help me.

The door opened. "Oh, it's you." Muriel crossed her arms and eyed me. "What do you want, Dimes?"

"First, I wanted to tell you I don't think the murderer was trying to kill you instead of Irene."

"What a relief." Her tone was sarcastic. "What convinced you?"

"Hatch was murdered too."

The snarky look dropped from her face. "Jiminy Christmas! What does that mean?"

"I think it means Frank Lake isn't guilty. He's been in jail this whole time."

"He wasn't in jail when Irene was killed."

"It raises reasonable doubt, don't you think?"

"Does it? Give me one good reason why Lake didn't do it."

"I don't have to, Muriel. You grew up with Frank. You know he's not a killer."

She made a sour face. "Yeah … I guess. Okay, Dimes. I'll give you that. I'll allow for a teensy-weensy bit of doubt." She studied her shoes. "Maybe I shouldn't have lost my temper the other night."

"And I'm sorry about not being upfront with you about my investigation. So truce?"

She nodded slowly. "Truce."

"Fabulous, because I have a question. If something shady was going on here at the house, anything suspicious, where would it be?"

"You mean other than Pete?"

"What's Pete doing that's shady?"

She shot me a don't-be-stupid look. "Him and his women. What a heel."

"Yeah, he's a heel all right, but that's probably not a motive for murder."

"His murder maybe … if the husbands and boyfriends ever find out. Wait. You think Irene was killed because of something going on here at the house?"

"We've eliminated about everything else."

"You're screwy, Dimes."

"It would be something you don't know about since you're still alive."

"Then why ask me?"

"I thought you might have half a suspicion about something … or somebody. Something you saw or heard. Maybe even an odd smell. Anything that struck you funny, that didn't fit."

She shrugged. "I haven't the foggiest idea."

"Can you at least point me in a direction?"

"I don't know. It's a big house."

"Is there an attic?"

"Sure. The pull-down ladder is in my closet."

"Oh. Hmm. The placement makes it less likely someone would hide anything there. Still, I suppose they would have access to it while you're at work. I wonder, could Irene have gone up there out of curiosity and found something?"

"Who knows?"

"Can I check it?"

She tilted her head. "This isn't some ploy to worm your way into my boudoir, is it, Dimes?"

I felt my cheeks flush. "What? No."

"Well, if Nellie catches us in here together, we're both out on the street. So I'm gonna take a walk around the block. That way she'll only kick *you* out."

"Yeah. And probably call the cops to boot." I hadn't had a police interrogation in nearly eight hours. They were probably missing me down at the station.

Muriel shrugged and swept past me. "Have fun."

The closet was right inside the doorway. I opened it and reached for the cord in the ceiling, pulling down a rickety set of wooden steps that swayed to one side like a hammock in a stiff breeze. Was this thing even safe? Stepping carefully, I climbed high enough for my head to rise above the planked floor and found a string hanging down from a light. I gave it a tug.

The space was filled with random items haphazardly placed — an old steamer trunk, a wooden barrel, an old boxy crank telephone, two ramshackle chairs that looked like they came over on the *Mayflower*, a rusty crank ice cream maker I wouldn't use on a dare. More importantly, a thick layer of dust covered everything. No one had been up there in months, if not years. This was not where Irene stumbled upon something.

I caught movement out of the corner of my eye and turned to see a family of raccoons not four feet away, staring at me with threatening fangs. Startled, I lost my footing and bumped down the ladder. I crumpled in a ball on the closet floor, then jumped to my feet and shut the trapdoor as quickly as I could.

As I leaned panting against the closet doorframe and warily eyeing the trapdoor for signs of movement, I decided I should check the line of dresses hanging on the wooden closet rod. I flipped through each of them, poking my hands into the pockets. I regretted the invasion of privacy, but I would have regretted even more leaving stones unturned. Three hat boxes sat on a shelf. I checked them also but found nothing.

Leaving the closet, I surveyed the bedroom. I probably should have checked the dresser, but that's where I drew the line. The thought of digging through my great-aunt's unmentionables was even scarier than the raccoons.

I cracked open the door to the hallway and took a peep. The coast was clear, and I slipped out.

I continued my search in the empty room across the hall from Muriel. It was as sparsely furnished as my room, so it didn't take long. I looked under the bed and in the dresser drawers. I opened a corrugated cardboard box I discovered in the closet, but found it filled only with empty canning jars.

At the foot of the bed stood a chest. I opened it to the scent of cedar and the sight of old sweaters. I dug my hands down through the stack with only a slight sense of foreboding for the possibility of more critters lurking within.

I said, "Oren, I'm not finding anything."

"Keep looking. Muriel told you something was bothering Irene. Do you believe her?"

"On that, yes."

"Then it is likely that what was bothering her was something she had discovered about someone — something the person didn't want known. That is what you are trying to find."

I headed down the hallway. At the end was my room on the left. To the right was the short hallway leading to the bathroom, another unknown door, and the back stairs. I entered the bathroom, closed the door, and rifled through the vanity under the sink. Nothing.

Oren said, "Dr. Hatch told you he was like a father figure to Irene. If that is true, then she might have confided to him about what was bothering her."

"In that case, then why didn't he tell me?" I left the bathroom and moved to the unknown door. It was locked. I had two more soft keys. I used one on it.

"Perhaps he had ulterior motives," Oren said. "Perhaps he wasn't as honest as you thought he was, and he tried to use the information to blackmail his way out of his money troubles."

The room was stacked with boxes and trunks. I shut the door behind me.

"And it got him killed," I said.

"The clue was in the doctor's office."

"What clue? Which clue?"

"You'll see."

"You know, I hate it when you do that."

"Do what?"

"Be all mysterious and smug." I lifted the lid to the first trunk. It appeared to be filled with books. This could take a while.

"It is a compliment, Gabriel. I am allowing you the opportunity to come up with the answer yourself."

"Yeah, right." I crouched, lifted out a stack of books, flipped through them at random, then slid the other stacks around the trunk to check for anything hidden.

"I will tell you this, Gabriel. It made more sense for the criminals at the Kit Kat Club to be involved. However, once we eliminated them and Carl Beck, that left only the people at the house."

I stood and closed the lid. "But who at the house?"

"That's what I don't yet know, though every indication is that it's —"

"Shhh." Someone had stepped into the bathroom next door. "I'll talk to you later."

I spent the next hour and change going through everything in the storage room. I found a whole set of boys' adventure books about boy scouts who somehow ended up involved with everything from rattlesnakes to bi-wing airplanes to Pancho Villa. I found Victorian dresses and newspapers from the 1800s. It all would have been a treasure trove to twenty-first-century archivists. But nothing jumped out as something blackmailable. I relocked the storage space and returned to the bathroom to wash the dust from my hands.

At the other end of the hall, I knocked on Peter Ryan's door.

"Come in."

Ryan was sitting up in bed, wearing pajamas. He looked up with a scowl from a little book where he was penciling in a note. "You, huh? Thanks to you I have to cross Evelyn off my list."

"Sorry. My bad."

Ryan shot me a confused glance. "Your bad what?"

"I mean, I had no idea she would be so excitable."

"She's a dame. They're sensitive about death and all. It's just the way they're built."

That certainly hadn't been my experience in the twenty-first century, especially with Sarah. Oh, how she loved a good autopsy.

"I heard you, by the way," Ryan said.

"Heard me where? When?"

"In Muriel's room. The Potters would love to know all about that."

I held up my hands. "Buddy, you grabbed the wrong end of the stick. We weren't —"

He smirked. "Sure, I did. And so will Nellie. I reckon I own you now, Columbo."

That piqued my interest. For what purpose did he need to own somebody? "Okay, let's say you do. What does ownership entail?"

"Simple. You cover for me. When the Potters want to know why I'm out late, you say we were playing cards and you got cleaned out early. Or you saw me heading into a movie while you were going out."

This guy, I thought. He worked more angles than a math teacher. "Sure, Pete. Whatever you say."

I had been planning to ask him if he had seen anything suspicious around the place. But so far, he was the most suspicious thing I had found. Was he just trying to cover up for his womanizing? Or was his womanizing a cover for something more sinister? I wished I could search his room, but that was out of the question with him there.

I said, "Well, I'll see you around." I started to go.

"Wait." It sounded like a command.

I froze in the doorway and twisted around to face him. "What?"

"What did you want?"

"Hmm?"

"Why did you knock, Columbo?"

"Oh … um … lunch. Are any restaurants around here open on Sunday?"

He shot me a look like I was whacko. "Yeah. Most of them." His eyes shifted back to the little black book.

I shut the door behind me. There was one other room opposite his on the other side of the stairs. I knocked. When no one answered, I opened the door, finding another empty bedroom, smaller than the others. Dresses and suits and an old Army uniform were hung in the closet. I thumbed through them all with no shocking discoveries. The dresser was also a waste of time except for the minute or two I took to read the newspapers lining the bottoms of the drawers.

That was the top floor searched. I slipped down the stairs and into the parlor, which was now vacant and silent. Through the door to the kitchen, I heard the clanking of silverware on a plate. At least one of the Potters was eating lunch, possibly both, though I couldn't hear any conversation to prove it one way or the other.

Moving as quietly as I could, I made a quick inspection of the room. I checked behind the console radio, eased open drawers, and felt along the bottoms of side tables. I was in the process of tilting a picture frame away from the wall to peek behind it when I heard footsteps on the stairs.

I let go of the picture, and it thumped against the wall. Turning, I saw Muriel in the doorway clutching a purse.

In a voice way too loud she said, "How's the treasure hunt going, Dimes?"

Chapter 30

The Motherlode

"Shhh," I said to Muriel.

Footfalls sounded from the kitchen. I whirled to the davenport, grabbing a magazine from the side table as I sat. It happened to be the *Ladies' Home Journal*, which isn't exactly my go-to periodical, but that didn't matter right then.

Nellie stuck her head through the door and gave me a funny look when she saw me with it. She shook a finger and said, "Don't you tear out any of those recipes."

I crossed my heart. "I wouldn't dream of it."

Mrs. Potter disappeared back into the kitchen. I rolled my eyes at Muriel, and she responded with a shrug.

"I'm going for lunch," she said. "Wanna come?"

I needed to search the kitchen, the Potter's bedroom, and the basement. I'd have liked a crack at Peter Ryan's room as well. None of those things were possible, though, with people there.

"Yeah. Lunch. Why not?" I joined her in the hallway, and we walked outside.

Muriel said, "On the way, you can tell me about all the fashion tips from the magazine."

"Sure. It's helmets. Everybody is wearing a helmet this spring. They call it war fashion. Of course, the War Department doesn't want to let go of all that steel, so most people are wearing leather football helmets. It's all the rage."

She laughed, and we walked on in silence. A half block later, she asked, "What are you looking for in the house?"

"I'll know it when I see it. Anything that could get somebody killed."

"Oh, you mean like sitting in Lester's chair?"

This time I was the one who laughed. "Remind me not to do that."

"You know, Dimes, what you said earlier about half suspicions? There *was* something. One night Irene was poking around the house looking for batteries. She might have found something she wasn't supposed to. It was when she came back that she started acting funny."

I stopped walking. "When was this?"

"Last weekend, I think. Yeah, it was Sunday evening, a week ago."

"Four days before she was killed, you mean." Long enough, I thought, for her to confide in Hatch and then confront the person. "That fits. We have to find what she found." I started to turn back.

Muriel grabbed my arm. "Without getting killed ourselves."

I thought about Nellie ensconced in the kitchen, Ryan up in his room. "Yeah."

"Besides, you promised me lunch, Dimes."

"I thought you invited me."

"Oh, I did. Doesn't mean it's going to be my treat."

We popped into Pop's Diner. Betty the waitress nodded to me as we entered. Seems I was becoming a regular. We ordered coffee and omelets with toast, bacon, and cups of fruit, making this a brunch decades before brunch became a thing. The food was great, and I even picked up one more item of diner slang when a waitress shouted out, "Adam and Eve." Muriel, who had some waitressing experience, explained it was two poached eggs.

I found it difficult not to gulp my food and hurry back to the house to complete the search. Reminding myself that we needed to allow time for people to shift rooms or leave the house, I forced myself to take it easy.

I hoped Lester and Nellie would go for a Sunday drive. I wished for Ryan to take a long walk although that seemed an unlikely activity for a door-to-door salesman to do on his day off. I wondered what I would do if they were still in the way when we got back. Maybe Muriel could distract them. We didn't have many more hours before Frank would need to enter a plea.

We were lingering over a second cup of coffee when Betty brought the check. It finished off the last of my change, and Muriel had to chip in to make up the tip.

We returned to the house with the clock on the hallway wall showing five minutes past one. We were greeted by the sound of snores and a radio announcer saying, "It's a swing and a miss." Both the Potters were asleep in their chairs, no wonder with the way the room was shut up and stifling hot. Lester's head listed toward the radio. Nellie loosely held a paperback on her lap, her eyes shut.

Considering her earlier expressed views on social propriety, the novel had a surprisingly salacious cover.

Muriel and I bypassed the room and tiptoed down the hallway. My first stop was the hall bathroom but not for any of the usual reasons. The only spot in there to hide anything was the built-in linen closet. I sorted through the towels and bedding without finding anything of interest.

Moving to the kitchen, I waved Muriel to the Hoosier cabinet while I focused on less obvious places — the undersides of the table and chairs, inside the fridge, the curtained area under the sink. We both came up empty.

"We need to check their bedroom," I whispered. I felt uneasy at the prospect of rifling through Lester's drawers (in multiple senses of the word). "You do it."

"Me? This is your operation, Dimes."

"I'll stand guard. If they wake up and start to come in here, I'll think of something to waylay them."

She stuck her tongue out at me and went, "Phhhtt," but she entered the room. I watched her check the dresser and the closet. "Dimes, you can see under the bed from the doorway there. I'm not getting down on my hands and knees."

I crouched and saw nothing. That left only the basement. Or rather the mysterious locked door in the kitchen, which I assumed led to a basement because I had heard voices coming through it as if from below.

I pivoted to the door and pulled out my last soft key while Muriel was still in the bedroom and couldn't see what I was doing. I inserted the strip, waited a second for it to harden, and then turned it. The door swept open, creaking out a long complaint as it swung away.

A black round knob was stuck on the wall inside where you would expect to find a light switch. I gave it a twist. A lightbulb affixed to the sloping ceiling flashed on to reveal steps down to a landing then more steps to the right. We descended.

A partial cinderblock wall rose on one side of the stairs topped with musty-smelling dirt and rocks toward the back of the house. To the other side, the basement stretched away in shadows toward the front.

At the bottom of the steps, another lightbulb hung from the low ceiling with a pull string. I tugged at it. The bulb's minimal wattage was not enough to illuminate the far corners. I flashed back to childhood fears in the dark cellar at my grandparents' farmhouse. It might have been the same for Muriel if the way she clutched my arm was any indication.

In the center of the space, a huge furnace rose from the floor. One could imagine it as a monster with pressure gauge eyes and vent pipe arms. A pile of coal extended from one side of the mechanism toward a wooden coal chute coming in from the side yard above.

In a corner, a tub washing machine with a wringer on top stood above a drain in the floor. Along one wall was a rough wooden shelf unit crowded with dusty canning jars and stacks of old magazines. On another wall, a wooden workbench sat underneath a pegboard hung with ancient hand tools.

There wasn't much here to search, except for a door set into a dark shellacked beadboard wall facing us at the end of the space. We moved to the door arm-in-arm, our footsteps grinding across the gritty, coal-dust-laden concrete. I tried the handle and found it locked.

I had used my last soft key on the basement door. Now what was I going to do? I wiggled the knob two or three times in frustration.

"Oh, for goodness' sake," Muriel said. "Step aside, Dimes."

She crouched before the door and pulled a bobby pin from her hair. Spreading the pin and popping off the plastic tip, she wiggled it in the lock.

"How is it you know how to pick a lock?"

"Shhh. I need quiet." She wiggled some more. "Bad relationship. This guy had some of my stuff and wouldn't give it back. I asked around. You'd be surprised what you can learn if you ask around."

And there it was — the gender roles changing before my eyes. She might have screamed in the movie theater. She, like all of her generation, might have been raised to see women as the weaker sex and dependent on men. But the war with its call for women to join the workforce was teaching them to be self-reliant, to not wait on men to do something they could do themselves.

Hollywood would continue through the rest of the twentieth century and beyond to make movies where men rescued damsels in distress, but a more nuanced reality was already beginning to emerge. Which, personally, I was all for, especially since Sarah had once saved me from being killed by a deranged robot.

The lock went *click*, and Muriel grinned up at me. She stood, twisted the knob, and pushed the door open. The light from the bulb by the stairs was enough to reveal another pull-string light fixture inside. I stepped forward and gave it a yank.

In the corner sat a heavy steel contraption the size of a refrigerator, all flywheels and gears. I recognized it as an old printing press, aided in that identification by what stood in the middle of the room — a butcher block table covered with foot-high stacks of sheets of paper. Each sheet contained sixteen images of George Washington. Not dollar bills. Beside each image of our founding father was printed: *One Unit Gasoline*.

Muriel whistled softly. "Holy Toledo. Ration coupons."

Which was exactly what Dr. Hatch had written in his spiral notebook ... except for the holy Toledo part.

I said, "These have to be counterfeit, right?"

"You know it, brother. Nobody gets issued this many."

"Irene must have stumbled upon these while looking for batteries. That is, if the doors had been left unlocked."

"No need," Muriel said. "She once told me she knew where the keys were kept."

So Irene found these. Realizing they were counterfeit and not sure what she should do about it, she probably asked Hatch for advice. That was when he made the note on his pad. And somehow both had ended up dead.

Muriel said, "What some people won't do for a few extra gallons of gas or another pound of sugar. Too bad we don't have a camera. We need a picture of this."

"On it." I pulled out my phone and snapped a couple of shots.

"What's that contraption?"

I winked. "A camera. I told you I was a spy. C'mon. We need to call the cops."

I pulled the light string to shut it off and closed the door. We headed across the basement and up the stairs. I took the lead, switching off the lights as we went.

I had legged it into the kitchen and spun toward the hallway door when it hit me. Literally. A swishing noise behind me was followed by a *thud* and a sharp pain in the back of my head. The room went dark as the floor rushed toward my face. My last thought before the blackness overtook me was that I should have known it. It was Muriel all along.

Chapter 31

Like a Box of Cracker Jack

When I came to, I found myself in the parlor sitting in Lester's chair with a headache so bad it made my eye twitchy. With a wince of pain, I twisted my head to the side and saw Muriel in Nellie's chair, tied with ropes, her face intense and filled with dread. I blinked. Turns out it wasn't Muriel all along.

I let my head fall back onto the top of the chair, then jerked it forward again, pain radiating from a tender spot on my skull. I went to raise my arm to touch it and found my hands tied, the rope between them running across the bottom of the chair. I tried to move my feet and found them also bound. Seriously, what was it with everybody tying me to chairs? I totally enjoy sitting and rarely require being lashed in as an inducement to stay in that position.

"He's awake."

I figured out how to focus my eyes on the source of the voice. Nellie was sitting on the davenport. She was untied. Lester stepped in from the hallway, a revolver in his hand. Apparently, it was the Potters all along.

I groaned. "What hit me?"

With his free hand, Lester pulled a palm-sized leather club from a pocket. "I sapped you good."

At least now, having been hit over the head with a blackjack, I was definitely a certified 1940s detective. Philip Marlowe, who rarely went a half dozen chapters without being similarly bludgeoned, would be proud.

"Sorry to be sitting in your spot, Lester. If you'll untie me, I'll be happy to move." The day had warmed. The parlor was hot.

"Shut your trap."

I became aware that my beloved fedora wasn't on my head. "Hey, where's my hat?"

Lester gestured with the gun toward an end table where my headgear was perched, seemingly none the worse for the clobbering.

Muriel said, "Your hat? You're concerned with your hat?"

"I like my hat." However, she had a point. What we needed was help. I said, "Oren."

"What was that?" Lester asked.

I said, "Oh, rats."

"Didn't sound like it."

"My brain's still a little mushy."

Oren's voice sounded in my head. "Yes, Gabriel."

"I see it all now," I said, hoping Oren took my meaning and connected to my translator bots to see what I saw and hear what I was hearing. I figured he would, him being a genius and all.

"What do you see?" Nellie asked with clipped, acidic words.

"I see two people who care nothing for the war effort, two people profiteering on greed and willing to murder to line their pockets."

"You don't know anything about us," Nellie said.

Oren said, "I'm receiving this all, Gabriel."

I peered down at my arms held in place by ropes.

Oren said, "You are fettered. I will send help."

I said, "Not Zastra in the middle of the day." A public sighting of her would cause such a commotion she might never reach us.

Lester said, "What did you say, boy?"

"I said it's not a disaster. It's the middle of the day."

"What are you talking about, Columbo?"

"Hmm?" I tried to pass it off as the concussion talking.

Lester said, "You thought you had me, sneaking around while I was asleep. Too bad for you Phil Cavarretta hit that homer. The crowd and the announcers woke me up with their yelling. I heard you talking downstairs."

"I'm the one who heard you," Nellie said. "He wouldn't hear a hand grenade. And you two, like Irene, should have minded your own business. If she wanted batteries, she should have asked us where we keep them instead of skulking around. There's a whole drawer full of 'em in the kitchen."

Lester touched his wife's arm. "Now, don't say anything."

She grimaced. "It don't matter a hill of beans now. We're gonna have to kill them same as we did to Irene. Same as you did to Hatch." She turned to us. "Can you imagine? A respectable doctor trying to blackmail people. It's a disgrace. What is this world coming to?"

I said, "It looks to me like it's coming to retired folks going into counterfeiting. I mean, I know everybody needs a hobby in their golden years to keep active, but couldn't you take up crafting or playing the guitar?"

Lester grunted. "You gotta understand, the rooming house business ain't what it used to be. All the men are marching off to war, and the women don't earn enough to pay regular rates. I'll be danged if we lose this house now in our old age after what we went through in the depression."

I thought he had made an excellent point in favor of pay equality, but this didn't seem like the best time to bring up politics.

Muriel spoke, her voice strained. "Sure. We understand perfectly. Lord knows all the big corporations are making a bundle off this war. Why shouldn't you make a little money on the side from ration coupons? It doesn't hurt anybody. There's no need to kill us. We won't tell, will we, Dimes?" In the heat, a bead of sweat ran down her cheek.

Judging from their expressions, I didn't think the Potters were buying it. I decided to go another way. "You know, the bigger the body count, the more likely you are to get caught. Detective Vukovich knows I was looking into this. What's he going to say when we turn up dead?"

Nellie shot Lester a worried glance.

Lester groused for a few moments. "Well, I don't see any other way. I reckon we'll just have to make sure you don't turn up. We'll say you two ran off together. Young love."

A small moan came from Muriel. Unlike me, she didn't know reinforcements would be arriving. If only I could stall Lester and keep him talking instead of shooting.

I said, "Could you at least indulge my curiosity before you bump me off? How did you manage to kill Irene right there in front of everybody?"

Lester chuckled a hollow laugh. "What do you think? It was dark. I passed behind her on the way to the bathroom and let her have it."

"What about the knife? How did you come by that?"

"That there was a stroke of luck. I walked up to the concession stand to buy popcorn and there it sat large as life. I didn't know who it belonged to. I pulled out my handkerchief while I was reaching for change and draped it over it. Then I pulled the bandana, knife and all, back into my pocket clean as a whistle. It was like an answer to prayer."

I wondered what kind of god he was praying to that helped him acquire murder weapons. This guy needed to brush up on his commandments.

"We had to do something," Nellie said with disgust in her voice. "Irene came to us a few nights before, that stupid, innocent girl. She told us she found the stash. She said she thought about going to the cops, but she was certain we had a reasonable explanation for why we had all those coupons."

"Nellie told her they came from a chain letter." Lester was grinning like it was all a funny joke. "She said we had mailed off one ration coupon and got all those others back."

"The girl swallowed it hook, line, and sinker," Nellie said. "But come the next night there she was again, looking at us all sideways and funny. It musta been from talking to Dr. Hatch. That man."

Lester said, "I had to do something. You see that, right? What else could I do? That dumb girl was gonna ruin it all."

Muriel glared at him. If she had been possessed of Superman's heat vision, Lester would have been charbroiled where he stood.

I said, "And you kept your handkerchief around the knife while you stabbed her, so you wouldn't leave prints."

Lester raised his chin with a gleam in his eye. "I'm not stupid."

I wondered how much longer I needed to keep him monologuing before the cavalry charged in. I figured it had to be Buad and Blan. With a chill, I remembered they hadn't been to the house on Olive Street. Would they be able to find us?

Nonchalantly, I asked, "By the way, what's the street address here?"

Muriel looked at me like I was insane. Lester fingered the gun, and I deemed it prudent to steer him back to bragging about his crime. "How did you know where to stab her?"

"What do you mean?" he said with a puzzled expression.

"The doc said it was one of the most quickly lethal places on the body. No chance to cry out."

He shrugged. "Huh. Lucky again, I guess. The only reason I stabbed her there was because I couldn't lean over to reach her throat. I'm not as flexible as I used to be."

Even if the Avanians could find the place, the windows and doors were shut tight. Would they be able to get in? Taloned feet aren't the best with doorknobs.

I said, "I'm hot. Are you guys hot? Maybe we should open a window."

Nellie said, "So you can yell bloody murder? I think not."

Lester cocked his revolver. "Any more questions? I don't have all day."

"Um, yes. Yes, I do as a matter of fact. I have gobs of questions. I'm dying to … ooh, poor choice of words … I'd … I'd love to hear how you did it. What about Dr. Hatch?"

Lester said, "Irene must have gone to him for advice. I didn't know until he called and demanded a piece of the action."

Nellie said, "I wish you had told me about all that."

"I didn't want to worry you, put another death on your conscience."

She wagged her hand at me. "Well, you shoulda 'cause when this one asked me where you went, like a fool, I told him. I didn't know. I was worried about your health."

He frowned. "What's done is done."

"I don't like all this killing, Lester. You should have just paid the doctor off."

He gave her a hard stare. "We'd have been paying him and paying him 'till the cows come home."

"Hey, you can pay me off," I said. "A one-time fee, and I'm out of your hair for good. You'd be surprised how affordable I can be."

"Zip it," Lester said. "Besides, it galled me, Hatch acting all high and mighty like we were doin' something terrible. Gas rationing doesn't even apply to doctors. What did he care?"

I said, "So you arranged to meet Hatch in his office and clubbed him to death. Then you ambled across the street and ate a hearty breakfast."

Nellie eyed Lester. "Breakfast? What did you eat? I hope it wasn't biscuits and gravy."

Lester said, "Good thing I had taken off my jacket because that time the blood got on my shirt something terrible."

"I had to throw that shirt out." Nellie shook her head as if it were a crying shame.

From the hallway came the *creak* of the front door opening and closing. A wild look flooded into Nellie's eyes. Lester, gun drawn, tottered hurriedly to the front corner of the room on the other side of the parlor entryway.

Quog strolled in, his eyes fixed on a brightly colored cardboard box in his hands. The lid showed a man in a 1940s conception of a spacesuit firing a blaster at a green squid monster with long fangs. Across the side in bold letters, it said: *MARS MISSION SUPERSONIC SPACE GUN.*

Quog glanced up, pretending somehow to not notice I was bound hand and foot. "Hi, Lou, look here at what I found for your nephew."

Lester stepped behind him and stuck the revolver in Quog's back. "Have a seat, Mr. Columbo. I gotta say, you sure picked a poor time to visit."

Quog shuffled to the davenport and sat with the box resting on his knees. Lester swung his gun from Quog, to me, to Muriel, back to Quog. "You better hand over the box."

Quog said, "What, this thing? Oh, this is merely a children's toy. Here, I'll show you." He pulled the cover from the package. Then, as if it were a box of Cracker Jack with a prize inside, he reached in and brought out a real live blaster.

Lester motioned with his fingers. "Gimme that thing."

Quog clutched the blaster to his chest and flashed me a look like I was supposed to do something at this point in the plan.

I said, "It was you, wasn't it, Lester, who tried to break into Hatch's office later? Guess what? I was inside going over the place at that exact moment."

Nellie said, "That was where he was a darn fool. After he took care of Hatch, he should have looked around right then and there to see if the doc had kept notes about what Irene had told him."

"Oh, he did keep notes," I said. "It's what put me on the right track." Technically, the notepad was probably what put Oren on the right track, not me, but why complicate the narrative?

Lester whirled to face me, revolver leveled at my chest. "You."

That was the moment Quog shot him with the blaster. Lester crumpled to the floor. With a gasp, Nellie leaped for the gun as it skittered across the wood floor. Quog shot her before she reached it.

Muriel shrieked, her eyes growing to the size of coffee cups. "What is that thing? What did you do to them?"

I said, "Don't worry. Calm down."

"Calm down? Calm down? Are they dead? What did you do?"

"It's all right, Muriel. Let me explain."

"Who are you people?"

Quog's brow wrinkled. "Miss, you really must be quiet. Please."

"I'm supposed to be quiet? With you shooting death rays at people?"

"Oh, gracious me." Quog sighed and shot her too.

Chapter 32

Loose Ends

"Quog! Why did you go and shoot her? That blaster *is* set on stun, isn't it?" I asked.

"Well, of course, it is, Gabriel." Quog held the weapon close to his face and studied it to make sure. "Yes. They've all only been stunned. As for the young woman —"

"Muriel. She's my Aunt Muriel."

"Is that right? My word, what a coincidence. But she was asking too many questions. We needed time to think of a reasonable explanation."

"I had one already. I've been telling her I was a spy. She would believe a spy would have a top-secret weapon."

He tilted his head to one side. "Would she? Really, Gabriel, if the U.S. had blasters, why wouldn't they issue them to the troops?"

"I don't know, but I could come up with any number of reasons. The weapons cost too much to pass out to every soldier. Or the government wants to keep them a secret. Or they don't want to risk them falling into enemy hands."

He extended a palm in my direction. "Well done. You have the story all ready for when she comes to."

I rolled my eyes.

"I must say, Gabriel, I would have thought you would thank me for saving you."

"Sorry, Quog. Yes, thank you. Awesome job. You were brilliant. I don't know how much longer I could have stalled him. You just surprised me, is all. I didn't expect it out of you. It was more of a Zastra kind of move."

Quog raised his chin. "I'll take that as a complement. Now, what about your landlords?"

"Former landlords at this point. Untie us, and we'll tie them up. Then we'll call the cops."

Quog unbound me, then Muriel. He helped me carry her to the davenport where we stretched her out and put a pillow under her head. We hauled Lester and Nellie into the chairs and trussed them up.

While I was retrieving my fedora, Quog slipped into the hall. I heard the pages of the phone book being flipped followed by the mechanical *whoosh* of the phone dial.

"Hello, police headquarters? … I would like to speak with Detective Vukovich, please … Well, of course, I know it's Sunday … Oh, he'll want to come in for this. Tell him it's Doug and Lou Columbo, and we've captured the killers … He'll know which killers … Just tell him … Sure, I'll hold."

Muriel came around first. Quog fetched her a glass of water while I fed her a yarn about Quog and me working for the FBI in anti-counterfeiting operations and being armed with experimental weapons. She was skeptical, but having seen the blaster in action, she bought the story.

When the Potters returned to consciousness, we told them the same thing. Lester and Nellie were still glaring at me when Vukovich along with two uniformed officers knocked on the door. Quog showed them into the parlor.

Vukovich said, "So what's the story?"

I turned to the Potters. "Do you want to tell him, or should I?"

Lester scowled. "I'm not saying anything."

"Have it your way. I'll tell him what you told me, and Muriel can back me up. You see, Detective, it all started because Lester here is a greedy snake in the grass who doesn't give a rip for the welfare of our great nation."

"Shut up," Lester snapped. "I was only trying to make ends meet. I didn't mean for any of this to happen."

I said, "Right, you're the victim here."

Vukovich said, "Why don't you tell it your way then, Potter? I'm all ears."

Lester spilled the beans, justifying his actions at every step, blaming everybody from President Roosevelt on down to this guy named Clarence who used to room there but enlisted and left them in the lurch financially.

When Lester had finished, Vukovich nodded to the uniforms to take them away. As they left, he dropped into Nellie's chair and rubbed his eyes. "Well, that's that. You all will need to testify at their trial."

I said, "Um … what if we aren't here?"

He gave me a sneer. "Planning on taking a vacation, are we?"

"I was thinking about enlisting. I enjoyed striking a blow for the war effort."

Vukovich went back to rubbing his eyes. "Eh. Sure. We have them with the confession ... and the counterfeit coupons ... and since he killed the doc only yesterday, I bet we can find that bloody shirt. Go ahead and enlist, Columbo. And Lord help your commanding officer."

He stood and lumbered toward the door, then stopped in his tracks and turned to point at me. "Wait. Enlist? I thought you just said you were in the FBI. And before that a lawyer. And before that a defense contractor. No, don't answer any of that. Ask me no questions, and I'll tell you no lies, right?"

I flashed my best grin. "How about giving me a ride to headquarters? I want to see Frank Lake released with my own two peepers."

Vukovich grumbled. "Sure. C'mon."

"Give me a moment." I put a hand on Quog's shoulder. "Dad, I'll see you back on the ... the thing."

I sat beside Muriel on the davenport. "I need to go. You won't see me again." Which wasn't exactly true because I could remember her seeing me when I was a little kid and deliberately ignoring me.

"Take care of yourself, Dimes. It's been a hoot."

She started to lean in. I could see where this was headed. She was going to give me a goodbye kiss, and from the gleam in her eyes, this was going to be the kind of kiss nobody wants to receive from a great aunt. I did a head fake and ended up in a totally appropriate hug. I stood and rushed out.

An hour later, after sitting on a hard wooden pew at police headquarters through an unbelievable amount of red tape and rigamarole, I heard a door squeak open. A cop escorted Grandpa Frank, once again in his Army uniform, out to me. He rushed up and began pumping my hand like he was churning butter, his grin stretching nearly to his ears.

"Mr. Columbo, you saved my life. How can I ever thank you?"

I said, "Frank, go fight this war. Keep your head down. Then come home and start a family. Live a good long life. That's all I ask."

"You got it. I'll have a whole passel of kids. And if I have a son, I'll name him Louis after you. How about that? What's the matter, Mr. Columbo?"

The matter was the cold shiver shooting down my spine on that warm May afternoon. Louis was my dad's name. It had always been my dad's name. Hadn't it? Had I influenced my father's name with the random choice of an alias? But how could I? He had been born sixty-some years ago from my perspective. It broke my mind thinking about it, and part of me worried that this was exactly the kind of future-causing-the-past thing that might blow up the universe.

Add to that the fact that my dad always said he never much cared for the name Louis. I wondered if I could fix that for him. I could suggest Mark or Jeff or even Gabriel. I started to say something to Frank but stopped, afraid of warping the timeline even more.

As we walked out of police headquarters together, I said, "You know, Frank, I think you could have gotten off sooner if you and your friends had told the police about leaving your knife on the concession counter."

He stared at his shoes. "You knew about that? Yeah, well, I thought one of them picked it up. I thought maybe Red killed Irene. She turned him down for a date too, and he was pretty sore about it."

"Why didn't you say something?"

"I didn't want to land him in trouble. Look, I knew I hadn't killed her, and I was confident I'd be freed sooner or later."

"Frank, buddy, your faith in the legal system is inspiring, but quit it." Of course, that was the twenty-first century talking. In a less skeptical age and in the middle of a war defending freedom, I'm sure it sounded way too cynical.

Grandpa headed for the bus station to return to Camp Atterbury. Despite all that had happened, he had only missed three and a half days. He would probably receive a chewing out he would never forget. But with a full exoneration of all charges, his Army career should soon get back on track. They needed soldiers too much.

As I set out along the streets toward Garfield Park, I contacted Jace to find out if I needed to walk, jog, or run to catch my ride. Buses and cabs were off the table as I had spent the last of my dimes on lunch with Muriel.

"Hey, Jace, I fixed the timeline ... I think. How will we be able to tell?"

"We won't. When you return to your own time, whatever happened will have always happened, and you'll never know any different. But as long as you're there, and Sarah and Lucas are there, it will be fine, right?"

"Right. How are you doing on fixing the *Shaymus*?"

"I'm nearly ready for a test."

"How do you test a chrono drive? Jump into next week?"

"Oh, I think we can take a bigger leap than that. I imagine it can make it all the way back to the night we picked you up."

"That is music to my ears, pal. I'll be there in about an hour unless you want to send Buad or Blan with a dime for bus fare."

Buad's voice sounded in my ear. "Not a chance, lamebrain. You can walk."

"Hey, are you listening in on a private conversation?"

"Who said the bot connection was private?"

"Gabriel." This was Oren's voice. "I wanted to express my gratitude to you for a job well done. I had to rely heavily upon you in this case, and you responded admirably."

Blan said, "Don't say that, Boss. You'll give him a big head. It's already fat."

"Thank you, Oren," I said, ignoring Blan. "You know, I've always dreamed of visiting this time. Of course, some of this whole shindig was more nightmarish than dreamlike."

"No doubt."

"I take it the jotting on Hatch's notepad about ration coupons was the clue you picked up on."

"Yes, it provided a motive connecting both murders. It made more sense that the gangsters would be involved with such a scheme, but once you eliminated them —"

Buad cackled. "Or the other way around. Those guys nearly eliminated Gabe."

"Yes," Oren said. "Another close call. But once we knew they weren't involved, and the theater manager wasn't either, then it had to be someone at the rooming house."

"Did you suspect the Potters?"

"There was the comment Mr. Potter made about being a printer in a past career."

"You're right. That one flew right past me. I guess that's why you're the genius, and I do the leg work."

Speaking of leg work, I was at that moment passing the pioneer sculpture in Fountain Square. I paused to take one last look at the centerpiece of my neighborhood as it once was.

"How did you know about gas rationing, Oren?" I asked.

I heard a child's voice behind me say, "Mommy, who is that man talking to?"

I jerked my head around to see a little girl in a yellow dress and brown pigtails staring at me bug-eyed. Her mother, with equal parts embarrassment and suspicion showing on her face, was hushing the girl and escorting her away, while at the same time casting accusing glances back at me.

In those days before Bluetooth headsets, walking down the street and talking to someone who wasn't there was a good way to end up with the guys in white coats coming to take you away. I had seen enough movies about the early days of mental health care to not want that to happen. I picked up my pace and walked on.

Oren said, "In answer to your question, Gabriel, I asked Quog about rationing. Evidently, his parents told him numerous family stories about life during the war. He was an excellent resource on this period."

"So do you think everything will go back to the way it was ... with my grandparents and all?"

"It is overwhelmingly likely. From all indications, your grandmother already had feelings for Frank. If anything, those emotions may have grown stronger through this ordeal. And since they both need to get through this war before they marry, your disruption will not have affected the timing."

"Speaking of marrying, you guys need to get me to the church on time."

"We are happy to do so, Gabriel. We can depart shortly after you return to the ship. Quog would like to speak to you when you get here."

"Oh? What about?"

"I will leave that to him."

Chapter 33

Time After Time

"You want to do what?" I asked.

Quog had kind of set me up. He had replicated two soothing cups of Maltese fruit tea for us to share in the galley while Jace made final preparations for the flight. Then he sprang his plan on me.

"I've decided to stay here in this time, Gabriel."

"No. Wait. What? After all we did to get you home?"

"You did get me home. I've been home ever since I arrived on Earth after decades away in other parts of the galaxy. If you recall, since then we've been trying to get you home."

"But —"

"Everything you've told me about the twenty-first century — cell phones, social media, streaming everything — those things aren't me. They're not the Earth I remember. At heart, I'm an analog guy. I belong in an analog world."

"Quog, you've been living in a high-tech digital world ever since you were kidnapped."

"Which is part of the reason I want to stay. Your century sounds too much like the advanced alien cultures I've come from. Not to mention the problems in your digital world with cyber-bullying and deep fakes and identity theft and doom scrolling. Gracious sakes, it's clear that human ethics haven't kept up with the technology." He spread his arms. "Here, in this time, everything is simpler and … and more like what I knew in the sixties. I feel at home here."

I said, "You know this time is far from ideal, Quog."

"Oh, I know. I remember all the protests from when I was a kid. In this period, racial and gender attitudes are still mired in nineteenth-century thinking. But be honest, is all that put right in your time?"

"No. No, it sure isn't."

"I'm hoping I can bring my galactic perspective to bear in this time period and prod people toward a better world."

I pointed at him like a mom talking to a kid. "Don't change the timeline. I just got it cleaned up."

"Don't worry. It is nearly impossible to move people ahead of what they're ready for. However, I might be able to improve a few individual lives here and there. I know all the rules. Live quietly. Don't kill anyone, which shouldn't be difficult. Don't marry. That won't be hard either. Don't introduce alien or futuristic technology."

"In ten or twelve years, you're going to be born, Quog. The original you, I mean. Jace said you can't meet yourself."

"I'll make sure I don't. Those Sam Spade stories have me thinking about moving to San Francisco."

"I hear it's a lovely place. Spoiler alert, you should probably purchase real estate there now."

He patted his pocket. He had enough diamonds to buy whatever he wanted.

I said, "And Oren is okay with this?"

"I have his blessing. Though if anyone from the galactic alliance ever found out, they would probably come to arrest me."

"Your secret is safe with me."

Jace's voice came over a speaker. "Everything is set."

Quog said, "I guess this is goodbye then, Gabriel."

"You won't …" I didn't want to say it.

"I know. I won't live to see the twenty-first century. I won't even live to see you born. But I might keep an eye on your grandfather and give his timeline a nudge if I need to."

"Thanks. Hey, what will you call yourself?"

"Douglas Columbo. I like it. Look me up on your Internet when you get home. I intend to keep a low profile, but you never know. I might write my memoirs and call them science fiction."

Quog extended his hand. I shook it and pulled him into a hug. "Take care of yourself … Dad."

"You too, Gabriel Lake. Remember …" His voice faltered and he shook off what he was going to say that he wanted me to remember. It didn't matter. I wouldn't forget any of this.

Quog broke the embrace and left the galley. I returned to my cabin, looking down at the mess my suit was in. It had been less than twenty-four hours since I pressed it. But during that time, I had been shoved in a car against my will, been tied up twice, been nearly shot by multiple people, rolled around on a warehouse floor, sweated through a police interrogation, sat in a filthy jail cell, and been knocked unconscious by a blackjack.

The suit was a shambles and obviously beyond what the pressing cabinet could fix. A good dry cleaning would be in order, except I wouldn't have time to have it done before the wedding. I could have sacrificed the suit to the replicator and then have it create an identical cleaned and pressed version, but I didn't want to do that to Grandpa's suit. Some things need to stay original.

Kah-Rehn's voice sounded in the cabin. "Are you ready to take off, Gabriel?"

"Give me a couple of minutes, okay?"

"Certainly. With a chrono drive, we have all the time in the universe."

I figured the sonic shower was a kind of dry cleaner, right? Only it uses sonic waves instead of solvents. I shrugged out of the jacket, pants, and shirt. I hung them each on separate hangers, hooked the hangers over the sonic shower walls, and turned it on. When it finished, I ran them through the pressing cabinet. They came out, if not perfect and pristine, at least in much better condition than they had been. Slipping on the shirt and pants, I told Kah-Rehn I was ready to head back to the future. I hopped into the comfy cockpit chair in the middle of the room and let it strap me in.

The *Shaymus* blasted off. Once the chrono drive kicked in, it only took one orbit around the planet to jump those few decades. One orbit for computers to become ubiquitous, for the Cold War to start and end more or less; for the space race to take humans to the moon; for disco to come and go; for cellphones to be invented big and boxy, then get smaller, then grow bigger again.

I thought about time and how the culture of an era shapes us. Quog and I both loved the 1940s but for different reasons. To him this was home in a way it could never be for me. I was raised with computers and summer blockbuster movies and big box stores. To me the forties were more like a fantasy world, like stepping into Frodo's Shire or beaming down with Captain Kirk to an unexplored planet. And like those fantastical worlds, that long-ago decade was a time of both hope and fear, a time when history called upon a generation to act with courage and sacrifice, and they responded.

We landed. I pulled out my phone to check the time, and all of a sudden it went off like an incessant alarm clock.

Ding … ding, ding, ding … ding, ding, ding, ding, ding, ding, ding.

The harness retracted, and I hopped out of the chair. I pulled up my notifications to see what all the hullabaloo was about. The first text from Sarah had been sent about an hour after we had taken off across space.

Sleep tight, baby. Thinking about you.

Obviously, that was something I should have answered right away. From there the one-sided discourse had slowly escalated, the messages coming in at intervals of anything from five to thirty minutes.

Good night.

I'm going to bed now.

Fun night, wasn't it?

Gabe?

Is everything all right?

Your phone is offline. Where are you?

Gabe??? Answer me.

I needed to text back right away. I typed:

Hi. Sorry. Phone off for the night.

I slipped on my suit jacket and fedora and heard a *ding.*

Why?

Excellent question. I texted back.

I thought it was bad luck to text the bride before the wedding.

The excuse was lame, but it was the best I could do without telling her that on the night before our nuptials, I had gone off on an adventure — something no bride wants to hear. Not that I intended to keep any of this from her, but now wouldn't be the best time to bring it up. My answer received no immediate response, which unnerved me more than the preceding twenty-some texts.

I went over in my mind everything I needed to do before the wedding — walk home, shower, shave, take a nap if I could fit it in, drink a huge amount of coffee if I couldn't, dress again, apply some ice to the bump on the back of my head, pack for the honeymoon, check Amazon for books by Douglas Columbo. Add to that list the most obvious and immediate task — I needed to call Sarah.

On my way out of the cabin, I tapped her picture in my contacts list. I was approaching the ramp with my thumb poised over the call icon when I stopped. I had something even more important to do first.

"Deploy stairs."

214

I climbed to the office. Along with everybody else, Jace was there, talking to Oren.

Zastra said, "Don't you have a ceremony to get to, Gabe?"

"Yeah, but I wanted to thank you … all of you. Thanks for helping me out of my fix."

Oren said, "You're welcome."

"As to your fee, I may have to pay you in installments." Oren was known to bill at astronomical rates.

"Consider it a wedding present."

"Really? Thanks! I was prepared to work off the invoice over the next twenty years."

"Even without a debt, I hope you can still accompany us on cases from time to time."

"I'd like that. Of course, I really should clear those with Sarah from now on."

"Naturally."

"Well, I'd better mosey along."

Zastra said, "Next time, Gabe."

Jace said, "Congratulations and good luck."

Blan said, "Tell Sarah we think she's making a huge mistake." Buad cackled and poked his brother with a wing.

I smiled and waved. I felt like giving them all a hug, but that probably would have been welcome only with Jace and not even possible with Oren. Before things could turn any more touchy-feely, I rushed down the stairs and out the ramp into the pre-dawn.

This time the parking lot was paved. The familiar murals were painted on the backs of the shops facing Prospect Street. I was home, and apparently, I was still me. I was ecstatic to be in a timeline I knew and was a part of, even if things today aren't as simple and black-and-white as they were in the 1940s.

As I walked toward my house, I pulled out my phone and placed the call.

"Hi, Gabe." Her voice sounded weary.

"Good morning, babe," I said. "Sorry about the phone mix-up."

She heaved a sigh. "You don't need to apologize. It just freaked me out a little when you didn't answer. I worried and let my imagination run. I thought maybe something had happened to you. I thought … I thought you were going to leave me at the altar."

"Hey. Never. Nothing in this world or any possible alternate reality can keep me away from this moment."

There was a pause.

"You say weird things sometimes, Gabe. I hope that isn't part of your vows."

"Listen, Sarah, I just got … um … I'm just starting my day. Let me drink some coffee before I say something else stupid."

"I understand," said the time traveler's soon-to-be wife. "You know what else I understand?"

"What?"

"I know you. There's something you're not telling me."

"Um …" I couldn't deny it. "Yes. There is. But it's not a problem. I'll tell you all about it."

"When?"

"Soon."

"I guess that will do. For now, the only things I care about are that you're safe and I'll be seeing you soon."

"Sarah?"

"Yes, Gabe?"

"It's good to hear your voice."

I was home at the beginning of what would be the most important day of my life, a day I would look back on for the rest of my years. Tomorrow too and the day after that. All these days. Every day. The good old days aren't only the forties or the sixties or the eighties or whatever. Good old days dawn every single morning.

I said, "I promise I'll explain everything after the ceremony … well, maybe after the honeymoon. We'll have other topics to talk about on the honeymoon."

"Like what?"

"The future. Our future."

How would you like to make my day?
Please review this book on Amazon and/or Goodreads.
Your honest words would mean the world to me.

Last Word and a Free Offer

Thank you for reading *Trouble in Paradox*. As someone fascinated with history and genealogy research, this story was a delight to research and write. I wasn't alive in 1943, but I'm old enough that traces of that world still existed in my childhood. I tried to describe 1940s Indianapolis as accurately as I could. I read old newspapers and dug into material at the Indiana State Library. When possible, I scouted real locations, though I had to take poetic license in several cases, especially with the Kit Kat Club.

I would love to hear what you think about the book. You can leave a rating or a quick review on Amazon and/or Goodreads. Please! It genuinely helps move the book up the algorithm.

I want to thank Kameron Robinson for another fantastic cover design. Also, a huge thanks to my readers who encourage me with reviews and just buying and reading.

Follow me on Amazon, to know when I have new releases. To do so, click the Follow button beside my picture on the Amazon page for any of my books. You can also follow me on Instagram at garyrandolphstoryteller and Facebook at GaryRandolphStoryteller.

Check out my website at grstoryteller.com. It has summaries of all my books and links to my blogs. I also do storytelling, and you can watch some videos of me singing songs and reciting poems.

While you're on the website, please sign up for my mailing list at the bottom of the home page. That way I can tell you when I'm releasing a new book, having price promotions, or doing a storytelling performance. I promise I won't abuse the privilege of having your email address. Nobody hates spam more than I do.

And something free for you. If you sign up for my mailing list, I'll send you *The Jewels of Eca*, an 8000-word story that tells how Zastra joined the Galactic Detective Agency. If you're a fan of the series, it's a tale you'll want to read.

Selected Other Books by Gary Blaine Randolph

The Galactic Detective Agency

Gabriel Lake is just a regular computer guy from Indianapolis … until he is recruited into this series of lighthearted murder mysteries in space. Under the guidance of the brilliant Oren Vilkas, the Galactic Detective Agency hops from one weird world to another to take on quirky aliens and solve interstellar crime.

The complete series is available on Amazon at amazon.com/gp/product/B08XN1BL1G

Book 1 – A Town Called Potato

Book 2 – The Maltese Salmon

Book 3 – Return of the Judy

Book 4 – The Big Sneep

Book 5 – Murder on the Girsu Express

Book 6 – The Cormabite Maneuver

Book 7 – Trouble in Paradox

Book 8 – The Wrath of Kah-Rehn (coming late 2024)

Pelham and Blandings

Pelham G. Totleigh is an unlikely hero. His species, Haplors, are smaller than most others in the galaxy. And as his Aunt Agutha constantly reminds him, he is hardly the smartest or most industrious of Haplors. He also has an unfortunate habit of stumbling his way into the most outrageous and hilarious predicaments. Fortunately, his faithful valet Blandings has enough brainpower for both of them and is always there with a brilliant idea and an excellent cup of tea. This series is a loving tribute to and re-imagining of the Jeeves and Wooster stories of PG Wodehouse. Join Pelham and Blandings on their comic misadventures through space.

The series is available in both paperback and e-book formats on Amazon at https://www.amazon.com/dp/B0BYPLWPBV

Book 1 – Viva Lost Vogus

Book 2 – The Importance of Being Pelham

Book 3 – The Code of the Totleighs

Alien World

If you were stranded, all alone on an alien world, if you had to hide your identity and try to blend in, how would you do it? What would it cost you? What would you long for most?

Not a comedy — well, there are some funny bits — *Alien World* is an exploration of what it would be like to be an alien stranded on Earth and forced to live out decades there, trying to blend in while staying one step ahead of the military that is hunting him.

Available on Amazon at https://www.amazon.com/dp/B085SYG3L7

Printed in Great Britain
by Amazon

44898071R00126